A Rancher's Surrender

Susan

A Rancher's Surrender

A Frontier Montana Romance

Michelle Beattie

Congratulations! I hope you enjoy Wade + Jillian's story.

*Best,
Michelle Beattie*

A Rancher's Surrender
Copyright © 2016 Michelle Beattie
Tule Publishing First Printing, September 2016

The Tule Publishing Group, LLC

ALL RIGHTS RESERVED

First Publication by Tule Publishing Group 2016
Second Edition

No part of this book may be used or reproduced in any manner whatsoever without written permission except in the case of brief quotations embodied in critical articles and reviews.

This is a work of fiction. Names, characters, places, and incidents are products of the author's imagination or are used fictitiously. Any resemblance to actual events, locales, organizations, or persons, living or dead, is entirely coincidental.

ISBN: 978-1-945879-35-7

Dedication

For my mom, my dad, and my brother, Normand. Knowing you're together brings me peace. Remembering the good times growing up brings me happiness. I love you lots, think of you always. I hope I've made you proud.

Acknowledgments

First to Dr. Jeff Serfas at the Forestburg Vet Clinic for help with the cesarean section on the cow. To Larry and Carol Uglem, best neighbors ever. Larry helped answer my questions about horses and wagons and Carol fed me coffee and cookies afterward! To my sister-in-law, Susan Beattie, for also contributing her horse knowledge. Any errors or omissions are entirely my own.

Chapter One

Montana Territory
May 1882

"They're not going to get here in time."

Wade Parker ran a frustrated hand under his hat. What was taking so long? He wondered. He'd sent for the veterinarian almost an hour ago. Once he'd realized he'd had no other choice.

"They'll be here soon, son. But the way the rain's coming down, it'll slow down old Doc and Scott." James rested a calloused hand on Wade's shoulder. "Go check on the cow again, and I'll have a look outside."

Wade had been taught from a very young age that no matter how bad things got, there was always something to be thankful for. And right now, he was thankful for two things. One, for James. Not only had James been foreman of the Triple P for as long as Wade could remember, he was also a friend. A friend who, at times like these, reminded Wade no matter how bad things got, he had family and friends to see him through.

The other thing Wade was damn glad for was that Doc

Fletcher's replacement hadn't arrived yet from Pennsylvania. Not that Wade hadn't helped choose the vet's replacement and not that he wasn't satisfied with the new doc's qualifications but, with the lives of his animals at stake, he wanted someone he knew, someone he trusted, tending what was his. Doc Fletcher would understand the importance of saving the cow and calf. But then, most everyone in Marietta would.

It was no secret the Triple P was neck deep in debt.

Wade made his way to the stall while James's steps made squishing sounds behind him. Wade blew out a troubled breath. They needed to get that new barn finished. Adding the cost of the vet, he ran figures in his head, refused to be defeated by the staggering numbers that filled the debt column. He'd manage. By God, he'd manage. He wasn't losing the ranch his pa had built.

Wade took a deep breath, braced his forearms on the top rail and prayed, not for the first time, that he wouldn't lose two animals before the night was over. While he knew he'd find a way to survive should the worst happen, it sure would be a hell of a lot easier if the cow and calf survived.

The animal's eyes were glazed with pain; her mooing was raspy where a few short hours ago it had been loud and strong. Though she struggled to get up, she wasn't able to do more than lift her head. He cursed, feeling an iron band of tension wrap around his shoulders. He'd already sold off part of his herd but he couldn't afford to sell it all. He needed enough heifers for breeding, enough to keep selling. And if nothing else happened, maybe, just maybe, he'd start thinking about starting that horse ranch.

"They're here!" James yelled.

Relief poured through Wade. "Hang in there, girl. Help's on the way." Wade ran to the door.

"Well," James said, pushing his hat further up his forehead. "This sure is an unexpected surprise."

"What's the problem?" Wade asked, stepping around James.

He stopped dead, felt his jaw slacken.

What greeted him in the yellow glow of the barn was not even remotely close to old Doc Fletcher, or the J. Matthews they'd hired to replace him. This wasn't the short, plump vet Wade had expected. Neither was he the tall, strapping man Wade imagined would cross a country to replace Doc Fletcher. Instead there stood a woman barely tall enough to reach Wade's shoulder.

She held her horse's reins in one gloved hand and saddlebags in the other. Though she didn't seem to notice, water streamed over the brim of her hat. Her eyes never left his and the directness of that gaze stopped him momentarily. Wade turned to Scott. Scott Taylor, the only ranch hand Wade could afford besides James, shrugged.

"She was at Doc's place. Told me she could help." He explained.

"Doc's place?" Wade shook his head.

That made no sense. If Doc wasn't at his place, then it should have been Dr. Matthews, as was the agreement made when they hired the new vet. He turned back to the woman.

Green eyes, a heart-shaped face. She was pretty, no question, but it wasn't pretty he needed at the moment.

He glared at Scott, then James. "This isn't time for one of your damned practical jokes."

He stepped out into the rain. Surely Doc Fletcher was waiting around the corner with his bag in hand. Surely any moment now Scott and James would laugh and gloat as he'd fallen for their prank. But there was nothing outside but darkness and sheets of rain and his ranch hand and foreman remained unnaturally silent.

The woman's voice cut through the silence like lightning. "Could you see that my horse is looked after?"

Wade spun round. She handed the reins to Scott then skirted past a wide-eyed James. She strode purposefully into the barn, saddlebags in hand.

"Wait just a minute!" Wade said as he loped behind her.

"What?" she asked, never once breaking stride.

"Where's Doc Fletcher?"

"He left town."

"Since when? He was still here last I heard."

"Apparently he didn't feel you needed to be apprised of his comings and goings," she said, slipping into the stall.

She tossed her hat and dripping slicker onto the clean straw. A thick braid of auburn hair fell down her back.

Stunned, Wade could only watch as she opened her bags, set a pristine white cloth onto a dry patch of straw, and began placing shiny medical tools onto it. None of what he was seeing made a lick of sense.

"What are you doing?"

Her hands stilled and her fiery green eyes snapped. "Exactly what you brought me here to do." She took her stethoscope, placed one end of the wooden tube on the hide and her ear to the other.

His gaze snapped right back. "I sent for Doc Fletcher."

"No, you sent for the veterinarian," she said, shifting to her knees. "And that's what you got."

"But—"

Her hands skimmed over the distended belly of the animal as she continued to talk. "I'm trained as a vet, and I'll explain afterward. But right now, this cow is my only concern."

He couldn't help it; his eyes roved over the woman. Her black belt cinched a tiny waist. Leaning over the way she was, it was only natural he noticed the way her skirt draped over her trim backside.

His mind told him she couldn't be a doctor. Her shoulders didn't look broad enough, nor did her hands appear strong enough to do what needed to be done. But, as she said, they didn't have the luxury of arguing. Time wasn't on their side. If Doc wasn't coming, she was his only hope.

She placed the stethoscope to the cow's brown hide. The

barn was silent as she worked except for the constant patter of rain, both inside and outside.

"Is this her first time?" she asked when the cow tried once again to raise her head, then gave up with a low moan.

"It is." Wade confirmed.

"Calf must be too big for her." She fixed those green eyes on his again. "I'll need clean towels, warm water and all of you to help hold her down while I do the surgery."

Wade took a breath, nodded. Whether she knew what she was doing or not, she was here and she was all they had. He, James, and Scott had tried everything they could think of earlier. He'd just have to trust she could get his animal through this crisis alive.

"I figured you might," he answered. He gestured to the corner of the stall. "We already got the rags and there's hot water ready on the stove. I'll be right back with it." He turned to James, who'd joined him at the stall. "Stay here in case she needs anything else."

Wade strode down the aisle, his pace increasing when the cow moaned again.

Scott, who was in the last stall tending the woman's horse, looked up as Wade approached. "You need me?"

"We will, just as soon as I get back."

"I'll be ready," Scott answered.

Wade ran for the house. His mother came running the moment he stepped inside.

Worry filled her eyes. "Did you lose them?"

"Not yet." Though with this unexpected turn of events, the possibility seemed more likely than ever.

Eileen Parker's shoulders fell. "Well, that's a blessing I'll take. You're ready for the water now?"

"Yeah."

"I'll get it."

She didn't have far to go; the house wasn't very big. Two bedrooms upstairs; one for him, the other his ma and his daughter, Annabelle, shared. Downstairs consisted of a kitchen to the left with a small enclosed porch jutting off of it to wash up and a parlor to the right. Since Samuel and Eileen Parker only had one child, there hadn't been a need to build a large house.

"Thanks, Ma," he said, taking the buckets from her grasp.

"I'll get some more going, in case you need it."

She opened the door for him. "Don't let Miles leave without coming in for a hot cup of coffee."

Wade paused. "Miles Fletcher left town."

Panic filled her eyes. "You don't have help?"

"We do. I think. I hope." He shook his head, thinking of the woman he was trusting with his animals. He hoped to hell she knew what she was doing. "I don't have time to explain, I have to get back. But don't worry; I plan on asking her a whole lot of questions once this is over."

★

LANTERNS HANGING ALONG the back and sides of the stall illuminated the little square. Other than the patter of rain on the roof and dripping into the puddles in the corner, Jillian worked in silence. She was relieved James didn't seem bothered by her presence and wasn't firing questions at her as fast as Mr. Parker had.

Did it matter where their precious Doc was or why she was there in his stead? Did Mr. Parker really think she'd follow a complete stranger in the middle of the night if she didn't know what she was doing?

Granted, since women weren't allowed in veterinary schools, she could understand his questions. She had, in fact, expected them. But she had the tools and she'd followed his ranch hand in the dead of night, surely that ought to prove something. But then, he wasn't the first man to look at her and not see past the fact she was female.

She'd grown and learned despite the abundance of such attitude toward her, and Mr. Parker, no matter his prickly attitude, would not deter her from doing what she was trained for, what she loved to do.

The owner returned and his men followed him in, making the already small stall even smaller.

"Okay, we're ready," she said. "I need her two front legs kept forward, her rear legs kept back as well as her head held down. I don't want to give her too much ether, that way she can stand and nurse sooner."

Scott took the back legs, James the front and head. The

owner's knee rested against Jillian's when he took his position at her side. Despite their wet clothes, his heat seeped through and made her skin tingle. Annoyed by her reaction, she immediately broke contact.

"We're ready when you are," James said.

Pouring some ether on a rag, Jillian held it briefly under the cow's nose until she felt its muscles relax. "That's it. We'll take good care of you." She switched the rag for her knife. "Here we go, hold her steady."

Carefully, Jillian cut an incision into the left flank of the cow. Its legs jerked, but the men held her easily enough. The sound that came from its mouth was low and pitiful. She heard the owner's quick inhale, felt the intensity of his stare on her. He didn't think she could do this. Well, he wouldn't be the first man she proved wrong.

Moving quickly, Jillian cut through the skin followed by layers of muscle. She reached inside the abdomen to get a hold of the uterus. When she felt the calf's legs through the tissue she pulled it toward the opening.

"I've got a hold of the calf's rear legs. Mr. Parker, I'm going to cut through the uterus, then I'll need your help to pull it out."

Jillian didn't wait for his answer; time was too critical. Holding the calf's legs in one hand, she cut through the uterus until they had enough room to pull out the calf. Water and blood poured out onto her skirt. A thin veil of vapor rose from the incision as the warmth of the animal combined with the cool night air.

"Now!"

Jillian dropped her knife in the bloody water at her feet and together she and Mr. Parker grasped a leg and pulled. The calf slipped out of its mother's womb and onto the floor. Jillian quickly pulled the mucus from its nose and mouth.

"It's not breathing!" Jillian scrambled up and as she grabbed the calf's rear legs, Mr. Parker leapt in and helped. Together they pulled the animal off the straw floor, gave it a few good jerks. Placing it back down again, she leaned over the newborn. Warm air blew on her hair as the calf exhaled. Hers wasn't the only sigh that filled the stall.

"Keep holding her." She reminded the other two men, though they hadn't made any move to let go.

Jillian dealt with the cord efficiently but the amount of blood worried her. Why was there so much?

Mr. Parker grabbed the calf. "I'll take him to another stall and clean him up. It will give you more room to work."

Jillian didn't look bother looking up. She simply nodded as she tried to determine where the excess blood was coming from.

"There's a problem, isn't there?" James asked.

"I think there's a tear somewhere, I just need to—"

She found it immediately. There, a rip in the uterus. It must have torn when they'd pulled out the calf. It wasn't an uncommon thing to tear something in a cesarean section, but it could be fatal. And if she hoped to prove herself, she couldn't afford for the animal to die.

Using all her skills and sending up a few prayers for good measure, Jillian sewed the tear and the cut. The catgut worked well as an interior suture material because it was eventually absorbed naturally by the body. Using some of the rags to wipe at the blood, she inspected her work. There didn't appear to be any seepage. Wiping the moisture from her brow with her sleeve, she then began closing the hide.

A precise row of sutures later, followed by a confirmation of a strong and steady heartbeat, Jillian pressed her hands to her lower back and stretched.

"Thank you, gentlemen, you can let her go now."

Scott immediately scooped up the bundle of straw that contained the placenta. "I'll take care of this," he said.

"Should I bring in the calf?" Mr. Parker asked from outside the stall.

Jillian looked up, saw where his gaze was aimed and dropped her hands to her side. "Yes, the sooner he can nurse, the better."

Though the mother had yet to stand, she nonetheless moved her legs aside to give her young access. The calf didn't waste any time and began to suckle.

With the crisis taken care of, Jillian had a chance to examine Mr. Parker a little more closely. He too had taken off his coat and his shirtsleeves were rolled up, revealing forearms sprinkled with golden hair. His wet pants clung to long, lean legs. Jillian had always thought a man looked more, well, manly in working clothes than he did in fancy suits. She'd always been drawn to the more rugged sort.

But she'd made that mistake once before, to heartbreaking results. A smart woman learned her lesson. And Jillian Matthews was no fool.

"Will she make it?"

"Infection is always a risk, as is internal bleeding. It's why many vets choose not to perform the surgery. Though I'll examine her again come morning, I'd say the worst is over."

The worry faded from his eyes. Yet he didn't say thank you, didn't acknowledge her skills. The omission stung because she knew good and well his old Doc Fletcher would have received a hearty handshake and likely a solid pat on the back.

She wasn't the kind of woman who needed pretty words. All she'd ever wanted was to be accepted for who she was, a woman who also happened to be a skilled doctor. Good Lord in Heaven, why was it so blasted hard for a man to accept that?

Annoyed, she hurried through cleaning her instruments, but was careful when she placed them back into her bags. Standing, she grimaced at the squishing sounds coming from her boots. Luckily her hat and slicker had remained dry. She settled her hat onto her head and slipped into her slicker.

Down the aisle, Hope's snuffle caught Jillian's attention. Scott had stepped back into the barn. He stopped as he passed the horse and spoke in a gentle way, his eyes locked with those of her horse as he scratched her withers. Jillian watched, mesmerized, as Hope nickered and leaned into Scott.

"He's got a way with animals, especially horses," James said.

Jillian marveled when Scott walked toward them and Hope stared lovingly at his back. He set a shovel against the wall.

"I buried it far enough away that it shouldn't attract any trouble."

"Thanks," his boss said.

Jillian gnashed her teeth. His ranch hand, who'd done nothing more than bury the afterbirth, got the man's thanks when she didn't get so much as a nod of gratitude? Her gaze went to the shovel Scott had returned. She was sorely tempted to use it.

"Miz Matthews"—James approached, his hand outstretched—"that was fine work. Thank you."

His hand was calloused, his grip firm. Because it was the same handshake he'd have given a man, Jillian smiled, knowing she'd gained someone's approval. And if she had his then hopefully—

Mr. Parker's head snapped back as though slapped. "Wait! Did you say Matthews?"

Seeing the shock in his eyes, Jillian braced for an even fiercer storm than the one raging outside. James's brow furrowed, then the wrinkles smoothed out as realization dawned.

"We introduced ourselves when you were fetching the water. Wade, this here's Jillian Matthews, she's the new vet."

Wade's mouth pinched.

Jillian crossed her arms. "I responded to the advertisement and was given the position."

"No. Miles and I read through the replies for our post together and we offered the position to the most qualified man who responded. Jared Matthews."

It was the first time Jillian had heard her father's name spoken since his funeral a month ago. For a moment, she cherished the sound, held it close as though, somehow, she was holding him.

"That's not possible. Jared was my father and he died last month."

"If he's gone how is it that—"

James put a hand on Wade's arm. "Let's go inside. We could all do with a cup of coffee and I'm sure Miz Matthews would appreciate a chance to get dry."

Extending him the same courtesy he showed her, Jillian ignored Wade and turned her eyes to James. "I'd love a cup of coffee, thank you."

She could almost feel the frost form in the air.

"I'm turning in," Scott said. Then he too extended a hand her way. "Thank you. It must have been a little scary following a stranger in the middle of the night."

"Well, the pounding on my door gave me a fright, but it's what I do. Thank you for taking care with my horse."

He shrugged. "She's a beauty." He tipped his hat to her, nodded to Wade and James and slipped out into the rain.

"Well, no point in us lingering here either. We'll finish this inside."

Lightning shot for the ground outside the open door. A thunderclap rattled the building. Lifting the collar of her slicker against the wind and rain, and hoping the menacing weather wasn't a sign of what awaited her in the house, Jillian trailed Wade across the yard and into the house.

The smell of fresh coffee greeted her like a warm blanket.

Mrs. Parker was there to take her slicker and hat. "I've set warm water and clean towels for you upstairs, the door on the left. Wade, dear, there's a basin and some dry clothes for you in the porch."

Cold and wet, Jillian didn't argue. She removed her boots then lifted the hem of her soiled riding skirt and padded up the stairs and into the bedroom on the left. Immediately the masculinity of the space hit her and she realized that she'd been sent to Wade's room.

A dresser displayed a handful of coins and a comb. A blue quilt covered the bed. At the end of the mattress was a pine chest with a pair of pants tossed over it.

She'd been courted by Clint for almost a year. They'd gone to dinner, gone dancing, gone to the theater. She'd seen him dressed in his best suit and dirty in his working clothes.

They'd kissed, held each other close. Yet none of those events had been as intimate as standing there, where the scent of leather, hay and man clung to the log walls; where his presence breathed in the room.

Realizing she was standing there like a ninny thinking of how Wade's room smelled rather than getting her wet, clinging clothes off, Jillian closed the door. She was here for one thing and one thing only. There was no room in her life for men, especially selfish, short-sighted ones who couldn't accept that a woman was capable of more than cooking and raising babies.

While Jillian hadn't had much experience with either children or cooking as they'd had a maid to cook at home and her sister Katie was only four years younger than Jillian was, she'd nonetheless always hoped to have a family one day. But that didn't mean she couldn't do more. Didn't need to do more. She was amply qualified to be this town's vet and she aimed to ensure, before this night was over, Mr. Parker understood he had hired the best doctor for the job.

★

THE MURMUR OF voices grew louder as Jillian—dressed in dry riding skirt, blouse, and stockings—descended the stairs. Light from the kitchen spilled onto the entryway floor, creating a pale glow on the worn wooden surface.

"We were just talking about you," Mrs. Parker said when Jillian stepped into the kitchen.

Jillian's gaze flew to the table where Wade and James sat. She acknowledged James with a smile, but it was Wade who commanded her attention. He'd taken off his hat but hadn't combed his hair. Damp, sandy brown waves fell onto his forehead. His jaw was dark with stubble. His accusatory gaze followed her to the table. Oh, she had little doubt they'd been talking about her. And even less doubt that Wade had anything positive to say.

Mrs. Parker pulled out one of the chairs that rimmed the table. "Sit. I'll get you some coffee."

Jillian had barely taken her seat before Wade leaned forward, arms braced on the table.

"I assume you have an explanation for misleading us about who you were?"

Mrs. Parker's simple calico skirt swooshed as she spun round.

Her honey-colored eyes flashed. "Your interrogation can wait until the poor woman's had a chance to get some coffee." She held her ground, finger still pointed until Wade slumped back in his chair. Only then did she turn back to the stove.

James, with a twinkle in his eye, gave Jillian a wink. Before long Wade's mother had placed a steaming cup before Jillian. Jillian wrapped her hands around the mug. Heat seeped into her chilled palms. Not caring that she'd likely burn her tongue, Jillian took a sip of the bold brew and sighed as it warmed her throat and belly. Her moment of peace was shattered all too soon.

"I'm still waiting."

"Wade!"

"It's all right, Mrs. Parker."

"Eileen. We don't stand much on formality around here." She shot Wade another glare. "As you can obviously see."

Wade once again rested his forearms on the table, intertwined his long fingers. The hard lines of his jaw said the little patience he'd been hanging onto was gone. "She lied to us and I want to know why."

Jillian set her cup down. Hard. Wade wasn't the only one losing patience. "I never lied to you or anybody else."

"Is that what you call never once saying you were a woman? You signed all your correspondence with the letter J. If you weren't lying, why didn't you use your full name?"

"Wade, it's late. I think this can all wait until morning."

"It's all right, Eileen, I can answer this." Jillian shifted forward in her chair. "I didn't sign my full name because you advertised for a trained veterinarian and that is exactly what I am. I suspected, rightly so as it turns out, that if I signed Jillian you wouldn't hire me. As to my father, I have no idea how you even came to know of him."

"When you first sent your letter of interest we telegraphed Philadelphia, asked for information on J. Matthews. Everything that came back about a vet in Philadelphia was for Jared Matthews."

Jillian finished her coffee, pushed the cup aside. "I'm not responsible for that. Clearly you sent away for this information prior to his passing."

"Which doesn't change the fact that you aren't what we are looking for or expecting."

"Wade Parker!" Eileen hissed.

Though James said nothing, his scowl said he didn't think too highly of Wade's words either.

"Ma, the town entrusted me and Doc to find Doc's replacement. They're not going to be happy about this and I don't have time to soothe feathers nor to start looking for another doctor. That took weeks as it was." He glared at Jillian, laying the blame at her feet.

Jillian grabbed the last edge of her temper before it snapped wildly. She'd come west to practice medicine. Nobody back east wanted a female vet. She'd believed moving west, where trained veterinarians were in shorter supply, would be the answer. That the need for her skills would matter more than her gender. That there might actually be a man out west open-minded enough to acknowledge her skills. That she wouldn't have to fight, every single day, to be accepted.

She took a deep breath, knowing she had to convince Mr. Parker he hadn't made a mistake. Moving back home wasn't a possibility. Not only would it mean giving up her dream of being a veterinarian, but it would also prove Clint right. And after the way he'd treated her, she'd never give him the satisfaction of seeing her back in Philadelphia.

She forced a smile she didn't feel. "I have no doubt my being a woman is a shock to you. I realize it's not common, but I assure you that I am everything I claimed to be. My father, as I'm sure you know if you sent for information about him, was the most highly sought after veterinarian in Philadelphia. He was schooled in London. He taught in many cities and towns in Pennsylvania. I learned at his hand and worked alongside him for years.

"I assure you, Mr. Parker, that you won't be disappointed in having hired me. All I ask is that you give me a chance to prove so." Jillian gestured to the darkness behind the windows. "Now if you'll excuse me, it's time I got home. Eileen, thank you for the coffee."

Jillian took her cup to the counter and almost bumped into the other woman when she turned around.

"Jillian, it's the middle of the night and the rain isn't letting up. I won't have you going home in this weather." As though to prove her point a gust of wind splattered a sheet of water against the window.

"It's fine. I'll be home in—"

Eileen held up a hand. "No, I won't have it. You've been through enough tonight. Not only has my son been unquestionably rude, but you've worked hard. Surely you must be tired."

"Exhausted," Jillian answered. "Which is why—"

"Then it's settled. You'll stay the night. Let me just

change the sheets on Wade's bed, and then you can go on up and get some sleep."

"What?" Jillian sputtered.

Wade leapt to his feet at the same time. "Ma!"

James chuckled and slipped out of the kitchen into the porch as Wade's mother ignored them all and went upstairs.

Chapter Two

WADE DREW IN a deep breath, filled his lungs with moist, mountain air. Exhaling slowly, he rolled his shoulders, willed his tight muscles to relax. As far as days went, he'd had better but he'd certainly had worse. And, with the cow and calf alive and breathing, he was fully aware just how worse things could have gone.

Of course that didn't change facts. The work that needed to get done multiplied faster than rabbits, while the time and money needed to accomplish it seemed to do the complete opposite.

It wasn't only the ranch that required his money and attention, however. He also had Annabelle, his eight-year-old daughter to consider. And now, thanks to Jillian Matthews, the added responsibility of having to hire a new vet, which would take yet more time away from the ranch.

He rubbed his brow, exhaled heavily. But it could have been worse.

Still, he could use a good shot of whiskey. Knowing his mother would be all too happy to discuss the woman who was nestled between his sheets, and knowing Scott wouldn't have any, Wade tugged his hat low and angled for James's bunkhouse.

He hurried through the downpour, past his mother's garden. The smell of mud and spring leaves followed him to James's door. There were three cabins in total; James occupied the first in the row. Scott, who'd been with Wade for five years, slept in the middle one. The last one was vacant and, other than needing to be cleaned, it would work for another hand when the ranch was doing better and he could afford to pay one. When. Not if. If wasn't an option.

"It's open," James called after Wade's knock.

Wade took off his hat, stepped in, and closed the door. The cabin was small but accommodated a table and two chairs, a stove, a few cupboards, a bookshelf and a bunk along the back wall. James sat reading a book under the lantern, which hung off a rusty nail just over his bed.

"Why do I get the feeling you were expecting me?"

James peered at him over the cover of his book. "I know Eileen. No way was she going to let that filly go home tonight. And I knew you wouldn't cotton to sleeping in the parlor."

Wade tugged off his muddy boots and dumped his wet jacket on top. In sock feet he unrolled the bedroll James kept by his door and laid it next to the table. His foreman was right. The couch in the parlor was hardly long enough for three small people to sit side by side. He couldn't cram his six foot tall body into it without having his knees pressed to his armpits all night. And, with his ma and daughter sharing the only other bedroom, that didn't leave Wade with a whole lot of options.

"Got any whiskey?"

"You know where I keep it."

Wade took a clean cup from the counter and poured himself a healthy dose. He downed it in one swallow.

The fire burned a swath clear to his stomach.

Sitting on the bedroll, Wade tugged off his socks and shirt then sprawled on the blankets. The wool was rough on his back.

"That was some fine doctorin' she did."

Wade sighed. *So much for getting any peace in here.* "I guess she did all right."

"All right? She sat in your decrepit barn, up to her knees in mud and blood and still managed to save two of your animals. I'd say she did a mighty fine job."

"Fine." He conceded, albeit grudgingly as it still grated on him that she'd misrepresented herself. "She saved my animals."

"It was a shock to see a woman come in when we were expecting old Doc, though, wasn't it?"

Wade stacked his hands beneath his head. "I was sure it was you and Scott up to your no good tricks again."

"Wish we could take the credit. Lord knows it would've been our best yet. But seeing as how it wasn't, I'd say we came out ahead of the bargain."

"How do you figure that?"

"Not only is Miz Matthews a fine doctor, but she's pretty as a picture, too."

"Hell, here we go," Wade grumbled.

"Amy's been gone for a while now, Wade. It don't hurt to look at other women."

"James, I get enough of this from Ma."

"Well, she's right. You haven't looked at another woman since Amy died."

"I don't have time. I have the new barn to finish before the wedding, a ranch to get back on its feet and a daughter to raise."

Besides that, there was no way in hell he'd ever get mixed up with a woman like Jillian. Sure she was pretty, but Amy had been pretty, too. He'd loved his wife, would have given his life for her. And still it hadn't been enough.

"Those are all fine excuses, Wade, but the wedding is mine and I'm paying for it. You're hardly alone raising Annabelle; you have your ma and me, not to mention Scott. And as for the barn, I told you that I'd help. Hell, I've told you since your pa died that I'd—"

"I'm not taking your money, James. This is my ranch and I'm—"

"Just as goddamn stubborn as your father was." James finished. "He wouldn't let me help him either."

"It's not help, James, it's charity, and I'm not taking it." Wade rolled to his side and jammed the pillow beneath his head. He'd make his own way.

The small bunkhouse fell quiet. The tension in his shoulders was starting to ease and his eyes were drifting shut when James's chuckle rumbled from the end of the cabin.

"Miz Matthews sure got under your skin. I don't think I've seen a fire give off more sparks."

"I don't appreciate being made a fool of, not to mention the position her lie has put me in."

"Or maybe you just don't appreciate the way she reminds you of what you've been missing."

Wade rolled to his other side, wide-awake again. He jabbed at his pillow some more in an attempt to get comfortable. The only reason Jillian had gotten under his skin was because of the misconception she'd deliberately created. It had nothing to do with the punch to the gut he'd first felt when her green eyes had met his. It had nothing to do with the heat that had licked along his skin when she'd stretched, when her breasts had strained against her blouse. And it especially had nothing to do with the fact that, even now, he couldn't help but wonder, was she naked in his bed?

★

"Who are you?"

Jillian dragged her way through a thick fog of dreams and pried her eyes open. A young girl with dark braids and sparkling blue eyes stood next to the bed, her small arms were crossed over her chest. Her foot tapped the floor as she awaited an answer.

Jillian pushed herself to a sitting position as last night's events streamed through her mind. Though it now made sense why she was in a room that wasn't her own, it didn't explain who this child was.

"Who are you?" She countered.

"Annabelle. Why are you in my papa's bed?"

Jillian blinked. "Your papa?" Wade had a daughter?

She looked around the room again in case there was something she'd missed last night, but it remained the same sparsely furnished, masculine room. If he had a daughter, where was his wife? And why wasn't she sleeping in his bed?

"Are you getting married? James and my grandma are getting married this summer."

"Oh. Well."

"Do you know where my papa is?"

"In the kitchen?" Jillian volunteered, figuring whether she was wrong or not it would at least send the girl looking and give Jillian time to make sense of things.

"Are you going to be staying in my papa's room again tonight?"

"Definitely not," Jillian answered.

"Why? Don't you like my papa?"

Good Lord, the child asked as many questions as her father.

"Annabelle!" Eileen strode into the room, took her granddaughter's hand. "I'm sorry, Jillian. Far as I know, since both Wade and I are up at dawn, she comes straight down in the mornings. If I'd known she'd barge in on you I'd have kept an ear open for her."

"It's fine, Eileen. After all, it is her home and she had no way of knowing I would be here."

"Well, be that as it may, she didn't need to linger and pester you with questions. What do you say to Miss Matthews?" Eileen asked.

"I'm sorry," the girl mumbled, looking down at her boots.

"We'll leave you to get dressed, dear. Come on, Annabelle, I've got your breakfast ready."

★

JILLIAN CLOSED THE front door behind her and leaned against it. Calling out a quick goodbye while Eileen's attention was focused on wiping up Annabelle's spilled milk was cowardly, but it was simpler that way. All she wanted was to check on the cow and get back to her own quiet house. Especially after last night. Even alone, there was something unsettling about sleeping in a man's bed.

The dust that had choked the air since her arrival in Montana a few days ago was gone. In its place was the clean smell of earth after a good rain. Around the yard site, newly formed leaves trembled in the breeze and above her the blue sky stretched forever.

Taking the boots she'd carried, she sat down on the step.

The laces were crusty with cracked mud when she bent to tie them. A moo in the pasture behind the corrals turned her attention to the herd of cattle. A hundred head, maybe more. Past the animals, green hills rolled toward the grey, snow-capped mountains. It made a stunning picture against the sharp blue of the sky.

Now that she could see the ranch in full daylight, Jillian scanned the yard with interest. Though she had no way of knowing just how much land the Parkers owned, the yard site was quite small. Jillian frowned as her eyes fell on the barn. Whatever color it may have been was long gone, exposing the cracked and worn boards beneath it. Some of them sagged like an over-burdened clothesline. As her gaze went to the roof, she grimaced. More worn and weathered wood there, no doubt due to harsh winters.

A few corrals were coupled between the old barn and the newly framed structure that must be its replacement while others jutted from either side. Her horse and several others stood proud in the morning light, their tails switching lazily. Behind the barn, three cabins marched in a perfect line.

Taking her bags and raising her split skirt to avoid the worst of the mud, Jillian crossed the yard. Wade met her at the door to the barn and she knew by the slit of his eyes and the pinching of his mouth that something awful had happened.

"What's wrong?" she asked, though a part of her feared she already knew. There had been all that bleeding.

"The cow's dead."

Even suspecting the news would be bad didn't lessen the blow. She hated losing any animal, but a mother always seemed so much worse.

"She must have bled out. I'll know once I- What are you doing?" she demanded when he took a step to the side and blocked her path.

"She's dead. Nothing you can do."

"But—"

"I have more than enough to do here without letting you play at what can't be fixed."

"Play?" She scowled.

Just then James came out of the barn with her saddle.

"James will saddle your horse."

"But if I could see her"—Jillian tried again—"it would help me understand—"

"Understanding won't change the facts and I've got work to do."

He turned, grabbed a shovel, and marched around the corrals, heading for the pasture, no doubt going to dig the grave.

Culpability settled heavily on her shoulders as she thought of the loss, of what, if anything, she could have done differently. For a long time, she simply looked into the barn and wondered. What had gone wrong?

"Miz Matthews?"

She turned to the foreman who'd not only prepared her

horse but had also managed to open and close the paddock gate without Jillian hearing.

James handed her the reins.

"Wade's not usually so coldhearted; he just has a lot on his mind."

He wasn't the only one.

Jillian looked to the dim interior of the barn. More than anything she wanted to see the cow; learn what had gone wrong. But Wade had made his feelings on the matter clear. Just as he'd made his feelings on her being the new vet clear last night. She could admit he had reason to be angry with her over her deliberate withholding of her first name but he had no reason to be angry about the cow. Not if he wouldn't let her see what had happened. She couldn't be sure it was her fault without doing a proper examination.

Yet despite her best efforts, despite believing she'd done everything right, an animal had died after she'd treated it. Jillian wasn't a fool. It didn't matter that she'd done her best; that she felt awful for the loss. She knew, despite both truths that what had happened here didn't bode well for her.

Not well at all.

★

LONG SMEARS OF crimson and mauve with an overlap of orange played peek-a-boo in the western sky as Wade rode into Marietta. At this time of day, Marietta's long, main street was mostly bare. Children were getting washed and ready for bed, the mercantile and most other businesses were closed until morning. Wade hardly saw a soul until he reached the end of the street and the two saloons that crowned the corners of Main Street, Grey's and Silver's.

There weren't more than five horses tied in front of his friend Silver's establishment. The same couldn't be said for Grey's.

Across the street, Grey's Saloon was doing a brisk business. Near a dozen horses lingered along the hitching rail, pans and picks dangling from saddles as their mining owners drank away their good fortune. Or drank for the lack of it. It was hard to say which.

On the balustraded balcony that perched over Grey's front door, whores paraded their wares. Through the swinging saloon doors, Wade heard the shrill giggles of the painted women and the deep chuckles of the randy miners and prospectors. It was a sight Wade didn't have a problem imagining as he'd spent many Saturday nights there before he'd met Amy. In fact, most single men were very well acquainted with Grey's Saloon.

Grey's Saloon, while not exactly the pillar of respectability, was nonetheless the heart of Marietta. Its owner, Ephraim Grey, had built it when the town was nothing but an old, fur trading post. From there, businesses and folks had moved in and Marietta had grown. It was only about two years ago that Silver Adams had come to town and turned an abandoned barn into Silver's Saloon.

Where Grey's was as much brothel as saloon, Silver kept a clean and tidy saloon. Gambling was allowed, but no whoring. She hired respectable women to serve the drinks and the rooms upstairs were all her own. To Wade's knowledge, nobody had ever been up there but Silver herself. Not that that stopped the townsfolk from judging and believing different. Still, while they talked, the wives still preferred their husbands to patron Silver's over Grey's. But as each saloon met a different need, scratched a different itch, Silver and Ephraim coexisted without any hostility that Wade had ever noticed.

Tying Whiskey alongside the other horses in front of Silver's, he loosened the cinch on the saddle and took a moment to scratch his horse's neck.

"I won't be long, boy," he said before giving the animal an affectionate pat and stepping onto the boardwalk.

"Well, look what the wind blew in."

Wade turned, grinned. "Out looking for trouble, Sheriff?"

"Why, plan on giving me any?"

Shane McCall's badge glowed silver and bright as it caught the light spilling from the saloon doors. Nearly everything else on Shane was black; hair, pants, vest. His shirt, which was laundered and starched by a widow who fed her brood of four growing boys by doing laundry and mending, gleamed white against the black.

Wade had known Shane since they were eleven. They'd

gone to school together, smoked their first cheroot together and gotten drunk for the first time together. He'd always considered Shane his brother, and still did, though he now also included Scott in that distinction.

"You're safe, tonight. I'm just here for a drink or two." And he wouldn't dwell on the fact he really couldn't spare the money for one, let alone two.

"Good. And now that you've finally dragged your sorry butt into town, you can tell me all about the pretty lady that slept in your bed."

Grey eyes danced as Wade's narrowed.

"Goddamn, Scott has a big mouth."

"He came to see me at home, so you don't have to worry about anyone overhearing. Although given your boring reputation, something like this wouldn't hurt."

Wade pushed open the saloon doors.

Wednesday nights didn't draw a big crowd at Silver's; it was one of the reasons he'd come tonight. A merry tune came from the piano that sat beneath the oak balustrade, which overlooked the array of tables and the polished cherrywood bar. Behind the bar was an assortment of bottles containing the best whiskey this side of Bozeman, gleaming glasses, and the woman who looked after it all.

Silver Adams's hair was as light as Shane's was dark. Slim and of medium height, she didn't look strong enough or tough enough to run a saloon, but Wade had seen her order more than one drunk out of her establishment. And while physically she wasn't strong enough to toss out anybody, the man who helped tend bar was. Bruce was near as big as the mountain that overlooked Marietta and his fists were rumored to be hard as granite.

Silver didn't tolerate anyone breaking up her place. If anyone proved to be more than she could handle, Bruce took care of them for her. Since a good portion of her patrons was married men whose wives wouldn't allow them to step foot in Grey's, Silver didn't usually have too much trouble.

Other than a table of three miners he'd seen around once or twice, there were only two other men—local businessmen—in the saloon. They were sidled up to the bar. Wade tipped his hat in greeting then he and Shane took the empty stools next to them.

"Evenin' gentlemen," Silver said, her smile bright. "I was starting to miss your handsome faces. Why haven't I seen you lately?"

"I had some late calves due, couldn't get away. Thanks," he added when she placed his drink before him.

"And here I'd been hoping it was 'cause you found someone pretty to spend your time with."

Jillian's face came to mind but he shook his head to clear the vision. "Nope, just work."

"Well, I'm not giving up hope on you, Wade." She then fixed her caramel-colored eyes on Shane. "Well, what's your excuse?"

Shane took a swallow of his whiskey. "Just because I

don't ranch doesn't mean I'm not busy, too."

Silver crossed her arms. "Well, I suppose I could have missed a stage coach robbery, or a gang of outlaws riding in. I live and work right here, but I suppose I could have been too busy to hear the hoopla."

Wade choked on his whiskey. When he'd recovered his breath he gave Silver a warm smile. "Thanks, Silver, I needed a good laugh."

She dropped one of her hands onto his. "Aw, something wrong, honey?"

It wasn't that he particularly wanted to talk about it, but he couldn't stop thinking about Jillian and the fact that if she hadn't lied about who she was, she wouldn't have been there to begin with. Either Doc or a new male doctor would have been and then maybe he wouldn't have lost an animal he couldn't afford to lose.

"One of my cows was having problems calving. I sent Scott for the vet."

Silver grabbed a glass, started polishing it. "Doc Fletcher couldn't save it?"

"Wish I knew," Wade said with a shake of his head. "Wasn't Doc Fletcher who showed up."

"Doc's gone? I knew he was leaving, but I thought he'd come say goodbye first."

"I did, too. But I suppose once his replacement arrived he couldn't get away fast enough."

"Well, he did say he missed his children and grandchildren."

"If only that were the case, Silver. I suspect he fled—and I do mean fled—because he knew we wouldn't be happy with his replacement and we'd want him to stay on longer."

"What's wrong with his replacement?" Silver asked.

Shane elbowed Wade. "Tell her."

Wade finished off his drink, nodded for another. "Doc's replacement is a woman."

Silver bobbled the bottle and amber liquid spilled onto the bar.

"The new vet's a woman?" she asked, drawing the attention of the two businessmen, "and you didn't know?"

"Of course I didn't know!" Wade argued.

"She's pretty, too. According to Scott," Shane answered when Silver's annoyed gaze fixed on his.

"Well," Silver said, focusing her attention on cleaning up the spill. "Unexpected as that may be, did she do a good job?"

"I wouldn't say so. The cow died." Wade took another swallow.

Silver's hand stilled. Murmuring to each other, the two men next to Wade slapped coins on the bar and left.

"What happened? She didn't know what to do?"

"She seemed to." And that was the part that was hard to swallow for Wade. Despite his misgivings and his anger, she *had* seemed to know what she was doing. Still, he couldn't help but wonder if things would have been different had Doc been there?

He told them what he knew of her and how she'd come to be at Doc's place. Then he described the surgery and how the cow had seemed all right when they'd left her.

"Oh, Wade, I'm sorry for your loss, but that doesn't mean it was her fault."

"Don't be defending her just cause she's a woman, Silver."

Silver stood hipshot. "And don't you be condemning her for it, neither. You said yourself she was trained by her father and you were more than happy to hire him."

"Maybe it was her fault, maybe it would have happened had Doc been there. I wish I could know what would have happened had it been Doc."

"Wade, honey." Silver soothed. "That kind of thinking will drive you crazy."

Wade pressed his fingers over his tired eyes. "You're right. Either way the cow is dead." And he'd taken yet another step back in his dream of moving from cattle to horse ranching.

"The calf lived. It could have been worse. You could have lost them both."

And he almost had. He remembered how the calf hadn't breathed, how upset Jillian had been. How she'd worked fast to get it breathing.

"What are your plans now?" Shane asked.

Wade dropped his hands, looked at his friend. "For the

ranch?"

"No, for the vet. You and Doc hired her but Doc's gone. It's just a matter of time before word gets out she's his replacement. When it does, folks will be coming to you for answers. What are you planning on telling them?"

"That I didn't know she was a woman either."

"I imagine they're going to want to know if you plan on keeping her on or if you plan on advertising for another one."

"Hell, trying to get another one could take months. Look how long it took to find her."

Shane held up his hands. "Don't shoot the messenger. I was just pointing out that when you hired this new vet you thought your problems for replacing Doc were over. But it seems to me they may have just begun."

Chapter Three

Steven Garvey was exhausted. His shoulders ached from a long day at the feed mill. His head throbbed from his wife's nattering, which had been incessant since he'd gotten home from that long day. Jacob, his eight-year-old son, had woven tales of exploits in between his mother's breaths. Was it any wonder Steven had tucked his whiskey bottle into his jacket and escaped to the barn?

His first few pulls on the bottle were fast, a desperate stab at relaxation. But now, with his throat and belly warm from the alcohol and with the sharp edges smoothed out, Steven settled into the straw and sighed. For the first time all day, things were blessedly quiet.

Horses, at least two by the sound of hooves pounding on dirt, broke his peace. Steven cursed his luck. He should have known it was too good to last. He contemplated ignoring the visitors but quickly dismissed the thought. Though most folks saw him at the feed mill if they had town concerns, a few preferred to talk to their mayor away from prying eyes and keen ears.

Besides, whoever it was that had come would likely go to

the house and his wife would end up screaming for him from the porch. No, he'd had enough of her shrieks for one day. Tucking the bottle into the straw—he was still mayor after all—Steven went outside.

The sun had tumbled over the Gallatin mountain range a good hour ago but there was enough light lingering to recognize his friends.

"Over here," he called out.

Bill and Robert looked over their shoulders, changed their direction. Steven had no idea what they were doing there as they didn't normally stop by. Usually, whatever they had to talk about was done either at the feed mill or at Silver's during their weekly poker game.

It didn't take long to learn the reason for their unexpected visit. They'd barely tied the horses before Robert turned from the rail.

"Wade hired us a woman vet."

Steven opened his mouth. Then shut it and opened it again. He shook his head. "He did what?"

"The vet Wade and Doc hired? It's a woman. Wade was just at Silver's talking about it."

He hadn't had that much whiskey, but he might as well have been falling down drunk for all the sense these two were making. "How is that possible? There's no such thing as a woman vet." And he knew damn well he'd never agreed to hire one at the town meeting where—to his frustration—he'd had to side with the rest of the folks and leave Wade and Doc in charge of hiring Doc's replacement.

"Well, apparently there is," Robert answered.

Bill wasn't tall; he was a brick of a man with thick shoulders and no neck to speak of. His eyes were like pistols, cold and hard, when they fixed on Steven. "I own the stable, what the hell am I supposed to do if an animal in my care needs a vet? I ain't calling no woman doctor. Especially one who has already killed one animal."

Blood was beginning to thrum in Steven's ears. "She killed an animal?"

"According to Wade, she killed his cow," Robert answered while Bill stood there, nostrils flaring and breath heaving like a raging bull.

Steven spun back into the barn, knowing they'd follow. Figuring it couldn't hurt at this point, he grabbed his bottle from the straw then dropped into the chair he used when oiling his tack. The whiskey sloshed in the bottle as he took a long drink. Bill and Robert strode in, Bill's spurs jingling. They took up on the opposite side of the aisle.

"How the hell did this happen?" Steven asked.

"I don't know," Robert answered. "None of the telegrams I saw gave any indication it was a woman wanting the job," Robert said, referring to his position at the post and telegraph office.

"I don't care if he knew or not," Bill said, frothing at the mouth. "Animal doctoring's a man's job."

"I don't rightly care, one way or the other, either. But he

will fix this. Didn't I say, when the town met to discuss replacing Doc, that I'd do the hiring? But, no, Wade had to step up and volunteer." He sneered, remembering the day well.

That was the day the town had trusted Wade over their own mayor. The day Steven had to graciously accept their majority decision all the while cursing the man who'd never stopped being a thorn in Steven's side. Wasn't it enough that Wade had had more friends in school? That he'd been better at ciphering and reading? That he'd turned Amy's head just when Steven thought he'd finally gotten her attention?

For years he'd lived in Wade Parker's shadow. Until he'd become mayor. Then finally, he'd had a say; he'd had respect. Until he'd been made a fool of, yet again, by the town's love for Wade. How humiliating it had been to hear them say, "Why don't we let Wade and Doc look after it? After all, Wade's a rancher and who better than a rancher and our own vet to know what we need?"

Swallowing the anger and the hurt had nearly choked him. Well, now they'd see, wouldn't they? They'd see just how bloody smart Wade was.

★

HE'D FORGOTTEN ALL about paying her.

Between the urgency of the surgery, the confusion of her being Doc's replacement and the cow dying, it had slipped Wade's mind. Regardless of his still being angry about being misled, he couldn't, in good conscience, delay bringing her the money he owed her. He'd called for a vet and though he'd lost one animal, he could have lost both.

Not that it made parting with the money any easier. He'd not only had to swallow his pride and ask James to make up the total amount since he hadn't had enough on his own, but he'd also had to dip into the little money he had saved to go toward a quality breeding mare.

James had offered to pay the whole amount and let Wade keep the money for the mare, but Wade had refused. As much as he could, he'd pay his own way.

No matter how much it hurt.

Yellow tulips marked the end of the lane. Old Doc Fletcher's place—well, hers now—wasn't more than a one-story house and a small barn. Two small corrals were nestled against the barn. One was empty; a beautiful chestnut mare grazed contentedly in the other. It didn't seem troubled by the blazing sun that sent waves of heat shimmering along the ground. Just behind the corrals, within a small pasture, a cow and calf basked in the sun.

Hearing them approach, the mare raised her head, pricked her ears, and pranced to the fence. With big brown eyes she watched as they walked by. Whiskey, smelling the mare, kept his eye on her as well, though he was well-mannered enough to keep to Wade's direction.

Wade didn't see Jillian anywhere, but figuring she'd be inside where it was cooler, headed for the house. He'd no sooner tied Whiskey to her porch when he heard footsteps behind him.

Her hair was once again folded into a thick braid and, like she'd worn in his barn, her sleeves were rolled to her elbows. She wore a dirty apron over her skirt and in her hand she carried a pitchfork.

Her skirt scattered dust as she moved. Green eyes never left his as she came to stand before him. She poked the tines of the pitchfork into the dirt between them.

"Mr. Parker."

He pushed his hat back. "Miss Matthews."

Freckles he hadn't noticed the other day danced across her cheeks and bridged her nose. He had the most ridiculous urge to trace them with his fingers.

Hell, Wade, you've got enough damn problems. A woman like Jillian—the likes of which he'd sworn off after Amy died—was the last thing he, or Annabelle, needed.

"Before you say anything," she said as he opened his mouth, "I'd like you to come with me." She yanked the fork from the ground and headed toward the barn.

His eyes fell to the sway of her hips. He couldn't deny, despite the tension between them, the view was amazing. And it stirred blood that had gone far too long without being stirred. Whether he liked it or not.

The damp coolness of the barn enveloped him as soon he stepped through the doors. He sighed in relief, tugged at the shirt that had clung to his back within moments of leaving the ranch.

The barn smelled of straw and hay and a menagerie of animals, several of which shuffled in their pens at his presence. Wade blinked as his eyes adjusted to the dim light. Since he'd never had reason to be inside Doc's barn before, what he saw surprised him.

"You couldn't have possibly brought all these with you from Pennsylvania," he said.

"I didn't. They were your Doc Fletcher's and I agreed to keep them since he didn't want to take them along."

The barn had a short aisle with stalls on either side. Jillian moved to the first one and Wade followed. The stall door was open and she stepped through it, lifted a cage off the ground and brought it forward. Inside a plump white rabbit twitched its nose incessantly. It backed to the far edge of the cage and thumped its back foot.

"Mr. Fletcher named him Whiskers. He's not used to me yet, but I'm working on bringing him 'round."

She poked her fingers through the cage. The rabbit thumped again. She put the cage down and moved to the next, slightly larger stall. A Billy goat came right over to the gate, its mouth reaching to nibble on her skirt.

"This is Zeke. Mr. Fletcher warned me he eats everything in sight, so watch your clothes." She gave the goat an affectionate scratch under the chin, then gently turned its face before it could gnaw on her clothes.

"You don't keep him outside?"

"I put all of them out during the day. I was about to move him when I heard you ride up."

A scuttling sound across the aisle drew their attention.

"Hello, Rascal," Jillian said. "According to Mr. Fletcher, Rascal here kept finding his way into the house and making a mess of things. He tried shooing him away but Rascal always came back. Miles figured the best way to keep his property intact was to keep the raccoon caged."

Jillian shrugged. "I'm thinking of letting him go. Doesn't seem right to keep a wild animal penned up."

"And if he makes a mess of your house?" Wade asked.

For the first time he saw a real smile from her and it knocked the breath from his lungs. Her hands were smudged with dirt, the bottom of her skirt was dusty and soiled from cleaning stalls, but her face glowed. Life filled her eyes and Wade couldn't help but stare.

"I guess if he does it more than once I'll have to rethink the decision to keep him caged. Come on, there's one last thing I want you to see."

Wade followed her to the outside paddock and the pretty little chestnut mare he'd seen when he'd ridden up. The horse leaned her head against Jillian and was rewarded with a scratch on the neck.

"This is the only animal I brought with me from home," she began, "and her name is Hope."

He propped a boot on the lowest slat, braced his forearms on the rail. Though he had yet to figure out why she was doing this, he was interested. And despite himself, he enjoyed the sweet sound of her voice.

"There was an old man who lived a few miles north of the city. He had a farm, a good one actually, at one time. But after his wife died, his own health started to deteriorate. He slowly began losing his mind. It was his doctor, a friend of my father's, who said the man had animals and wasn't looking after them properly. Honestly, most times I think he believed he'd fed them already. He had a few arguments about that when my father commented on how thin some of them were. He swore he'd only just come back from feeding them.

"Anyhow, my father did his best to look in on him, but he had other people depending on him, clients as well as family. Time began to stretch between visits. He'd bring feed with him, but each time he brought more, it was to find the last bags he'd brought were still mostly full.

"The last time we rolled into that yard, the stench was terrible. Animals lay rotting in the snow. We found the old man dead in his bed. We tried to save the animals that were left, but they were too far gone. Most had starved or were too close to death to bring them back.

"Hope was the last standing and I took her home with me that day. It took a while, and there was a time we weren't sure she'd ever recover, but she did."

"How old is she?"

"Three."

Wade looked the filly over. She was gorgeous. Nice lines, solid confirmation. "Do you know her pedigree?"

"Since she was born before his mind was too lost, he had all the papers in his house." Jillian gave the horse another pat. "She has excellent breeding."

Had circumstances been different he'd have offered to buy the mare then and there. The picture of the colt that could come from this animal and Whiskey was clear as the Yellowstone River which ran through his property. Wade's heart filled with longing. If only...

"Why did you show me these animals?" he asked.

"Because, Mr. Parker, I love them. All of them. And even though I've only been here a few days, I'd do anything to protect them and keep them healthy. It's not only what I do, it's who I am."

She squared her shoulders. Considering he knew he was in for a lecture, he shouldn't have noted how it made the cotton stretch over her breasts.

"I'm terribly sorry about your cow. I swear to you, I did everything right. Sometimes these things just happen, despite our best efforts. Medicine isn't perfect, Mr. Parker. I know you think things may have been different had Mr. Fletcher been the one to operate, but this wasn't my first cesarean. My father was well respected in veterinary medicine and I learned at his side. I'm not here to play at being a veterinarian; I am one."

Part of him admired the gumption it took to stand up

and defend herself. Part of him thought she was damn pretty. The rest of him warned not to be swayed by either fact. She'd never be content with a man like him, a simple rancher.

"I suppose I partly deserved that."

She raised her brows. "Partly?"

Wade pushed away from the corral.

"I stand behind the fact that you deliberately misled us when you accepted our position. Because of that, and due to the dire circumstances, I was angry and upset."

"You accused me of killing your animal."

"I know, and for that I'm sorry. I've cooled off since then. I know things could have been worse, that I could have lost them both if you hadn't been there."

Her shoulders eased. He expected her to say something about how she was glad he'd come to his senses. How she'd told him from the beginning she knew what she was doing. Instead she simply nodded.

"I know that I wasn't completely honest when you hired me but, Mr. Parker, I can do this. I've trained for it my whole life. All I ask is that, despite what happened at your ranch, I be given a fair chance."

Wade took off his hat, clasped it between his hands. "I can't speak for how folks around here will take the news of you being a woman."

"About as well as you did, I imagine," she said with a smile.

She really was a spitfire. His mouth curved. "More than likely. They're not going to be happy with either one of us, I'm afraid."

"Tell them you didn't know I was a woman; that should leave you blameless."

Maybe he hadn't known at the time, but he sure as hell couldn't deny she was a woman now. Wade blew out his breath. "I'm not sure that'll be enough to pacify them all. At any rate, I can't force them to call on you."

"You're acceptance would go a long way to reassure them."

"Well, that puts me in a hell of a position."

"Why? You just acknowledged that I wasn't to blame for your cow. All you have to do is say the truth. That I did good work and you'd call on me again should the need arise."

A kick of breeze spun between them. It brought along Jillian's scent, an intriguing mix of soap, sun and the unmistakable smell of a woman's heated flesh. He swallowed hard as his heart lurched and his groin thickened. Well, the need was arising right now, but it wasn't the one she was speaking of.

She regarded him closely, her pretty green eyes probing his. "You do stand behind your decision to hire me, don't you?"

Hell. If he supported Jillian, he'd rile at least half the town. But how could he not support her, considering he'd brought her here? She'd moved across a country, for Pete's sake. How could he simply tell her to turn around and go back? And, as he'd witnessed, she did appear to be a fine doctor. It was just as Shane had said, however, that his problems where the vet was concerned were just beginning.

"Yes, Jillian. I stand behind my decision to hire you."

She blessed him with another smile, this one even more potent than the last. He needed to leave before he fooled himself into thinking it would be safe to explore the desire drumming through his blood. She was a woman hell-bent on following her dream regardless of the cost. Since Wade had already paid that price once, he refused to pay it again. No matter what his body wanted.

Fishing into his pocket, he took the folded bills and handed them to her. "I never asked what your fees are, but James and I reckoned this should be close. If it's not, let me know." He jammed his hat back onto his head and crossed the yard to fetch his horse.

He put his foot in the stirrup. Her small but firm hand closed around his arm. It was the first time she'd touched him and it grabbed him 'round the throat. Slowly, he turned.

Lord, she was close. Close enough to see the gold flecks in her green eyes. Close enough to hear her breathing. Close enough to grab and yank her against him. He cleared his throat, hoped to hell she didn't look down.

"What is it?"

"When my father died, he left me a small inheritance,

enough to get me here and, if I'm frugal, enough for the basic necessities for three to four months. This is my livelihood, Wade, I'll do whatever it takes to get folks to accept me. It means a lot to me that you're on my side."

Of all the things she could have said, those were the most effective. He may not want to get close to her but he couldn't deny her words touched him. Wasn't he, too, simply trying to earn a living? Trying to keep food on the table? While she might have lied, might have chosen an unconventional way of going about it, Wade knew how hard it was some days to just make ends meet. Who was he to make hers any harder?

"I'll stand behind my decision to hire you but, Jillian, I really don't have time to seek out each rancher and farmer around these parts."

Her smile lit her face, captivated him until he had to remind himself to blink. The hand resting on his arm squeezed gently. For two, three beats, their eyes held, questioned. Wade shifted his gaze from to her hand and back again. Her eyes widened, almost as though she'd forgotten she was touching him.

With a fresh, pink flush brightening her cheeks, Jillian lowered her hand. "Thank you."

Afraid if he opened his mouth he'd give in to the urge to wrap his arms around her small waist and pull her in for a kiss, he tipped his hat, mounted Whiskey, and headed for home.

★

DAZED AND CONFOUNDED by her reaction to Wade, Jillian wandered back to Hope's corral. Animals didn't talk, but she definitely understood them better than she understood herself. Jillian grabbed the brush from the bucket in the corner and, with long slow strokes that soothed Hope as much as they did her, brushed her horse.

She'd gotten a silly flutter in her belly when she stepped from the barn and saw Wade at her porch. Considering his last words to her, she shouldn't have felt anything toward him but anger. Not that she hadn't felt that as well, but underneath the fury had been an undeniable, completely female and nonrational flicker of attraction.

The flicker had turned to flame when she'd touched him. In his barn, they'd touched due to confinement and though she'd felt a reaction then, it didn't compare to the pull she'd felt this time.

"Nothing like it," she murmured, remembering the feel of muscle beneath her hand, the way he'd looked at her.

But then she knew looks could be deceiving. She'd been fooled by them once before. She'd given Clint her heart, almost shared her body, only to learn he'd expected—no, demanded—she give up her silly desire to remain a vet once they were married.

She'd given him back his ring and he'd laughed. Laughed and told her no man would ever want her as long as she was a vet. Laughed and said he couldn't wait for the day she realized that and came home begging to have him back.

His laughter echoed in her ears, continued to sting in that part of her heart that had yet to heal. It was the reminder she needed. Handsome or not, desirable or not, she wouldn't open her heart again to that kind of rejection. She'd do whatever it took to prove Clint wrong, because, as God was her witness, she wasn't ever going back to Pennsylvania. Even though she'd never take Clint back, even if he begged, she'd never give him the satisfaction of seeing her back home.

Hope's head lifted. Jillian looked over as another rider turned into her lane. Tossing the brush into the bucket, giving a quick glance to ensure there was water in the other, Jillian set her soiled apron over the rail and slipped from the pen.

Could it be someone needed her already? Or, had word gotten around about Wade's cow and the fact that their new vet was a woman and they'd come to demand she leave?

She placed a hand over her belly in an attempt to still the nerves and stood tall. Whoever it was, for whatever reason, she would only let them see her confidence. She smoothed her skirt and waited by her porch as the man in black slid out of the saddle.

He was almost as tall as Wade and appeared to be close to the same age. Equally as fine-looking, too, she realized when he took off his hat and she saw his midnight black hair and grey eyes. Catching the glint of silver and unable to miss the gun belt riding low on his hips, Jillian wondered what reason the sheriff had to call on her.

"Afternoon, Miss Matthews."

"Sheriff." She cocked her head to the side. "Should I be concerned that you already know my name?"

His lips curved into a very nice smile. "It's not a bad thing. Word gets 'round in a small town."

"I imagine it does." She gestured to the porch. "Would you like to sit? I can get you some sun tea."

"No, thanks. I won't be staying long."

"Then what can I do for you?"

He leaned against the rail of the porch, crossed his arms. "Town's beginning to buzz about you."

Well, she'd expected it but nevertheless her stomach clenched. "That didn't take long."

"Never does. Anyhow, I thought I'd let you know it's not good."

"I didn't expect it would be, Sheriff, but I'm prepared to stay so I hope it's not running me off you were after."

"Nah. We're mostly harmless around here." He extended his hand. "I never introduced myself. Shane McCall."

"A pleasure, Sheriff," she said as she took his hand.

"Or Shane. Whichever you prefer. Just don't call me Mr. McCall; that was my father."

From the shadows that crept into his eyes, Jillian gathered that Shane had some hard feelings toward the man.

"All right. Shane it is. Are you sure I can't offer you anything?"

"No, I'm fine. I need to be heading back. Just wanted to come introduce myself and let you know where you stood." He placed a boot in the stirrup. "I don't expect anyone around here to give you any real trouble, they're mostly just jawing. But should that change, you be sure to let me know."

"I will, thank you."

He tipped his hat, swung the rest of the way in the saddle. "Good day, Jillian."

"Shane."

She watched him ride away, tall and handsome. His dark hair and clothes, along with the six-shooter he carried, gave him a commanding presence. She imagined if he weren't married he'd have any number of eligible young women swooning. Yet, no matter how much she thought Shane attractive and pleasant, the sizzle of attraction she'd felt with Wade hadn't been there with Shane.

She gave herself a mental shake. "You have more important things to worry about, Jillian, than handsome men." If the townsfolk were starting to buzz, then it was time she threw herself into the hive.

★

HEAT CLOAKED WADE as he made his way home, and it wasn't all due to the outside temperature. Jillian's smell, her touch. Everything lingered and teased him until riding became damned uncomfortable. He'd had women approach him at church, on his errands in town. He'd known by the way they smiled or found reasons to touch him they'd been interested. The problem was, he wasn't.

Oh, he'd looked. Considered, even. But as much as he wanted a woman who'd be happy to take care of his home, help raise his daughter, attraction was a necessary ingredient in a healthy relationship. And the more of it, the better.

And wasn't it just his luck that the first woman who'd stirred his desires since Amy had died was a woman who, he knew from experience, would never be happy to simply be a wife and mother. A woman bold enough to move across a country for what she wanted wouldn't give it all up for anything. Or anyone.

The fact he hadn't been enough for Amy still stung. The ranch, the family they'd built, hadn't been enough to keep her happy. She'd still wanted more. And, to this day, he didn't have more to offer.

Not with the bills his father had accumulated.

The first time Wade had seen them, he'd been sure there was a mistake. But a closer review showed they were correct. What he hadn't been able to figure out was why. Though not a huge spread, they had a fair-sized herd and the beef prices had been strong. It was his mother who'd finally filled in the blanks one night while he poured over the ledgers at the kitchen table.

"Wade, your father was a kind man," she'd said as she shook her head. "But he was a little too soft-hearted."

She'd gone on about the times his neighbors and friends, in one predicament or another, had come to him in desperation. And Samuel Parker had come through. The problem was he'd gotten himself so far in debt that there had been no one left to help him. The pressure had finally been too much and his heart had given out. Wade had buried his father next to Amy, who'd died only a year before. Who wouldn't have died at all if she hadn't found her husband lacking.

He crested a hill. Seeing the ranch, Whiskey shook his head, whinnied to announce his presence to the horses waiting in the corral.

"Almost there, boy. Are you ready for a drink?"

Lord knew Wade was. Every time he swallowed, he tasted grit. All he wanted was to get a glass of water from the well then dump a bucketful over his heated body. After that he needed to quit stewing over his problems and get to work. Pity wasn't going to pay the bills.

Outside the barn, he swung off Whiskey, whose tail swished as the usual assortment of flies homed in.

"Let's get you brushed inside where it's cooler."

He patted Whiskey's neck, his hand leaving a dark imprint on the wet hide. Whiskey tossed his head, as though agreeing. Suddenly, Wade caught a whiff of something vile. The pungent smell burned his nostrils. He grimaced. Had the smell been this bad last night or was it the heat of the day that had ripened it?

His frown deepened when he saw chicken feathers scattered in the aisle of the barn. He let go of the reins, knowing Whiskey would stay close. What the hell were chicken feathers doing there? The chickens never came into the barn; they stayed in the coop behind the corrals. Irritated, he stomped forward.

"Now!" Scott yelled.

Wade's gaze jumped to the right. There was Scott, on the floor, one boot propped against a post, the end of a rope in his gloved hands. Wade felt it across his ankle at the same moment he realized just what that meant for him. His gaze zinged to the left and sure enough, there was James holding the other end.

With Wade's momentum already going, his balance slipped out of his control. No matter how he tried to step out or over, they adjusted the rope. He flailed his arms to try and keep on his feet, now knowing why the barn stank and what lay beneath the feathers, but it was no use. Falling forward, all he could do was keep his mouth and eyes closed and use his arms to keep from falling face first.

Shit!

Chapter Four

THE WAGON CLATTERED loudly as Jillian made her way to town. Though anxious to see Marietta for the first time, she wasn't going in with any expectations about the townsfolk. She'd seen her share of men and women who frowned upon her being a doctor and Shane had warned her she could expect more of the same here. But her father had taught her if she wanted to follow in his shoes, she'd have to fight for it. Well, she planned on doing just that.

Jillian grunted as the wagon bounced through a large rut. She tightened her grip on the reins. She'd handle the town, but first she had to navigate this route. The road—if the two dirt furrows cut in the field could be called such—was riddled with rocks, bumps, and ruts. Perched on the edge of the seat with both feet braced on the floor, Jillian figured she'd be lucky to arrive in Marietta without having jarred every tooth out of her jaw.

Fluffy clouds dotted a sky that stretched between the mountain range on her left and the one on her right. The sun was warm in the valley and Jillian imagined several birds would be out singing jubilantly, not that she could hear them for the constant rattle of the wagon and the jingle of the harness.

The sun was at its highest when she rolled into Marietta. Tidy little buildings with painted false fronts lined the wide street and at the end, in the distance, a stunning snow-capped mountain rose above it all. Her stomach fluttered and her surly mood drifted in the breeze. It was so pretty.

She drew back on the reins and, not wanting to miss a single detail, jumped down. Curling her fingers in Hope's halter, Jillian led her horse up the street.

The road was wide enough to turn a team around and it cut between two rows of charming buildings joined by a long boardwalk. She passed the stable and blacksmith, the tailor, the barber, the cobbler, and the doctor.

A mother and two children stepped out of the doctor's office. The woman paused when she saw Jillian. Before she could respond to Jillian's greeting, her youngest broke free of her grasp and ran up the boardwalk, his little feet slapping the planks. His mother grabbed her skirts with one hand and her daughter with the other and gave chase while ordering the young man to stop right that instant. The boy turned the corner and disappeared from sight.

By the time Jillian reached the corner and looked down a short street that connected up with another, the boy had been caught and his mother was blistering his ears. There didn't appear to be any businesses down that way, only houses.

Turning back to Main Street, Jillian saw her destination was just ahead on the right. She tied Hope to the post in front of the mercantile and stepped inside. After the brilliance of the sun, it took her eyes a moment to adjust. The store was surprisingly large and the shelves were lined with more food items, sweets, pots, pans, and bolts of material then she'd imagined a small town would have. Everything smelled crisp and clean, and even the wood floors gleamed with a recent polish.

She'd never been the kind of woman who needed all the fancy trappings that came with a big city but she admitted to liking some pretty things around her. And she was more than pleased to see Marietta wouldn't disappoint her in that regard.

Two women with baskets tucked in the crook of their arms peered around the shelves to see who'd come in. Jillian smiled at them but they looked away and went back to shopping.

"You must be the new vet."

Jillian turned. Standing before her, arms crossed over her white apron, smiled a woman who seemed to be about Mrs. Parker's age. While her graying hair was drawn back into a bun, her face was smooth and her eyes bright as any child's. Jillian couldn't help but respond to the warmth in them.

"I am." She held out her hand. "Jillian Matthews."

The woman clapped both hands around Jillian's. "A pleasure. I'm Letty Daniels and if you need anything you don't see here, let me know, and I can bring it in. 'Course it may take months the way the stage works around here, but the town's working on getting the train to come through so hopefully things will move faster after that."

With her hand still holding Jillian's, Letty pulled her to the back of the store, only releasing her hold to step behind the long counter. Mrs. Daniels opened a large glass bowl and took out two peppermint sticks. At her nod, Jillian accepted one, smiled as the sweetness rolled over her tongue.

Letty leaned forward, her own candy stick still in hand. "You've sure got this town hopping. People haven't stopped cackling all day."

"The sheriff said word had gotten around. I must admit that surprises me. I only got here three days ago and I didn't come through town."

"Marietta isn't big so you'd better get used to the fact that if you sneeze, it'll be town's business by sundown."

"But when I was called to the Parker ranch they had no idea Doc Fletcher had left, let alone that I'd arrived."

"Well…" Letty smiled. "Eileen only comes in once a week to do her shopping and I don't expect her until tomorrow. Wade was over at Silver's last night. I suppose folks heard him talking about you and word spread from there."

"Silver's?"

"Silver's is the respectable saloon down the street. Grey's is the other, across from it and, unlike Silver's, it attracts an unruly bunch. You'll like Silver. She not only owns the saloon, she runs it. And despite what folks around here think, she's a good woman."

One of the women shopping harrumphed.

Letty fisted a hand on her hip, tilted her head to look down the aisle. "Did you need anything, May Bell?"

"No, just had something in my throat," the woman answered and made a show of clearing her throat. "It's better now."

Letty rolled her eyes, turned back to Jillian. "Silver and the Parkers, they're good people."

"Eileen seems very nice." Jillian conceded.

She wasn't sure yet what to make of Wade.

Letty stuck her candy in her mouth, sucked on it for a moment. "Eileen was the first woman who befriended me when we moved to Marietta. I'm glad you met her first. I can't say, from the grumblings I've heard, that the rest will prove as friendly."

Jillian bit her lip. "When I was at the ranch, there was a problem."

"I know, dear, and I was sorry to hear that."

"Word has gotten out already?"

"As I said, it's a small town."

"How bad is it?"

"It's not going to help, you, I'm afraid. But I have to say, even without that poor cow dying, you would have had a hard time. Folks, especially those who've been here since Marietta was founded, tend to think the town belongs to them. So, as an outsider, you wouldn't have been readily accepted anyway. But an outsider doing a man's work? That just makes it worse.

"Now don't get me wrong, Jillian, I'm not one of those. After all, if folks hadn't come, this place would still be nothing but a trading post. New blood keeps a town thriving, brings in businesses. Otherwise, we'd all become stale like week old bread. Unfortunately, not everyone's as open-minded as I am." She nodded toward the front of the store.

Jillian turned around. The two women ducked down, pretended they weren't listening to every word.

"Go on and find what you need, Jillian. I think those women are about done here."

There was pretty yellow material she'd love to sew into curtains, and a simple rug that would look perfect at her front door. But knowing she couldn't be extravagant in her spending, she kept to the basic necessities.

By the time Letty had rung up purchases and walked the women to the door, Jillian had carbolic acid, beeswax for her salve recipe, laudanum, and other medicines for her supplies. Fifteen minutes later Jillian and Letty were loading her purchases in the back of her wagon.

"Thank you for all your help."

"Well, that's what I'm here for." Suddenly Letty's eyes widened and she snapped her fingers. "The church is having a picnic after this Sunday's service. The whole town usually comes and they have races and games for the children, a baseball game for the men as well as a craft and bake sale for the women. It would be a good chance to get to know the people around here."

"Actually, I was thinking of riding around some of the farms, introducing myself."

Letty arched a brow. "You carry a gun?"

Jillian's eyes rounded. "Are you saying I'll need to protect myself against this town?"

Letty shook her head, popped her candy out of her mouth. "Nah, and I'm not sure what stories you've heard back home, but you won't get scalped either. Still there are rattlesnakes and such around here that you don't have back east. Besides, if you were my daughter, I'd tell you to carry a gun. I believe a woman ought to be able to take care of herself."

"I agree. And I can. As it happens I have a rifle tied to my saddle."

"Good girl. Now then, don't forget the picnic. Eileen and I will be there, so you'll have friends to talk to."

Friends. Jillian smiled. Those had been in short supply back home. "I'll look forward to it, then."

"Don't get too excited. While I expect most around here will accept you with time, the truth is some may never. Speaking of which, here comes just the sort."

A very prim-looking woman about Letty's age clipped along the boardwalk, her shoulders thrust back. Jillian wouldn't have been surprised to see a plank holding them that way. Her head was tilted so high it was a wonder she could see where she was going. As she approached them, her gaze flitted over Jillian. Her brow furrowed and her mouth pinched as though someone had just stuck a lemon into it. Angling her body away from Jillian, she fixed her gaze on Letty.

"If you have a moment, I need to make some purchases," the woman said. Her voice matched her expression perfectly.

"Of course, Angela." Letty held open the door, letting the woman precede her. "Nice meeting you, Jillian. See you Sunday!"

From the mercantile, Jillian passed Shane's office and moved to the post office. Though she was able to send off a letter to her mother and sister, Katie, informing them she'd made it safely, the man behind the counter—she had no idea his name as he didn't bother introducing himself—hurried her along as though he couldn't get her out fast enough.

Undaunted, Jillian said hello to everyone she passed. They could ignore her all they liked, but she wouldn't make it easy. She made a point of going into several businesses and introducing herself. Cold politeness met her at every turn. It wasn't long before her anger was simmering. Deciding to let it go for today, she guided Hope to the feed mill. She'd get what she needed and go home.

Inside, a boy about Annabelle's age greeted her. Since it was, other than Letty's, the first real smile she'd seen thus far, she strolled over to the boy.

"Hello."

"Hello. Can I help you?"

"You work here?" Jillian asked. Most of the bags that lined the wall weighed more than he did.

"My pa owns the mill. I do chores after school and we were let out early today. I'm Jacob, Jacob Garvey."

He had tousled, blond hair and smudges of dirt on his cheek. She'd never spent much time around children, but one thing she could say about both this boy and Annabelle was that they were honest and open. If only the rest of the town were as smart.

"Nice to meet you Jacob. I'm Jillian Matthews. I'm the new veterinarian."

His brown eyes widened. "Really? You can fix animals, make them better?"

"No, she can't," came the reply from the back of the mill. Striding forward was a tall, wide-shouldered man with a stern face.

"I beg your pardon?"

"You weren't able to save Wade's cow, were you?"

"That was entirely—"

"Your fault. Now what do you want?"

Jillian snapped her mouth closed. Was this really how the man conducted his business? Then he could take his superior attitude and—

"There isn't another feed mill. Closest one is a full day's ride away. In one direction. Now, did you want something or not?"

She swallowed her pride. For now. But she'd be sure to ask either Letty or Eileen just where that other feed mill was. Losing two days was a bargain compared to giving this man her hard-earned and, with a wagon of supplies, her quickly depleting dollars.

She told him what she required and grudgingly handed over the money. He sneered as he pocketed the bills then jerked his chin toward the wall. "Bags are right there." He pointed. "Come on, Jacob. We have work to do."

It wasn't that the bags were too heavy for her to carry. They weren't, though she did strain under the weight as she awkwardly carried one out to her wagon. But she knew, she just knew, he would never let another woman carry them out by herself. She hefted the bag into the wagon. If he expected to break her by a little hard work he had another thing coming.

Jillian was breathing heavy when she set the last bag on the ground behind her wagon. She took a few breaths, wiped her brow, and grabbed the corners.

"Oh, for heaven's sake, let me help you with that!"

Of the people that lingered on the boardwalk—including Mr. Garvey who, despite his claims of having work to do, stood in his doorway—the one person to offer help was a woman no taller than Jillian herself was. She snapped a fierce look Garvey's way before settling her gaze on Jillian.

"I'm Silver. Let me help you with that."

Before Jillian could respond to the name, the woman grabbed the bag by two corners. Hurriedly, Jillian grasped the bottom and together they lifted it up. Silver slapped the dust off her hands.

"Is that the last of it?"

"It is; thank you for your help."

"Well, it wasn't as though anybody else was willing," she said with another cutting glare toward Mr. Garvey. He sneered and disappeared into his mill. "How does a cold glass of sweet tea sound?"

Considering her throat was drier than sand, Jillian smiled.

"Sounds wonderful."

"I'm just at the end of Main Street." Her gaze never wavered. "I own Silver's Saloon."

"Letty told me. I saw the sign when I was at the post office."

Silver nodded. "I saw you looking, figured who you were, and decided to take a walk."

"You followed me?"

"Nothing as sinister as that." Silver reassured. "Let's just say I thought perhaps you could use a friendly face."

"I appreciate it, thank you."

"And you have no problem coming into a saloon? Even one that hasn't yet opened for the day?"

Jillian had never been in a saloon. She knew if she went she'd be judged—yet again—by her decision. Still, it wasn't a hard choice. This woman had helped her where others hadn't. She'd offered kindness and hospitality. Saloon or not, it spoke of Silver's character.

"Lead the way," Jillian answered.

★

JILLIAN FOLLOWED SILVER into the back door of the saloon to a spacious kitchen that, surprisingly, looked as modern as some she'd seen in Philadelphia. Silver pushed open another door and Jillian found herself, for the first time in her life, in the middle of a saloon.

Sunlight poured through the large windows and splayed its glow over the polished wooden floors. Midnight-blue velvet curtains, pulled back with gold sashes, flanked the windows, allowing the natural light to tumble in. Through the sparkling glass, she saw Grey's Saloon. Like Silver's, it was closed at this time of day.

Turning in a slow circle, she took in the round tables with the chairs tucked in tight, the piano beneath the most gorgeous staircase she'd ever seen. She couldn't help herself. She stepped over and ran her hand over the smooth wood.

"It took me months to get the handrail the way I wanted it."

Jillian turned. Silver was about her size, though slightly shorter. Combs pulled her blonde hair away from her face, revealing delicate features reminiscent of fairies. Loose, gold curls coiled down her back. The dress she wore was modest, but Jillian recognized it as being the same high fashion women wore back home.

"You did this?"

Silver smiled proudly. "I didn't build it. When I bought this saloon it was nothing but a beat-up old barn. I fixed what I could, bought what I couldn't." Her smile was nearly as bright as the sunlight. "It's not beat-up any longer."

No, it certainly wasn't. Letting her hand slip off the balustrade, Jillian's gaze fell to the bar. Judging from its luster, Jillian didn't doubt it would be smooth as the banister. Wine bottles, whiskey bottles, and others of varying shapes and sizes lined the glass shelf they rested on. Behind them a gilded mirror reflected her surprise.

"It's pretty."

"Thank you. That was my goal."

Silver slipped behind the counter, poured the sweet tea and passed Jillian a tall glass.

"I imagine big cities like Philadelphia have the luxury of serving ice in its drinks but Marietta doesn't have an ice house. However, I made that just before stepping outside and the well water is cold as any mountain spring."

"It's fine, thank you." Jillian took a long swallow, couldn't help but look around again before she faced her hostess.

Eyes the color of rich coffee laced with a touch of cream watched her closely. At first glance, Jillian imagined many people took in Silver's pretty face and little else. But Jillian had learned to examine the eyes and what she saw in Silver's was a woman who, quite likely, people underestimated. There was more to Silver than a pixie's face.

A fact soon confirmed.

"Jillian, a lot of folks in this town will talk behind your back rather than to your face. As much as that fact annoys me, I can't seem to change it. There are a few, however, that prefer to tell it like is, so I'll be up front with you.

"Being seen with me won't help you. I don't own a brothel, that's what separates mine from Grey's. The only rooms upstairs are my own and no man has stepped foot in them. Still, it's assumed I must be a whore, as why else would I have wanted to build a saloon.

"Much as I think we could come to be friends since we seem to be about the same age and we're both outsiders, I'll understand if you choose to walk away."

Silver's words struck Jillian speechless. Here was a woman who'd made this saloon the stunning establishment that it was, who'd very likely, by stepping forward and helping a stranger, further segregated herself from a town that already shunned her.

While Jillian's younger sister Katie had always been surrounded by friends, Jillian herself had never made any close acquaintances. Sure, when she and Clint went out the women were polite and cordial, but they never called on her for tea nor made any effort to get to know her better. Though she'd been busy working and learning at her father's side, she'd always secretly envied Katie's large circle of friends.

Experience had taught her not many people changed their minds once they were set. Jillian had seen firsthand today just how set many of those minds were. She was willing to be friendly and even put up with the rudeness, but she wouldn't bow to them and to what they thought she ought to be any more than she had back home.

"You mustn't be a very good poker player."

Silver's smile was confident. "Actually, I've been known to win my share as I can bluff when I need to." She shrugged. "There was no need to here."

Jillian took another sip of the sweet drink. "I appreciate your honesty."

"Good, then I have a little more for you. I know what happened at the Parker ranch."

Jillian hadn't been sure how to broach the subject of Wade and couldn't believe her good fortune that Silver mentioned him first. She fussed with her glass a moment then asked the question that had been foremost in her mind since leaving the mercantile.

"Letty mentioned Wade was here and speaking of me. Did he—well—did he have anything good to say about me, or was it all bad?"

Silver leaned a hip against the bar. "As I'm sure you know, he wasn't happy to learn that the vet he'd helped hire was a woman."

"Yes, he made that clear both the night of the surgery and again this morning when he was over."

With brows raised, Silver studied Jillian over her glass of lemonade. "He paid you a visit?"

"He paid me. For the surgery."

"Oh. Well, at least he doesn't blame you for the animal dying. I feel I should tell you he did at first."

"That's how word got round then, isn't it? Wade was here blaming me?"

Silver placed a hand over Jillian's. "Once he'd talked it out, he came to realize you weren't at fault."

"By then, the damage was done, wasn't it? Others must have heard him blaming me."

Silver's pained expression confirmed that he had, in fact, been overheard. Jillian took a deep breath. It was done; all she could do now was move forward and work at changing folks' opinions. Hopefully the fact that Wade now understood she'd done everything she could, would help sway them.

"Was the man at the feed mill one of the men who overheard Wade?"

"Steven wasn't here last night, but some of his friends were. I'm sure they didn't waste any time running to Steven's house."

"Steven?"

"Steven Garvey. He doesn't only own the feed mill, he's the mayor."

He was mayor as well? Her future in Marietta suddenly looked even bleaker than it had moments ago.

"Truthfully, Jillian, Steven would have been just as mean to you whether that cow died or not. He and Wade have known each other for years and apparently they've never gotten along. He'll make a ruckus about this because it was Wade's decision to hire you. That you're a woman will only give him more ammunition."

"But Wade didn't even know I was a woman when he hired me."

Silver shrugged. "That won't matter to Steven. As I said, he hates Wade. If he can make Wade look bad, he'll jump at the chance."

Jillian clasped her hands together. "I can't afford to lose Wade's support. He's the only one who's seen what I can do."

"Once Wade gives his word, it's ironclad. If he said he'd support you, then he will. But Steven will be as dedicated in ensuring nobody else comes around to Wade's point of view."

Had she really believed moving west would be simpler?

"What are you going to do?" Silver asked.

Jillian sat tall. "What I told Letty I'd do. I know Wade doesn't have time to smooth feathers and, frankly, it's not up to him. So I will. I'll visit the farms and ranches, make myself known. Make myself clear that they hired me for my qualifications."

Silver lifted her glass. "To fighting for what you want, no matter what."

Thinking of Steven at the feed mill and the man at the post office and hoping things wouldn't come to "no matter what", Jillian tapped her glass to Silver's.

★

THE IMPACT OF driving home the nails sent tremors up Wade's arm. Added to that his sweaty palm was making it harder and harder to hold his grip. He dropped the tool into the grass and wiped his hand on his pants. He squinted at the sky, praying for a cloud, anything to give him some relief from this heat. Normally their valley was breezy but this spring had been unusually calm. Grabbing the shirt he'd abandoned hours ago, Wade lifted it off the ground and wiped his face.

Hearing a rider coming in, Wade tensed. After their prank, James and Scott had gone up to check the high country, to ensure everything was ready to move the cattle up. They shouldn't be back unless they'd run into trouble.

But it wasn't Scott or James; it was Jillian. His first reaction was a hard kick of his heart, followed by an equally swift rush of desire. He crumpled his shirt and flung it aside. If only his lust could be as easily discarded.

Sighing, he faced the oncoming rider. What struck him first was her dishevelment. Considering the lack of breeze, even a little horseback ride wouldn't toss her hair like that.

Half her braid had come undone and the other half barely hung on. She had a smear of dirt on her cheek. Her blouse was dirty and—

The horse had barely come to a stop when Wade stepped forward, grabbed her mare's halter. "What happened?"

She had a large tear at her elbow and there was some blood. A crazy fury swept through him.

"I lost a wheel on my wagon." She shoved some hair behind her ear. "I know to check the wheels, make sure they aren't loose. But I had a lot on my mind and…" She slapped a hand over her skirt. A poof of dust floated up from the fabric. "Anyhow, if I'd checked, I wouldn't have taken a tumble."

Knowing she hadn't been manhandled didn't ease his tension. Losing a wheel unexpectedly often threw a driver and spooked the horse. It wasn't uncommon to be knocked to the ground by the unexpected jar then trampled by the wagon when a frightened horse took off. It was the reminder he needed to cool his blood. A woman like Jillian would constantly be in harm's way. And those who were foolish enough to care for her would always worry, would always be at risk of losing her.

"Front or back?"

"Back, luckily. I took a fall. Some of my supplies were tossed about, but it didn't hurt Hope or spook her as much as it could have."

"You were lucky."

"I know. And I can see you're busy…"

Her eyes slid over him and for a day that was already sweltering, the temperature suddenly shot up another ten degrees. He felt a bead of sweat skip down his chest and roll over his belly. He nearly swallowed his tongue when her eyes tracked it to the waistband of his pants. Her throat rose and fell as she swallowed. Blood roared in his ears.

Her face looking as hot as he felt, she said, "I know I'm imposing, clearly you were hard at work, but I can't get the wheel on by myself and coming here was closer than going back to town."

Hell, with the way his body was reacting, being alone with her wasn't a good idea. But neither could he refuse her help.

"All right." He sighed. "Just let me get a drink and a clean shirt." He turned and had to do some fancy footwork to keep from knocking his daughter to the ground.

"Annabelle!"

"Papa, can I come?"

"What?"

"Can I go with you? It won't take me long to get Peanut ready and—"

"Whoa, Button," Wade said, kneeling before his daughter and cupping her chin in his hand. "Did you finish your chores?"

Her little shoulders drooped as she realized she'd lost her chance. "No."

"Sorry, Button. But we had a bargain, remember? If you finish your chores like Grandma asked, after supper we'll go catch frogs."

Blue eyes so like Amy's it never failed to break his heart, filled with tears. "But I wanna come."

"Well, if you come with me now, then you'll have to finish your chores later and we won't have time for frog catching. So, you can choose. Come with me now, which is nothing but fixing a boring old wheel, or do as you were asked and we'll have all sorts of fun later."

"And you'll let me keep one like you promised?"

"Yes." Though he feared for the poor critter's life. He knew by her smile which choice she'd made.

"All right, Papa. I'll go finish my chores right now!"

"Wait!" he called before she bolted away. "What do you say to Miss Matthews?"

"Hello, Miss Matthews," Annabelle said hurriedly before skipping away.

Wade watched his daughter disappear behind the barn. He heard the chickens cluck and squawk as she burst into the henhouse. Jillian's giggle turned his head. The sound captivated him, as did the warmth that filled her eyes when she smiled.

"She must keep you hopping."

Wade shook his head. "You have no idea."

★

WADE SECURED WHISKEY to a nearby tree and grabbed the fallen wheel. It wasn't broken, which meant he'd be bringing back the spare he'd brought along.

He passed her the wheel. "I'll push up the corner, you slip it on."

She nodded and within moments the wheel was in place and secured. Silently they worked to load the supplies back into the wagon. Despite her protest that she could do it, he re-harnessed Hope to the wagon.

Wiping his hands on his thighs, he faced her. "That should do it."

Her green eyes met his and she stepped forward, her hand outstretched. "Thank you. I couldn't do this alone and you saved me from having to go all the way back to town. I know I'm likely the last person you want to help and I appreciate that you did it anyway."

He grimaced. "I suppose I gave you more than enough reason to think that." He accepted her hand. "You ever need help again there'll always be someone at the Parker ranch who can help."

Her hand was small and delicate within his. Soft. Silky soft. It conjured up all sorts of thoughts he shouldn't be having. But they bombarded him mercilessly. Flickers of images filled his mind. The way she'd looked at his naked chest. The way her cheeks had flushed. The way she'd made him feel as she looked at him. The way she was making him feel again.

He pulled his hand away but it burned as though branded. He hadn't looked twice at any woman since Amy died. Certainly Jillian was pretty, but there were a lot of pretty women around Marietta, take Silver for example. Maybe it was the combination of Jillian's green eyes and reddish-gold hair that made him want to touch her so badly his fingers twitched with need.

He knew by looking he could span her waist with his hands, could fill those same hands with her breasts. Knowing it, wanting it, drove him to distraction. He had to physically drag all the reasons she was wrong for him back to the forefront of his mind, where reason, not lust, reigned.

"Wade? Everything all right?"

"Yeah, sorry." He wiped his mouth with his sleeve. "Heat must be getting to me."

Despite knowing better, he helped her into the wagon. His fingers sank into the soft flesh at her waist. How long had it been since he'd felt the give of a woman's flesh?

She's not the right woman for you.

Yet he stood there, aroused and overheated, until Jillian rode out of sight.

Chapter Five

For hours he stared at the ledgers, scratched out numbers and shuffled them around. All he had to show for it was a crick in his neck and a thumping headache. The debt was still staggering and the horse ranch was as far away as it had ever been. He closed the books, rubbed his eyes. All he could do was take it one day at a time. Eventually, so long as he kept putting one foot in the front of the other, kept putting in an honest day's work, he believed he'd come out from under the burden his pa had left him. It was just going to take longer than he'd hoped.

And it was going to take innovation, such as making deals like the one he'd struck with Liam, who owned a spread not far from Wade's ranch. In much the same predicament Wade was in, they'd agreed to trade bulls. It would breathe new blood into each of their herds without the expense of buying a new bull.

From the open window he heard the porch swing creak. He'd forgotten his ma had gone out after making him coffee. He looked at the empty cup, wondered how long ago that had been.

"Long enough," he muttered, coming to his feet.

He knew his ma wouldn't go to bed until he did. And though she hadn't spent the last few hours stewing over the ledgers, he didn't doubt she worried about them as much as he did.

The porch swing dipped with his weight as he settled next to her.

"Make any progress?" she asked.

There wasn't any point in lying to her since she was smart enough to see what surrounded her on a daily basis but he could give her hope. "I have a few ideas up my sleeve."

Her hand found his, held on. "Let James help, Wade. He wants to."

Before the words had fully left her lips, he was shaking his head.

"Ma, I've already had this discussion with him. I won't take his money. He should be using it to build you a house, or saving it in case something happens to him the way it did Pa, that way you wouldn't—" He stopped, unable to say the rest. He'd loved his pa, but the man had left them a mess. Still, it somehow felt disrespectful to say it aloud.

She squeezed his hand. "I think we all learned your father's lesson. If James is offering to help, he's doing it within his means."

"I'll be all right, Ma." He kissed her brow. "I'll be just fine."

Wade wrapped an arm around her shoulders, leaned

back in the swing. With his heel, he set it in motion. Frogs sang; crickets chirped a steady rhythm. The moon hung plump and bright and the stars dotted the sky like his cattle would soon dot the foothills.

"Let him help you, Wade. Even a little."

"He already did with Jillian's bill. Tell James to build you a house if he's got money to spare. I've tried telling him but he won't listen to me."

"We don't need a house, Wade."

"Ma, I don't feel right having you two live in his bunkhouse after the wedding."

"It'll just be me and James in it. Besides, we'll still have our meals together here in this house, same as always. The bunkhouse suits us, Wade."

"It's not very big."

"What do we need big for? We have a table to sit and have coffee; we have a bed to—"

Wade held up his hand. "Ma, please."

Chuckling, she snuggled into his side. "You know what I mean. This house is yours now. Yours, Annabelle's. Your future wife's," she added with a smile in her voice. "I hear Jillian called on you earlier."

"I knew it was only a matter of time," he muttered.

Knowing he couldn't stop it, that if she didn't get this out tonight she'd only corner him another time, he tipped his head back and closed his eyes.

"I like her. She's smart. She's beautiful with all that fiery gold hair, those eyes green as a spring meadow." She nudged him. "I know you're not blind."

"No, Ma, I'm not blind." Even without Jillian there he could see her, hear her voice. Feel her softness.

"You know she could have gone to town, it's not that much further. But she came here. To you."

"She didn't come to me," he said, looking her in the eye. "It could have as easily been Scott or James who was in the yard."

"But it wasn't; it was you. Almost as though it was meant to be."

"Meant to be" were three of her favorite words. It wasn't that she didn't get angry, sad or frustrated with life. She'd cried and mourned for her husband. But, in the end, telling herself it was meant to be had allowed her to accept his death and move on. In that instance he'd been glad for those words, as it had been hard watching her in such pain.

He wasn't nearly so glad when she used those words on him.

"Ma, it just happened. It wasn't God's will."

"You hired her, didn't you?"

"Because I thought she was a man."

"But she's not. The most qualified person turns out to be a woman. Then it rains and she has to sleep in your bed."

"Because you told her to." And, though the sheets had been washed, he could still smell Jillian in his room. Not that he'd tell his mother that.

"Then," she continued as though she hadn't heard him, "her wheel breaks and she needs help. Of all the days you're working the range, today you were in the yard. At the exact moment she came calling."

"It's not fate, Ma," he argued. If he thought it was possible that they could have arranged it, he'd blame Scott and James.

"How do you know? Amy was sweet on Steven Garvey until the day she got a cramp swimming and you jumped in the river to save her. From that day on, she had eyes only for you."

He remembered it well. A handful of them had decided to go swimming in the Yellowstone River. Steven and his friends were diving beneath the water and showing off for the girls. Wade and Shane had been on the bank, talking about and staring at those same girls. He'd been watching Amy at the time; fate, as his ma would call it. She'd been swimming along with her friends, taunting Steven and his group when she'd suddenly grimaced and begun to sink.

At first Wade had thought it was a game to get Steven's attention. Heck, he'd seen Steven feign injury often enough to get Amy to come running and figured she was doing the same thing. It soon became apparent she wasn't. Amy thrashed; her head dipped below the surface. He was racing in when her friends yelled for help.

Wade didn't break the surface until he had Amy in his arms. By then Steven had realized she was in real trouble and was racing toward her. Wade had swum to shore, Amy clinging to him, her face buried in his neck. He'd held, soothed, and, when she'd finally stopping shivering, when she'd peeled her soaked, black hair from her face and thanked him for saving her life, she hadn't even looked to see where Steven was.

Not that Wade had cared either. Once the fear of the situation had passed and Amy remained in his lap, arms clutching his neck, nothing had mattered but how she'd felt in his arms.

"You and Amy started building a life together that day, Wade. You might not have known it would lead to marriage, but it did."

"I'm not marrying anyone, Ma, least of all Jillian." Wade shoved to his feet, turned and leaned against the railing.

"I know loving again is scary. The thought of losing James like I lost your father—" She stopped, her fingers going to her throat for a moment. "Life is meant to be lived. It's meant to be shared. Otherwise all you have is this." She gestured to the ranch that lay sleeping in the darkness.

She stood, placed a warm hand on his stubbled cheek. "I'm not saying you have to marry her, all I'm saying is don't close yourself to the idea of falling in love again. You've been doing it since Amy died."

For good reason. It wasn't that he regretted marrying Amy, because he didn't. He'd loved her. Together, they'd made Annabelle. But in the end, she'd broken his heart. Not by dying, though that had been devastating, but by looking elsewhere for fulfillment. By telling him, without words, that he wasn't enough.

He'd never told his ma he'd felt less of a man because of Amy's choices. It was easier on his pride that she continued to think he was simply too scared to love again.

"I know you mean well but, for me, once was enough."

"Why won't you give yourself the chance to be happy again?"

"I am happy. I have what I need."

"But do you have what you want?"

He thought of Jillian, how soft her skin was. How she'd felt when he'd lifted her into the wagon. How he'd yearned to kiss her and how that yearning had scared him.

"Other than my horse ranch, I have everything I want. Goodnight, Ma." He kissed her cheek then sought refuge in his room.

He didn't bother lighting the lamp. Lying on his back, Wade closed his eyes. Two women formed behind his lids. One with dark hair and blue eyes, the other with red hair and green eyes. Both independent. Both strong. One had already broken his heart.

He vowed he'd never give the other the same opportunity.

★

JILLIAN'S TEMPER WAS running hot as Hope's sweaty hide.

When she'd set out that morning, intent and eager to make introductions, she'd known it wouldn't be easy, that she'd meet with more than one stubborn man. It had been that way back east, even with her father at her side.

Yet she'd hoped she'd have something to show for her efforts.

Six farms since she'd begun that morning and the only thing she'd earned was a dusty blouse that clung to her damp back, a sweaty horse and a burning sense of frustration. Why were men so close-minded? Why were they willing to put their animals at risk for the sake of their pride?

Not that she'd seen any animals in need of tending. When she'd looked over corrals, been greeted by tail-wagging dogs and swaggering cats alike, she'd seen no evidence of her skills being required. If she had, she'd have been prepared, as she'd brought along her saddlebags. It would have made her case stronger if she could have shown her skills, rather than simply talk about them.

Jillian snorted. There'd been little chance of talking, let alone proving anything once she'd stated her name and the reason for the visit. The men that had been in the yard closed their mouths as she imagined they closed their minds. Well, she acknowledged with a fresh wave of bitterness, they did open their mouths long enough to tell her she wasn't welcome on their land and that it would be a cold day in hell before they ever called on her in a doctor's capacity.

A single man, and there wasn't any doubt he was a bachelor considering his foul mouth, had told Jillian he had only one need, and it wasn't for a veterinarian. He promised, with a lecherous grin, that should she ever be willing to dispense that kind of medicine, his door would always be open.

"I'd sooner gouge my eyes out," she muttered.

Hope agreed with a shake of her head. It was something, Jillian supposed, to have Hope listen, but how she longed to talk to her father. With each farm she'd left, she'd caught herself turning in the saddle, ready to discuss what had happened only to realize he wasn't there. Wouldn't be again. The void he'd left when he died had been great, but never more felt than it was as she rode along the quiet countryside of this unfamiliar and unwelcoming place. To simply have him there as support, as someone to talk to so she wouldn't feel as though she were alone in the world, would have made all the difference.

Emotion welled up fast and filled her throat. She missed him. The long discussions regarding their profession, hearing his opinion, knowing her own thoughts and ideas were accepted and not only because she was his daughter.

Jillian blinked to bring the narrow path back into focus. Overhead a hawk's scream sounded as mournful as she felt. All of a sudden her father's last words filled her ears as surely as if he were right beside her.

"Nobody can take your dreams, Jillian. The only person who has the power to snuff them is you."

How often had he said that to her?

"Every time I felt like giving up," she whispered in the breeze.

And every time, he'd reminded her what she wanted most, and that she alone was responsible for making it happen. She swallowed back the sorrow and pity. She put some starch in her spine and sat upright as another small farmyard came into view.

When she rode into the yard, her eyes were dry and her determination was once again firmly in place. Jared Matthews would be proud. Knowing that, Jillian slid from the saddle. It had been a long day of riding and her thighs lamented when her feet hit the dirt.

Whoever lived there lived a simple life. The house was no bigger than of one Wade's bunkhouses. The rest of the yard consisted of the privy, a small, well-trodden paddock and a barn that listed heavily to the right. It didn't appear the farmer grew anything but yellow-flowered weeds and patches of clover. Nor did he appear to be home.

Since it seemed she'd garnered her determination for nothing, Jillian didn't see that the trip needed to be a total loss. Both she and her horse were thirsty. Leading Hope, Jillian walked the small yard in search of a well.

She found the silver-handled pump and a shed, which was built into a small hill behind the house. Jillian pumped water into her hand, drank until her mouth no longer felt like the dirt she'd ridden on for most of the day. Not seeing anything she could use to water Hope, Jillian secured the mare to the well and headed for the shed. Surely there was something inside she could use as a bowl for her horse.

The door was closed and held shut with a thick plank braced against it. As Jillian wrapped her hands around it and began to tug, a putrid smell slithered around her. Wrinkling her nose, she freed the plank and set it down. With an eerie squeak the door fell open.

The smell of blood and death assailed her. Jillian choked, covered her nose and mouth with her hand. Dear Lord, what had she stumbled into? Squinting into the darkness she couldn't make out anything but strange shapes on the walls and dark shadows hanging in midair.

Inching her way forward, Jillian crept inside. Cool air, like the whisper of a ghost, brushed her face. Breathing through her mouth, Jillian stood there until the light from the doorway and her own adjustments allowed her to make out what she was looking at.

Skins of beaver, cougar, deer and squirrel hung stretched on the wall. Dangling from the cross brace were four headless rabbits, gelatinous red puddles where their heads used to be. Swallowing hard, Jillian backed away. Even if there were a bowl or bucket inside she'd never use it to water her animal. She knew, of course, people trapped, but she'd never seen it firsthand. Never seen for herself the lifeless carcasses hanging, the skins stripped and stretched. She hoped she'd never see it again.

With the grizzly images filling her head, Jillian turned for the plank she'd tossed on the ground.

And came face to face with a man's narrowed black eyes and snarling mouth.

Jillian screamed. The sharp pitch of it screeched through the small yard and filled her ears. She staggered back, realizing her mistake instantly as it brought her to the mouth of the shed. She forced her limbs to still despite every instinct that told her to run. Her breath soughed through her cold lips as she faced the stranger.

Damn it, why had she left the rifle tied to the saddle?

He wore blood stained clothes that matched his bloodied hands.

A pile of lifeless fur-covered carcasses lay at his feet. His eyes were small and as cold as the shed at her back. The russet mustache matched his hair, thick and unkempt.

Afraid he'd use those bloodied hands on her, Jillian hastened to explain. "I didn't mean to intrude, but it didn't appear anyone was home and my horse needed water. I was just looking for a bowl or bucket to water her."

"You're trespassing."

"Yes, well." Jillian wiped her hands on her riding skirt. "I didn't mean to, as I said. I actually came to introduce—"

"I know who you are."

"Oh. I see." She pushed her mouth into a smile. "Well, should you ever require my skills—"

"I won't."

"You might." She gestured to the horse that was sniffing

Hope. "He could get sick."

"Then I'll deal with it."

"What if you can't? What if—"

He gestured to the shed behind her. "Don't it look like I know what I'm doing?"

"You can't skin a horse!"

"What I do on my own land is my business." His mouth curved into a frighteningly twisted smile. "You want to stick around and see what exactly that is?"

Her gorge rose up her throat. Despite not wanting to show the man fear, she knew it showed as she hurried toward Hope. It took her two attempts to get her foot in the stirrup.

His evil cackle chased her down the lane.

★

STEVEN GARVEY WENT to Silver's saloon every Friday night. Not only was it a chance to get away from his wife's incessant nagging, it was also the night he and his friends gathered together for a few friendly games of poker.

The saloon was neat and tidy; spills were wiped as fast as they happened. Spittoons were strategically placed around the room and those who missed too often to be an accident were known to have their liquor cut off. If anybody else were the proprietor, he'd come in more often, but once a week was as much money as he was willing to give that whore Silver. And his wife would skin him if he ever stepped foot in Grey's.

Sure, Silver claimed she never took anyone to her rooms, yet many a man had professed to find relief between those thighs. Course, most were piss-ass drunk at the time, or had been ordered out by the bitch herself. Still, Steven was inclined to believe the stories. After all, no respectable woman would run a saloon.

Robert arrived not long after Steven had sat down. Bill, still smelling of the stable, arrived next. Harvey, a newcomer to town—if one considered a year new—followed shortly after. Harvey owned a plot of land north of town and trapped for a living. Justin was late, as always. As blacksmith, he always had work that needed doing.

Steven gnashed his teeth when Silver sidled up to their table. Despite the fact she employed other women to wait tables, when he came in it was always Silver who came for their drink order. He knew the bitch did it just to goad him.

Tonight, her golden hair was long and loose. Her face, devoid of the heavy rouge and charcoal many harlots painted themselves with, shone with energy and health. Her deep blue dress pinched in an already tiny waist and her corset pushed up an impressive pair of tits. If she wasn't a whore he'd eat his hat.

"What can I get you gentlemen?" she asked.

Then she grinned like a damn cat that'd just caught the fattest mouse. 'Cause she knew what they wanted to say. And she was smart enough to know they wouldn't.

"Why do you bother askin'?" Bill asked. "We always get

the same damn thing."

"Do you?" she asked, batting her eyes. "Well, I'm just a simple woman, how'm I supposed to remember all these things?"

The blasted woman laughed as she spun from the table and sashayed to the bar.

"I swear if there was another place to drink besides Grey's, I wouldn't step foot in here," Steven grumbled.

"She knows it," Bill said. "And she loves rubbing it our faces."

"And now she's gone and made friends with the lady doctor."

All eyes flew to Steven. He explained how Silver had helped Jillian the other day and how the two of them had come to the saloon afterward.

"It'll take more than a friend to keep her here. Have you heard of her getting any work?" Bill asked.

"I haven't. But I know she did get to at least a few farms today," Robert said.

Damn. That was all Steven needed, her going around making friends, making herself likable. He'd have a hell of a time getting her out of town if folks started to like her.

"And?"

Robert shrugged. "I can't speak for them all, but the ones I heard about didn't cotton to her being there and mostly told her to leave."

"That's what I said when I found her at my place," Harvey said.

Steven cut them a warning glance as Silver came back with their whiskeys. The sound of their coins jiggling in her hand was as irritating as her chuckle as she strolled away.

"You told her to leave?" Bill asked as soon as Silver stepped far enough away.

"I didn't have to," Harvey answered. "I gave her quite the fright when I arrived with some fresh meat. Then I told her what I'd do to any animal of mine if one got sick."

"You told her you'd kill it?" Steven asked, impressed with Harvey's gumption.

Harvey took a drink, licked the moisture off his mustache. "I just told her I wouldn't be needing her services."

Steven whistled, wished he could have been there.

"I don't think we have to worry too much. By now everyone's heard of Wade's cow dying. They won't be in any hurry to call on her," Bill said as he shuffled the cards. They snapped as he dealt each man five cards.

"Still, dire situations sometimes make folks do drastic things. Look at Wade. We know he couldn't afford to call the vet but he did anyway. What if someone else finds themselves in a situation like that? Might be they'd end up calling on her." Justin reasoned.

Steven had thought of the very same thing. It was like sitting on dynamite. Any minute there could be a real need for a vet and then where would they be? Forced to hand over their money to her the same way they were forced to patronize Silver's. Worse, Wade would once again be the damn savior.

Over Steven's goddamned dead body!

He signaled them to lean in. "We can always encourage her into thinking Marietta isn't the best place for her."

Understanding, Justin frowned. "I'm not hurting a woman."

"I'm not saying you have to hurt her. I'm just saying…"

"That maybe we should show her that it would be in her best interest to mosey along?" Bill suggested.

Harvey pulled in his cards, looked at them then tossed in his bet. "Sounds good to me."

Chapter Six

JILLIAN SLID THE barn door open and followed the sunbeam in. Her rabbit thumped when she stepped into his stall.

"Now don't be rude, Whiskers, I'm bringing you a treat after all."

Working around him, she replaced the soiled straw with clean bedding until the cage was clean. She'd picked some dandelions and placed them into the corner of the cage. He remained on the other end, his nose twitching madly.

"One of these days you'll realize I mean you no harm."

She'd barely turned her back before she heard him crunching the leaves. Smiling, Jillian grabbed her pitchfork with one hand and a handful of oats with the other before slipping into Hope's stall.

"Morning, angel. How was your night?" Hope nuzzled her shoulder, daintily took the handful of oats from Jillian's hand.

"Once I get the chores done, we're going to town for a picnic. How does that sound?" Hope snuffled as though she thought it was a great idea.

Humming as she worked, Jillian secured Zeke outside on the grass. By the time everyone was out, fed, had fresh water to drink, and the barn stalls were clean, Jillian was dirty and smelled nearly as bad as the wheelbarrow full of soiled bedding. Once that was disposed of, she pumped two buckets of water and took them inside to wash. When she was clean and dressed, she strolled into the barn to fetch Hope's saddle.

It wasn't there.

She frowned. She knew for certain she'd left it there yesterday. She looked around. The black halter and bridle were hanging on the same rusty nail they always were, the coarse brushes were side by side on the ledge of the dusty window. Even the saddle blanket her father had given her was draped on the rail, right next to where her saddle was kept.

"Where is it?"

Going stall to stall didn't produce any results either. It wasn't anywhere and it didn't make sense. She always put it in the same place. Could someone have stolen it?

"But why?" she asked aloud.

Though she would have been devastated had Hope been taken, it would have made more sense. She was a pretty, little filly and worth more than the saddle Jillian had used for years. Thinking she might as well check outside, though finding it there would make even less sense than having it stolen, Jillian stepped into the sunshine.

It was a typical morning with birds flitting about, their

songs joyous and carefree. The grass sparkled with the last of the dew and the sun warmed her face.

She felt like a fool looking for a saddle in the long grass, especially when Zeke raised his head to watch, but she wouldn't be able to accept it had been stolen until she ensured it wasn't anywhere else.

Having made a full circle around the barn, and of course finding nothing, Jillian shook her head. Then something caught her eye.

There, straddling the railing of her porch was her saddle. The brown leather shone with polish and the stirrups swayed gently from the brush of breeze. Stymied, she simply stood there. She hadn't put it on the porch. Why in heaven would she unsaddle Hope then carry the saddle across the yard when it was simpler—and made more sense—to leave it next to her stall?

Because she hadn't, she acknowledged suddenly feeling sick.

And it hadn't been there when she'd stepped from her house to do chores and neither had it been there when she'd finished washing and dressing. Her porch wasn't that big; there was no way she could have missed seeing it. Which meant the saddle was taken when she was inside the house and it was placed on the porch when she'd went in the barn to get Hope.

Which meant it had all happened just moments ago.

A lump came to her throat and a shiver skidded up her

spine, puckering her skin with gooseflesh. Were they in the house? In the trees? What did they want? And, dear Lord, were they armed?

Well, if they were, she couldn't have presented an easier target standing there, unarmed and alone. While she didn't want to give whoever it was the satisfaction of seeing her afraid, she couldn't continue to stand there, completely vulnerable. But should they be in her home, she couldn't go inside either.

Spinning on her heel, she raced back to the barn. It wasn't much, but the pitchfork would have to do. Standing in the coolness of the barn, her neck damp with fear, Jillian took a moment to compose herself. Surely if they wanted to hurt her, they'd had the chance. Therefore, it must be scaring her they were after.

"Well, they accomplished that," she muttered.

But she wouldn't give them the gratification of cowering in her barn all day. Gripping the fork, she went back outside, her gaze hunting the tree line.

Nothing moved but the silvery leaves and the grass, which swayed peacefully in the wind. Her yard was empty. No curtains moved inside the house. The thought of going inside, knowing someone could easily be waiting there, made her shudder. But she had to do something.

Snapping her spine, she marched to the porch. Her heart thudded louder than her boots on the dirt. The closer she came to the house, the higher she drew the fork. When she reached the porch, the sharp smell of oil grabbed her around the throat. She kept her tack in great condition, but she hadn't polished her things since arriving in Marietta. With a trembling hand she traced her finger down the center of the saddle, yanked her hand back. The polish was fresh.

Still managing to stand despite her jelly-like knees, she struggled to make sense of it. On the surface, it wasn't a threat. A farce maybe, someone playing with her, but Jillian couldn't help but feel it was more menacing than that. Whoever had done this was letting her know that if they could get this close to her without her knowing, they could do worse.

Her eyes focused on the saddle again and she forced herself to calm down. She could do one of two things, tuck her tail and hide or hold her ground. Had she really come all this way only to wilt now? Her heart thudding in her ears, she opened the door. It opened silently.

"I know what you did," she called out. There was no point in being quiet. If whoever was trying to scare her remained inside, they'd have already heard her on the porch. The house remained still, silent. It didn't take long to confirm she was alone. She leaned against the doorway to her bedroom, pressed her forehead to the wood and gave thanks.

She didn't linger. Marching across her house and outside, Jillian set the fork aside, picked up the smooth saddle, and stepped off the porch.

She had a church picnic to get to, after all.

THE CHURCH WAS on the far edge of town, on a side street behind and down from Grey's saloon. Other than the church, only the boardinghouse and school fronted that end of the dirt road. A spattering of houses huddled down at the other. The grassy area surrounding the small, whitewashed church buzzed with activity. Children dashed here and there, their mother's arms raised high so their pies and cakes wouldn't get knocked to the ground. Tables bulged with baking, needlework items, and quilts for sale. In the shade of the church, more tables were weighed down with food for the afternoon meal.

A group of men talked in the shadow of a large weeping willow. More were busy setting up games for the children, who, in their excitement, ran around and yelled for the adults to hurry. There were more people than she expected given that Marietta was only a two-street town.

Coming from a large city, Jillian was used to crowds, but this was different. In a large city nobody paid her any attention. Here, everyone knew each other. Here, she was an outsider. Feeling it, along with several stares directed her way, she lingered over securing Hope.

"You really like animals, don't you?"

Recognizing the voice, Jillian turned to Wade's daughter. Like the first time she'd seen the girl, Annabelle had her hair in two tight braids and those blue eyes of hers latched fearlessly onto Jillian's.

"Yes, I do."

"I like horses best. Cows stink."

Jillian laughed. "I supposed so."

"You don't think so?" Her eyes widened as though she couldn't imagine such a thing.

"Well, yes. But all animals smell, really."

"Nothing as bad as them cows," Annabelle said. "If all animals stink, then why'd you become a doctor for them?"

"Because I don't mind the smell, really. And because I like being around them."

The girl smiled, revealing gaps where she'd lost a few teeth. "I bet they're quieter, too. Not like people. Some just talk and talk. Like me, I guess. Grandma says I can talk the bark off trees some days."

"Hey, Annabelle! Come on! It's your turn to count."

Annabelle looked away from Jillian long enough to yell back at the boy Jillian recognized from the feed mill. "I'm coming!" Then she turned back to Jillian. "I gotta go. Boys don't like waiting on girls. Bye!"

And with that, the child ran off to join her friends. Jillian figured it was time she joined the group as well. The few women who were standing at the food table scattered as she approached. Nevertheless, Jillian smiled as they looked back over their shoulders at her. The sting of their rebuff was soon forgotten when she reached the fancy pastries and treats that had been brought. The smell of cinnamon, lemon and berries hovered over the table.

"Go ahead, take one. I won't tell anybody."

Jillian turned around, a smile upon her face. "I'm afraid if I start, Letty, I won't be able to stop. It all looks and smells so delicious."

Letty eyed Jillian's small waist and harrumphed. "Jillian, you could eat the whole table and it wouldn't show. Me? One look at these sweets and my hips can barely squeeze through a door. Not that Mr. Daniels minds," she added with a wink and a pat to her hip.

"I haven't met him yet, is he here?"

"John? He's over there getting the sack races ready. Honestly, sometimes that man is more of a child than the children."

But the loving smile as she watched her husband take off after a squealing boy who'd stolen a sack said she didn't mind one bit.

"Hello, Letty."

Jillian recognized the woman from her first trip to town. The woman's mouth was as pinched as the last time Jillian had seen it.

"Angela," Letty smiled despite the woman's frown. "Have you been introduced to Jillian yet? Jillian Matthews, meet Angela Hollingsworth. Angela runs the boardinghouse. Angela, Jillian is our new veterinarian."

"Yes, I know." Mrs. Hollingsworth set down her cloth-covered contribution next to the others. "Good day, Letty."

"Is she always so rude?" Jillian asked once the woman

had shuffled away.

"Mostly. She's stiffer than an over-starched shirt. Always wants to be called Mrs. Hollingsworth. I make it a habit to address her by her first name. She hates it," Letty answered with a mischievous grin.

Eileen joined them and pulled Jillian into a hug. "I'm so glad you could make it."

"Did you come alone?" Letty asked Eileen as she moved behind the table where she sorted the pastries. Pies went to the right, cakes and cookies in the middle and bread to the left.

"You know Wade, he hasn't been to a picnic since…well, he doesn't care for it," she added with a sad smile. "I brought Annabelle along; she's been nagging me since breakfast so we came a little early. I imagine Scott will come once the baskets are all through and he figures it's safe to be here without being wheedled into bidding."

"Bidding on baskets?"

"Every year the unmarried women make up picnic baskets and the bachelors bid on them. With the amount of prospectors and miners in these mountains, the bachelors outnumber the available women. Add in the ranchers and farmers looking for wives, and those baskets go for a hefty price. Of course, all the money raised goes to the church." Letty looked puzzled. "I'm surprised you didn't know about that. Eileen said she'd tell you."

Eileen coughed, tugged on the strings of her bonnet. "I

was going to. I'm sorry, Jillian. I plumb forgot to tell you that you should bring a basket."

"You forgot? You said you were going to ride over and—"

"Good afternoon, Eileen, Letty. And who might you be?"

Caught up in Letty's explanation of the auction, Jillian hadn't noticed the man approach. He was very tall. His black hair was generally sprinkled with grey. Creases fanned from the corner of his eyes when he smiled and Jillian saw nothing in their sky-blue depths but gentleness. The white band at his throat immediately set her at ease.

"Reverend Donnelly, this is Jillian Matthews."

"And so we meet at last. How are you finding Marietta so far?"

Since she wasn't about to tell the minister that most of the folks she'd met so far were close-minded and rude, and since she couldn't lie to him either, she simply said, "It's a lovely town."

"A good way to meet people, Miss Matthews, is Sunday service which is at ten every Sunday," he added with a knowing wink. "Ah, terribly sorry, ladies, but I'm being called over. Enjoy your day."

He strolled off, and Jillian couldn't help smiling after him.

"He's not very subtle, but he's a great preacher. You'll like him. Well, I'm thirsty. Let's get some sweet tea and sit down."

Several conversations hushed as they walked past. Despite that, Jillian made a point of looking at folks and nodding her head in greeting. Not all the women were unfriendly but Jillian noticed the only ones who smiled back were those whose husbands weren't standing next to them.

At a distance from where the children raced about, where they could converse without screaming at each other or being overheard by the busybodies, Jillian, Letty, and Eileen sat and enjoyed their drinks.

Jillian took a sip of the tea, which was liberally laced with sugar, and watched the children run about. Wagons pulled up steadily. Children jumped over the edge before their fathers had set the brake. With a wave of their hands, ignoring their mothers' warnings that they remain clean and out of trouble, they blended into the growing cluster of rambunctious bodies.

"Oh, to have that much energy again." Letty sighed wistfully.

Eileen smiled at her, placed her half empty glass down on the grass. "And what would you do if you had it?"

"Well, I suppose that would depend if John had as much." The grin Letty shot them equaled that of a naughty child.

Eileen shook her head, obviously used to her friend's openness. "Tell me, Jillian, have you been called on since the ranch?"

Jillian sighed. "Not yet. I did ride around to a few farms,

tried to introduce myself. For the most part I was practically run off."

Their disappointment was clear in their frowns, but it was only half of what Jillian felt. She'd come across the country to be a vet. It wasn't a matter of lack of work. Doc Fletcher had said in his advertisement that there was a great need. And having ridden around, she knew she was surrounded by farmers and ranchers. No, need wasn't the problem. Her being a woman was.

"It just burns my goat!" Letty said, finishing her glass of tea in one swallow. "If you were a man, they'd be lining up at your door."

"I know," Jillian agreed.

Her gaze drifted over the crowd. As expected, several women were staring at her as they participated in closed-circle discussions. Most looked away the moment Jillian saw them.

Past them, where the men were gathered, Jillian saw Steven with a handful of men, most she recognized as merchants in town. The one, the trapper, had her shuddering as she remembered his bloody hands.

Unlike the women who looked away when Jillian caught them staring, Steven was far bolder. His unblinking stare held Jillian's, until, feeling disconcerted, she broke contact.

"Grandma!" Annabelle ran over, eyes bright as the sky. She flopped onto the ground next to Eileen.

Eileen's smile was soft and full of love as she took her

granddaughter's hand. "What's got you so excited?"

"I was hiding behind that tree," Annabelle pointed to the tall willow Steven and his friends were gathered underneath, "and I overheard Mr. Garvey. He's blaming Pa for us having a woman vet and wants to have a meeting right away. Tomorrow morning." Blue eyes latched onto Jillian's. "He really hates you," Annabelle added with a whisper, "and he wants you out of town."

Letty muttered a curse. Jillian felt an upsurge of indignation. Just who did Steven think he was?

"You're sure?" Eileen asked.

"Positive." Annabelle's head bobbed with confirmation. "And he said to make sure everyone kept it quiet so Pa wouldn't know about it until after."

"Can Steven do this?" Jillian asked.

"Sure can. He's the mayor."

"He may be the mayor," Letty said. "But the rest of us have a say."

"Thanks, Button," Eileen said to her granddaughter. "You go play now. But," she added and grabbed Annabelle's hand before the girl could run away, "don't tell Jacob you heard, all right? He'll just tell his pa."

"I won't. Bye!"

And as though she hadn't just delivered news that had shaken Jillian's world, she scampered away to resume her game.

"That sneaky devil." Eileen seethed. "Trying to have a

meeting without telling us. He'll be blaming Wade for—" She caught herself, bit her lip.

"It's all right, Eileen. Wade didn't know he was hiring a woman. It's not his fault."

"Well, be that as it may, you're here and you know what you're doing. Seems to me that's all that should matter," Letty stated.

It took all Jillian's willpower not to march right over to Steven and give him a piece of her mind. Of all the self-righteous, pompous—

She inhaled deeply, reined in her temper. It wasn't only Steven she had no worry about; it was the town. One thing was certain, she needed to stand her ground, needed to fight for what she'd come for. If she didn't, then it would only be a matter of weeks before her money ran out.

And then what would she do? Clint's smirking face came to mind, but Jillian shoved it aside. She wasn't giving up; Clint wasn't going to win.

"What are you going to do?" Letty asked.

Jillian's hands clenched and unclenched in her lap, her thoughts ran faster than a wildfire. Her eyes, she knew, burned with determination.

"I'm going to the town meeting." She decided. "Steven may want me out, and he might not be alone in that, but I'm prepared to fight."

"It's not that we don't love having you here, dear, and not that we aren't prepared to fight right alongside you, but it must be reassuring to know you can always go back east."

Jillian thought of her bedridden mother, who'd been happy to stay in bed and bemoan her many ailments for the last several years. She'd worked as hard at discouraging Jillian to be a doctor as her father had encouraging her. Francis Matthews wanted both her daughters close by her side, where she could fuss over them and they could tend to her every need.

If Jillian's father hadn't put in his will that he was giving Jillian money to pursue her goal of being a doctor, Jillian was sure her mother never would have given her a cent to follow what she'd always called a ridiculous notion for a woman to undertake.

As for her sister… Jillian shook her head. They hadn't been close since they were children. Once Jillian had set her mind on being a veterinarian, she'd been busy with studies and working alongside her father. When she had free time, she'd taken her turn at her mother's bedside. The few occasions Jillian and Katie had had to sit down and talk they'd had little to say to each other and after a few such attempts, they'd each stopped trying.

While she loved her sister, their strained relationship wasn't enough to get her back to Philadelphia.

"No, Eileen," Jillian answered honestly. "There's no going back."

★

WHY DID SHE always do this to herself? Silver wondered as she walked into the churchyard.

The women were already clustered around tables or on the grass, heads together in conversation, their circles closed. A group of men leaned on the hitching post, smoke from their cheroots pluming over their heads. Low rumbling from their discussions stopped when she walked by. She didn't belong here. She felt it to the depths of her soul. She was Silver, the saloon owner. Silver, the woman who would never be more than a whore in their eyes. Even though she'd never bedded any of them. Even though most had tried.

Her heart hammered in rhythm with her steps. Her hands were damp where they clutched her basket. Doubt trailed alongside her like a lost puppy that didn't know where else to go. Despite it all, she kept her eyes forward, walked straight for the table that held the other baskets. She felt like a fool. But, by God, she wouldn't let it show.

"Miss Adams."

"Reverend. How lovely to see you."

And it was. Because he was one of few who never judged her. She'd asked him why, once. Why he didn't shun her as the others did. His sad smile had undone her nearly as much as his words.

"Silver," he'd said, "I'll not judge you or anyone else. That's God's task, not mine. There are enough folks doing that; I don't need to be among them."

"Is that chicken I smell?"

How he could smell it over the aroma of the pig being roasted was a miracle in itself. But then, if Silver were to believe in miracles, she'd believe this man capable of them.

"It is." She offered him a grateful smile. "You don't have to bid on it, Reverend."

"And let such fine food go to waste?"

He'd bought her basket every year she'd brought one, which was ironic, as the only reason she bothered coming in the first place was because of him. Other than Letty, Shane, and the folks at the Triple P, nobody else paid her the time of day. Well, the miners and prospectors had fallen over themselves when they'd first come to town but when she'd refused their advances, tossed more than one out of her saloon for grabbing where they had no business grabbing, they'd shunned her like the others.

But Reverend Donnelly was always nice to her. To have his support for herself if not her saloon—he never stepped foot inside—was a godsend. Coming here, putting up with the stares and the rebuffs was a small price to pay to return that kindness.

"I met Miss Matthews today. She seems very nice."

A smile curved Silver's lips. "She is. I asked her to come into the saloon for some tea."

He arched a brow. "Did you now?"

"The saloon wasn't open, Reverend. It was only the two of us."

"I'm glad she didn't refuse the opportunity to get to

know you. That speaks well of her character, doesn't it? Ah, and here comes another with great character. Good day, Sheriff."

Silver's stomach leapt to her chest. She'd known Shane since she'd come to town. He came into the saloon often enough that she should be over this darn reaction to him. And yet every time she laid eyes on his sculpted face, his secretive grey eyes, it was like the first all over again.

"Good day, Reverend." He tipped his hat. "Silver."

"Shane."

"I hope you have your money handy, lad. This lady's basket will fetch a fine price."

A flush the likes of which she'd never felt enveloped Silver. Shane had never bid on her baskets, ever. It was a sore spot with her because she always secretly made them with him in mind. A truth she'd take to the grave.

"Well, then"—he looked at Silver, his face unreadable—"I may just have to do something about that."

It took an iron will and her toes curled tightly in her shoes, but Silver kept her smile from blooming like an overrun patch of dandelions.

"Hello, Shane."

At the sound of the woman's melodic voice, Silver's joy sank and her toes uncurled. Silver knew Melissa Lake. The woman had been a thorn in Silver's side since she'd first laid eyes on her. Her father was the cobbler in town, though with the amount of cookies and sweets she delivered to Shane's office, a person would think her family ran a bakery. More than once Silver had bumped into her on the street holding a plate of treats and every time Melissa made a point of telling her whatever she was carrying was Shane's favorite.

Tall and willowy, she was Silver's physical opposite. With hair as dark as Shane's, she looked striking standing by his side. She turned her eyes toward Silver.

"Oh, hello, Silver. Saloon closed today?"

Silver bristled. "As it is every Sunday." She set down her basket.

"Goodbye, Shane. I'll see you next time you're in."

He opened his mouth, but in the end shut it without a word.

The reverend announced the bidding would start in five minutes. Silver had only enough time to race over to Jillian, Letty, and Eileen for a quick hello. When she heard about the town meeting, she vowed she'd be there as well.

She took her place next to the others who had brought baskets and gritted her teeth when Melissa took her place beside her.

"I just know Shane will want mine." Melissa purred.

After four baskets had been sold without Shane bidding on any of them, Silver dared hope, dared actually think that this year Shane would come through. She could easily picture them under the lazily drooping branches, laughing and talking about everything, anything. Then he'd look at her, a darkening in his eyes she'd always hoped to see, and he'd lower his mouth—a mouth she'd coveted for too long—to hers.

"And now," the reverend said, "we have a basket donated by Miss Silver Adams."

It was mortifying to stand there. Mortifying to know everyone was staring at her. She heard the whispers, those hushed words that weren't meant for her ears. There was nowhere to look that would make standing under their scrutiny and gossip any easier. But she wouldn't look down, wouldn't look at her feet as though she was ashamed. And she wouldn't look at Shane, even though she knew exactly where he was standing.

Picking a branch on a tree, she imagined sitting underneath it with Shane as silence stretched over the gathering. Why couldn't she have simply donated some money to the church rather than subjecting herself to this scrutiny and misery? Why did she do this to herself, year after year? Because she was foolish enough to hope that, one day, Shane would bid on it.

"I'll bid two dollars," the reverend said. "Do we have any other bids?"

Silver's stomach sank. The prick of tears hit her eyes.

As a bid, it wasn't the most generous since some of the others had fetched upwards of four dollars, but Silver wasn't concerned about how much her basket sold for. It was whom it sold to that mattered.

The silence was interminable. The wind slipped its warm

fingers over her face, but it wasn't a pleasant feeling. Instead it only reminded her of how alone she was. An unhappy baby began to wail. From the hitching post a horse whinnied. Nobody else countered the reverend's bid.

"Then it looks like I'm the lucky winner."

Silver drew deep within her heart for a smile. The reverend had been kind, and he deserved to see her smile. Turning, she grabbed her basket from the reverend and took it to a shady spot by the church. He'd join her once the rest of the baskets were sold. As she settled herself on the grass she heard Melissa's basket being auctioned.

And her heart ripped open when she recognized the man bidding.

★

"HE DID WHAT?" Wade asked around a mouthful of buttered potatoes.

"He called a town meeting for tomorrow morning."

Since his ma had already given him "the eye" for talking with his mouth full, Wade waited until he swallowed before asking, "How come we didn't hear about it before now?"

"He said he didn't want you to know," Annabelle answered.

Wade's supper slid greasily in his stomach. It wasn't a complete surprise that Steven would call a meeting. The man had been livid when the town had let Doc and Wade search for a vet. Steven had wanted to do it. As mayor, he thought it was his responsibility and had taken the town's decision to let Wade and Doc do it as a slap in the face. So, no, the fact Steven called a town meeting wasn't a shock. Neither was the fact Steven was deliberately trying to keep it from Wade. That didn't mean it sat well with him, however.

"I'm sure he's just itching to rant about how I messed up."

Annabelle was all but bouncing in her seat, happy to be the one who knew things nobody else did. "He said it was you who got the town into this mess, but he'd be the one to fix it."

"By running her out?" Scott asked. "That'd be a darn shame. I think she's a he—"

Eileen cleared her throat, causing Scott to blush. "She's a fine doctor," he continued. "I don't see how any man could do better."

"I agree," James added. Then with a wink added, "Of course it don't hurt any that she's pretty to look at."

Wade cut into his beef with more force than necessary. James chuckled.

"I think we should all go tomorrow." His ma suggested.

"Me, too!"

"You have school." Wade countered.

"Awww. I never get to do to the fun stuff." She whined.

"You won't miss any fun, Button, just a boring adult meeting."

"That's what you always say." She pouted. "May I be

excused?"

They waited until Annabelle had thumped up to her room before continuing.

"I mean it, Wade," his ma said again. "I think we should all go. It'll be stronger than if only you went."

Wade set his fork onto his half-full plate. "I can't spare everybody. I'll go. And since Annabelle's at school, you can come with me."

"No, I think it has to be all of us."

James laughed around a forkful of asparagus spears.

"What's so funny?" Wade demanded.

"It's inevitable, son. You know she always manages to get us to do her bidding."

"She does not," Wade grumbled, though he couldn't think of an instance when she hadn't.

Across the table, Scott choked on his supper. He dropped his fork and thumped on his chest, coughing as though he was going to bring up a steer. When he'd regained his breath, he scooped up a biscuit and lathered it with butter.

"You agree with him?" Wade asked.

Scott dished up more food. "I didn't say anything."

Wade muttered a curse, softly so his mother wouldn't hear, though the look she gave him said he hadn't fooled her. Ignoring everyone, he filled his mouth. The beef was tougher than boot leather but the taste of the onions his mother had fried it in came through. With money as sparse as it was, the only beef they ate was what was too old to be of any value.

Swallowing it down with a tall glass of water, Wade considered his mother's request. And, dammit, had to acknowledge she was right. There was strength in numbers and if they all went, as well as Letty and John Daniels and Silver, they'd present a stronger defense. But it would mean losing a half-day's work. He pushed the food that was left out of his way.

"You gonna eat that?" Scott asked, his eyes as hungry as Wade had been an hour ago.

Wade shoved the plate to him then both he and his mother watched Scott devour the leftovers. While his mother looked pleased, happy to cook for an appreciative man, seeing that much food eaten in one sitting turned Wade's stomach.

His ma, not about to let her argument go, speared some asparagus then pointed the loaded utensil at her son.

"She needs work and we all know she's capable. Besides that, Steven needs to know he represents the whole town, not just his friends."

"I can work later tomorrow night to make up for the morning," Scott volunteered.

"Me, too," James added, spurs jingling as he got up to pour more coffee.

Wade ran his fingers through his hair, dropped his hands to the table.

"Fine." He sighed. "We'll all go."

Chapter Seven

DARN IT!

There were a dozen horses already tied to the hitching posts next to the church. She'd hoped to be one of the first to arrive. The twitching in her stomach turned to hard shudders. She hadn't been as nervous going to the individual farms, but knowing she'd be facing everyone at once...

Blowing out a breath, Jillian tied Hope among the other horses and marched straight up the church steps before the anxiety that had kept her up and pacing most of the night took over.

The door creaked open. Apparently nothing about this was going to be easy. Sure enough every head turned toward the sound. Seeing who it was, a few of those heads bent toward each other and within seconds hurried whispers skipped over the pews to taunt Jillian.

Well, they could talk and gossip all they wanted. She wasn't going anywhere. Hoping to display bravado she didn't feel, she met the remaining gazes dead on. She didn't recognize everyone. That was a blessing. Maybe those folks weren't already set against her. But when they didn't return her smile, only turned back to the front without any sign of encouragement, Jillian feared she was wrong.

Steven was already in the front pew and the gaze he shot over his shoulder hit her with the force of a cold winter wind blowing off the Ohio River. Not about to back down, the smile she returned held the same lack of warmth. She held it long enough to prove her point—he didn't intimidate her— and then took one of the many pews that wasn't yet occupied.

It didn't take long after that for the small church to fill. And, as more people filed in, the temperature climbed several degrees. The small rectangular windows on either side of the wooden structure offered pitiful, if any, relief.

She'd deliberately slipped to the far edge of the pew, leaving plenty of smooth wood beside her for her friends, but so far only Mrs. Hollingsworth dared sit there. Of course she remained at the opposite end and didn't deign to look Jillian's way.

Had Letty, Eileen, and Silver changed their minds about coming? Eileen had promised she'd get Wade to come, and Jillian knew his presence would make such a difference. She could, and would, face everyone alone, but it would be so much easier with someone on her side when she did.

It didn't help her discomfort any that she felt the stickiness of everyone's stares. From the women who looked at her over the top of their fans, which worked hard to stir up the stuffy air, to the men who glowered at her as though she'd single-handedly ruined their lives. A few of those men she recognized. The blacksmith, the thick-necked man who owned the stable. Feeling the pull of an especially potent glare, Jillian shifted her gaze to the left.

It was the trapper. Did she know his name? She didn't think so. But his ice-blue eyes raked over her from underneath his thick ruddy brows. He wasn't covered in blood today, but it was hard not to remember him that way. Something he must have sensed by the way his mustache twitched.

Jillian decided it was time she stopped looking around. All she was accomplishing was stretching her already taught nerves. She clasped her hands tightly in her lap to try to control their trembling.

The door creaked open; a slight breeze snuck inside. The air brushed her shoulders, a light caress that was gone as quickly as it came.

"Excuse me," Silver said, wading through the crowd.

Jillian let out a deep breath. Thank God, a friendly face!

Mrs. Hollingsworth's lips puckered as she inched her knees to the side, allowing Silver to step into the pew.

"Sorry I'm late." Though she sounded out of breath there was a look of determination in her eyes. "I haven't missed the lynching yet, have I?"

"No. But I'm happy to see nobody is armed."

The door opened again and soon Mrs. Hollingsworth's

pucker came back full force. Eileen and Letty took their places next to Silver. Though Jillian didn't see Wade, and she couldn't help feeling disappointed about that, she felt better than she had since sitting down. She had friends at her side; she'd be fine.

"I shut down the mercantile when Eileen arrived. I see we're just in time," Letty added when Steven took his place behind the lectern.

The crowd shifted with anticipation. The energy in the room vibrated in Jillian's ears and flowed through her body from there. Whispers and murmurs escalated until Steven cracked his gavel against the wood.

"I know you're upset, and you've reason to be." His gaze skimmed over heads until it latched onto Jillian. "But we'll all have the chance to be heard."

Silver grabbed Jillian's hand and squeezed. "That goes for you, too," she whispered.

Eileen looked to the door. "He said he'd be right in," she muttered.

"As Doc is no longer here and Wade didn't deem your feelings important enough to show up this morning, I guess that leaves me to settle this matter."

His greedy eyes scanned the church. Steven was already a tall man, but he seemed to grow taller as he addressed the people of Marietta.

"Now, then. I've been thinking on the matter and I am prepared, as you'll recall I was prepared to do the first time," he added with a self-serving smile, "to be the one in charge of hiring a new veterinarian.

"I have the advertisement ready. Robert will send the telegrams out later today. Harvey"—he gestured to the trapper—"will, out of the goodness of his heart, ride to Bozeman and see to it that advertisements are put up around the city." Steven puffed up like a bullfrog. "This time we'll get what we need."

Comments erupted about the room.

"Damn right!"

"About time!"

"Shoulda been Steven who hired one to begin with."

"Let's find us a real vet!"

Steven's smile was wide and overflowed with satisfaction.

"Pompous weasel," Silver muttered.

Jillian couldn't agree more. But he'd said folks would have a say so she came to her feet. It was past time she was heard. The gathering erupted again, throwing accusations and insults her way faster than she could absorb them all. However several words shoved through the melee to be heard. No-good, useless, and the worst, animal killer.

Every time she opened her mouth to defend herself, she was bombarded with insults. Seeing nothing for it, Jillian grabbed her skirts and, with a hand on Silver's shoulder, stepped onto the pew. She had a good view from there and the astonished looks on everyone's faces would have been funny if she wasn't so angry. She did, however, use their temporary shock and silence to her advantage.

"I believe you said everyone would have a chance to be heard." She reminded Steven. "And I have something I'd like to say."

"We don't want to hear what you have to say, missy. You've done enough damage already."

Feet stomped in approval. Hands clapped, the sound sharp as a bullwhip. Though Steven held the gavel, he did nothing but tap it against his palm. Jillian glared at him but all he did was sneer. Darn it, he could have kept the crowd under control if he'd a mind to.

Jillian clamped her hands on her hips, sucked in a breath, and tried again. "I—"

"Miss Matthews has a right to defend herself."

Mouths went silent and bodies shifted as a wave when Wade, flanked by James and Scott, with Shane taking up the rear, stepped through the door. Jillian's breath came out in a gush of gratitude. He came!

With her standing on the pew, she was easily spotted. He pressed his lips together briefly, but not before she saw them tremble into a smile. Her face flamed; she couldn't imagine what she must look like, perched the way she was. She was thrilled he'd come, but her pride wished he'd have done so when she'd been a bit less…conspicuous. Yet, now that the damage was done, she kept her position. She really did have a good view and the height advantage made her feel more in control. They'd have to look at her now, wouldn't they?

Steven used his gavel now and he rapped it soundly on the lectern. "You've done enough damage here, Parker."

The gathering, slightly calmer now that the sheriff was there, nodded their agreement.

"So's she!" someone called out. "She's already killed one animal."

"No, she didn't," Wade began. "She—"

"That's not what you said. We heard you admit that she killed your animal." This from the man who ran the post office.

This wasn't news to Jillian, though Wade had no way of knowing that. The look he sent her was humble and apologetic. Her chest filled with warmth.

"How many more do you want her to kill before you admit you were wrong in bringing her here?" asked the man from the stable.

"I didn't—"

"Jillian," Wade interrupted, "let me say this first."

Since it seemed the least she could do seeing as how he'd come to her defense, she remained quiet. Wade threaded his way up the aisle. James and Scott held back, though they stepped aside to allow Shane to pass and take his place next to Wade at the front. Steven's face went crimson when Shane gestured for him to move back from the lectern in order for Wade to take his place.

Jillian pressed a hand over her thumping heart. His words, she knew, could make every difference for her.

"First of all, I'd like to apologize for being late this morning. It seems I was one of a handful who, mysteriously," he added with a pointed look at Steven, "hadn't been told about the meeting. However, I'm glad I could attend as I know there's been a whole mess of scuttlebutt about Miss Matthews and what took place at my ranch. Yes, I lost a cow. But no, it wasn't her fault."

"How do you know?" someone yelled.

"Because I saw her, covered in blood and soaking wet from the ride out, do everything she could to save that animal. Ask James and Scott if you don't want to take my word for it alone; they were there."

Both men's gazes went around the room as they nodded their agreement.

"She did a bang up job," James said.

"As good as I've seen Doc do," Scott added.

"Well, obviously not, as the cow died!" Steven took a step forward, clearly trying to reestablish his position as leader.

Wade turned to Steven. "And no animal ever died after Doc tended it?" Wade's gaze moved across the church. "Bill? Where's Bill at?"

A few hands raised and pointed and finally Wade seemed to see who he was looking for. Jillian followed the direction and saw the thick-necked man. He looked about as happy as Steven.

"Bill, as owner of the stable, I know you've called on Doc

before. Wasn't there a time when you had a sick horse and the night after Doc saw to the animal it died?"

"That horse was old. Doc said he might not make it."

"And you trusted him?"

"Hell, yeah. He knew what he was doing."

"So does Miss Matthews."

Wade's words gave her courage. As did the fact that folks seemed to be listening.

"Jillian? If you're ready."

She nodded, dried her hands on her skirt. She'd done it so often she was surprised it wasn't wringing wet by now.

"Thank you. And like Mr. Parker, I'd like to take this moment to apologize. I deliberately misled him and all of you when I responded to the advertisement."

"I knew it! She's nothing but a fraud!" Steven yelled. Of course this got the crowd all wound up again and within two breaths the sound was enough to wake the dead.

Wade grabbed the gavel from Steven and smacked it down. He waited until the noise had subsided before he spoke.

"Let her finish," he said.

She swallowed the knot of nerves that had formed in her throat. "I am a vet. My father was one of the best in Pennsylvania and I learned everything at his side. I've had years of training and practice."

"Then why didn't you stay there?" Someone demanded.

The crowd murmured and chuckled. Jillian pushed her

shoulders back.

"Because my father died. And most people back east aren't interested in a woman doctor."

"Neither are we." The voice was familiar. The trapper's.

She glanced down at her friends, was reassured by their encouraging nods.

"Well, I'd hoped you folks would be more open-minded. But in case you weren't, I replied to the advertisement using only my first initial, which is the same as my father's. Mr. Parker assumed he'd hired my father and I didn't do anything to dispel his belief. So he's as innocent in this as the rest of you. However"—she raised her hand to let them know she wasn't done—"it doesn't, or shouldn't, change the fact that I was hired for my skills. And those haven't changed."

"She's right," Wade concurred from the front. "We hired her based on her skills, not on her name."

"Be that as it may, she is a woman, and that isn't what we hired. At least I know it's not what I agreed to," Steven added, his words intended to once again rile the crowd.

"Even if we let Robert send out the advertisements, it could be weeks, even months until we find another vet. Dr. Matthews is already here, I say we give her a chance to prove herself."

Mrs. Hollingsworth, red as the ripest tomato, stood up. "I think this is preposterous. What kind of example are we setting for these children? Especially the girls."

"Amen to that," chimed in the trapper.

While Jillian knew it wouldn't help her cause to be argumentative, she wouldn't let them attack her character either.

"I've never stolen or cheated anybody. I've accepted eggs, bread and chickens when that was all the families could afford. I work hard and have never disrespected my family. Is that the kind of example you mean?"

"Well, I never!" Mrs. Hollingsworth sputtered, clearly not used to being spoken back to.

"Well, maybe it's time you do!" Jillian answered, gaining a few snickers from those assembled.

With the heat now unbearable, Jillian wiped the moisture from her lip, tugged at the collar that suddenly wanted to choke her. She didn't know what more she could do to plead her case but ask the same question she'd posed to the trapper.

"Is your pride really worth the life of one of your animals?" Her eyes touched on as many faces as she could. "Would you truly let them suffer, die unnecessarily, because you're not happy I'm a woman?"

She shook her head. "That's not only mean, it's short-sighted and, quite frankly, I expected more from people who've carved a life out here, where the winters are cold and long, where the land can be unforgiving. I imagined those folks to be the kind who band together, who do what's necessary to survive. Was I wrong?"

"No," Eileen said as she came to her feet. "You weren't. That's exactly the kind of folks we are. We raise good children, we work hard. We go to church."

Letty stood up. "We stand behind our friends."

"We don't give up, no matter the odds against us." Silver stood as well.

"I say we not only give Miss Matthews a chance to prove herself, but we give her a chance to see who we really are."

Tears burned her eyes at Wade's words. He'd said more than she'd hoped and as many sets of eyes fell to the floor, as heads nodded and a few folks verbally agreed to give her a chance, she knew his words had made a difference.

He hadn't swayed everyone, far from it, but he'd given her a start. With gratefulness pressing hard against her chest, Jillian's eyes met Wade's. Held. Her legs wobbled.

And she knew, when he tipped his head toward her, that gratefulness wasn't the only emotion swelling within her.

★

"WE NEED TO do more," Steven said. "That little trick you pulled with the saddle didn't even stop her from coming to the picnic. And now look at the mess we have."

Steven once again held the gavel. Wade had tossed it back to him once he'd managed, yet again, to get the town to listen to him. Well, he hadn't swayed them all, but Steven had seen the moment when some of them had shifted their support back to Wade. Goddammit!

"Shit," Bill agreed, "that saddle was a lame idea anyway. I told you," he said, pointing a sausage finger at Justin, "that it would take more than that."

Justin crossed his arms. "And I told you I wouldn't hurt her, neither. Besides, it scared her. Even from where I was hiding in the bushes, I could see her face was white as milk."

"Well, clearly she's not so easily rattled."

"I won't have it," Steven said, thumping the gavel into his palm. "I won't be made a fool of. We need her out of this town before she and Wade convince the rest of them."

"What about Wade?"

Steven looked over at Bill. "What do you mean?"

"Maybe if Wade stood to lose something, he'd reconsider supporting her."

"Well, hell, Bill, now you're talking!" Steven said. His mouth salivated at the thought of Wade finally getting some comeuppance.

"It's all fine to have Wade reconsider and all, but we can't ignore the Matthews woman either." Robert reminded them.

Harvey snickered. "Don't you worry, we haven't forgotten about her. If she's still around when I get back from Bozeman, you just leave her to me."

★

IT TOOK WADE longer than he expected to get back to the ranch after the meeting. First, his mother caught him outside, launched herself in his arms. Silver and Letty patted his back, told him he'd done the right thing. Then, as he knew she would, Angela Hollingsworth told him how disgusted she was with him; how she hoped he was using better judgment raising her granddaughter.

Feeling the sting of his mother-in-law's words, Wade told his ma he'd stay in town to take Annabelle—who would be ecstatic when she saw him waiting for her—home from school. Wade then asked Shane to join him at the restaurant for dinner.

By the time they ate and Wade brought a chattering Annabelle home, it was midafternoon. With a few hours yet before supper, Wade joined Scott and James, who'd been working on the barn while Wade stayed in town. Filling his pockets with nails, Wade carefully climbed into the rafters. A few more supports and they'd be ready for the roof.

"We did good today," James said after pounding in a nail. "I'd hate to think what would have happened if Annabelle hadn't heard about the meeting. Hell, can you imagine the damage Steven would've done?"

"It's what he'd hoped for," Scott said. "I don't know him as well as you do, but it made me happy to see his face when we walked in."

Wade chuckled. Looking at Steven hadn't been as rewarding as looking at Jillian, but it had given him satisfaction to see the shock, and then understanding creep over Steven's face.

"Your mother-in-law wasn't very happy with you either," James commented.

"You got that right," Wade answered. He'd tried. From the time he'd begun courting Amy, he'd tried to win over her mother. A widow, she'd fussed over her only child and had wanted much better for Amy than to marry a rancher. Then, Amy had gone one step further and pursued midwifery… well, that was just one more thing his mother-in-law blamed Wade for. As though he'd encouraged her—which he hadn't. As though he'd wanted her to be a midwife—which he hadn't. As though he hadn't been enough to keep her daughter happy.

"Well, I'm proud of you, son." James leaned forward, slapped his shoulder.

Wade, who'd just positioned himself on a beam, tensed and tightened his grip on the rough wood. Just that little tap by James had sweat breaking out along his forehead. Wade hated heights.

"You think they'll come around?" Scott asked. He was perched on a beam parallel to Wade's.

"I have no idea. But I'd like to think folks are going to be smart enough to call on her when their animals need help."

Time, and only time, would eventually tell in the end. And with nothing more to say on the matter, they got back to work. Soon, sweat was stinging Wade's eyes. The pounding of three hammers echoed in his ears. The vibrations made his palm tingle and itch at the same time. Nevertheless he enjoyed looking around—around, not down—and seeing progress. Loved the smell of freshly cut wood. Taking another nail, Wade drove it home.

"What do you suppose Jillian will do next?" Scott asked between hammering.

Wade lowered his arm. "What do you mean?"

"Do you think she'll leave Marietta if she doesn't get work?"

He hadn't considered that option but he supposed it made sense. She needed income to survive. Still, the idea of her packing and moving didn't sit well with him.

"I don't know," he answered simply. "I suppose she could."

"Be a shame if she did," James said. He straddled the wood, rested his hammer on his thigh. "Who knows when we'll get another one?"

"And one as pretty," Scott added.

Scott had moved into a position that would have made a monkey proud. With one leg wrapped around a beam, he reached into his pocket, drew out some nails and placed them between his lips.

"Be careful. I don't want you falling or we'll be picking nails from your cheeks for a week."

Wade looked down, a good fifteen feet. His stomach clenched. Not a good idea. Feeling the world tilt, he wrapped his hands around the wood, hammer and all, and looked up. Through the frame of the rafters, small puffy balls of clouds floated by lazily. He concentrated on their movement until his stomach settled back into position.

"Hey, are you going to daydream all day or are you going to carry your weight?"

Wade pulled himself together and looked at James, who seemed as comfortable on the narrow board as he would in a saddle. He took the jab for what it was, a distraction from his fear. James had known since he'd offered to build him a tree house when he was six that Wade couldn't stomach heights.

"Yeah, keep your shirt on. I just need to get some more nails."

Scott, having stopped to dig some out of his pocket, leaned over as far as his arm could reach. "Here, take these. It's almost suppertime anyway. That'll get you by for a few minutes."

Not daring to look down, Wade stretched to take the nails. It wasn't enough. Though only a few inches separated them, it may as well have been a mile. Grunting, Scott shifted and tried again, but lost his balance. The nails in his hands dropped to the dirt below.

"Shit!"

Instinct, not logic, had Wade reaching for Scott's hand. Managing to rotate and grab, Scott was able to stay up. Wade wasn't so lucky. In a matter of seconds his balance shifted too far to be righted. It happened so quickly he didn't have a hope. As his upper body swung down, his legs slipped from around the wood. His stomach plunged right along with the rest of him. The ground came up fast and all he could do was brace for impact.

Despite bending his legs he landed hard and his ankle turned as he rolled to the ground. His head smacked something cold and sharp. Breath knocked out, Wade gasped and wheezed for air. From above he heard shouts and shuffling.

"Wade! Wade, you all right?"

He worked hard on getting his breath back but it seemed his lungs weren't working. It was as though someone had smacked him across the chest with a wooden beam. He tried inhaling but he sounded like a donkey braying. Panic engulfed him. His lungs burned. The harder he tried, the more panicked he became and the less air went in.

Suddenly strong arms lifted him from behind. Propped, Wade was at last able to draw air. He took several long breaths, letting whoever was behind him support his weight.

James moved into his line of vision, his face was pale. "Are you okay? You're bleeding."

"I think so." Testing his theory, Wade looked from side to side. Well, he hadn't broken his neck. His arms were heavy and stung on the shoulder he'd landed on, but otherwise they worked. His ankle, though, if not broken, was sprained. As the rest of James' words sank in, something warm trickled past his eye and over his jawbone.

"How bad is it?" Scott asked over Wade's shoulder.

Luckily Scott didn't loosen his grip or else Wade would have fallen again. He was too dizzy to support himself.

James leaned forward, his eyes narrowing. "Too much blood to tell for sure. Let's get him in the house. Once he's cleaned up we'll have a better idea." He sat back on his haunches. "Are you ready to get up or do you need a few minutes?"

Wade felt like he'd been stampeded over, and his boot already squeezed his ankle. If he waited much longer they'd never be able to get it off.

"I'm ready. But I don't think I can walk on my left ankle." Keeping his foot off the ground, Wade stood up. Scott moved around to his side.

Hobbling, they staggered through large yellow rectangles the sun cast on the dirt floor. Each hop was excruciating for Wade. His ankle throbbed and his head pounded. Judging from the trickle, which was creeping into the collar of his shirt, the blood wasn't subsiding.

Somehow they shuffled along and it was with great relief when they reached the house. But one thing stood in the way of him, a chair, and a long swig of whiskey. The porch. Raising his head he looked at the two steps as though they were tall as the mountain that overlooked Marietta. They may as well be. Horses stomped in his head and he was light-headed. His swollen ankle pressed against the leather of his boot and every time he inhaled he smelled blood.

The front door flew open. His mother gasped. "What happened?"

"Papa!"

Though he felt like he was wading through mud, Wade forced himself to talk. He didn't want his daughter frightened. "Button, I'm okay," he managed through teeth clenched in pain.

"Eileen, we'll need some water and a cloth or two. Once we clean up the blood, we'll have a better idea how bad it is."

"Annabelle," Scott said in the same gentle voice he used for horses, "could you get some pillows for your pa? We're going to set him on the couch."

Though his vision wavered, Wade saw his daughter nod solemnly and run up the stairs.

"I'm okay," he managed again. "I just need to sit a spell."

"We won't know for certain until you're cleaned up. Might be we'll have to take you to town for stitches."

The idea of being jostled the whole way there and back had his ankle screaming and his head thumping.

"First, though, we have to get you up the porch. You let us take your weight, just jump when we tell you."

Oh, hell. With his arms around their shoulders, they made it to the bottom of the steps.

"Okay, jump."

They took his weight and he landed on the first step. Pain exploded between his ears when he landed.

"Once more." Scott encouraged.

Gritting his teeth, Wade did as he was told. Though he landed on his good foot both times, the jarring ripped through his body like lightning.

"Hard part's over," James said.

Easy for you to say. Together they staggered through the entryway. Suddenly that hard couch was looking mighty good to him. And once he got there, no way in hell was he getting off of it to go to town.

"I'm not going," he muttered.

"Going where?" James asked.

"Town. I'm not going."

Finally they made it into the parlor and Wade sprawled on the couch. Exhausted, the pain getting the best of him, Wade closed his eyes and sighed as the world went black.

Chapter Eight

Jillian stood on the Parker's porch, her heart drumming in her chest. She'd needed to go home after the meeting, needed to calm down. Her mind had been racing and she'd been trembling with emotion. Going home had been her only thought. She wasn't a stranger to narrow-mindedness, but it never failed to infuriate her.

After spending the rest of the afternoon with her animals and feeling much better for it, she'd washed, changed, and ridden over to say her thanks. But now, the idea of seeing Wade again made her nervous. She hadn't stayed to see how he'd been treated, hadn't lingered to offer her thanks. Did he think she hadn't appreciated his gesture? Had the townsfolk unleashed their resentment on him and did he blame her for leaving him to deal with it alone after he was kind enough to come to her defense?

Well, she wasn't going to find out standing here. She straightened her navy riding skirt and knocked on the door. While she could hear voices inside, nobody came to answer her call. She knocked again, louder. The door swung inward. Jillian gaped at Scott's appearance.

His hair was disheveled. A streak of blood slashed across his cheek. More was smeared on his shoulder. Jillian immediately thought the worst.

"Jillian." He breathed as he grabbed her arm and pulled her inside. "Your timing is perfect. Eileen, Jillian's here!"

Eileen ran from the kitchen. Her face was ashen and there were bloodstains on her blouse. From the parlor Jillian heard Annabelle crying. Dear Lord, what had happened?

"Oh, Jillian, thank goodness you're here!" Her friend exclaimed. "Wade's been hurt."

She went cold all over. Wade was hurt? Had he been beaten after the meeting? Would Steven and his friends have stooped so low? She didn't hesitate when Eileen pulled her into the parlor. The first thing she saw was Annabelle, on her knees with her father's hand clasped within her own, her head resting on his chest. At the front of the couch, James leaned over Wade's head, a handkerchief pressed to Wade's temple.

She moved closer, sucked in her breath at the sight of the blood seeping from underneath the kerchief.

"What happened?"

James ran his free hand through his hair. "We were working on the rafters of the barn. He slipped and fell to the ground. I'm pretty sure he twisted his ankle 'cause he couldn't walk on it."

"He hit his head against a rock, got the breath knocked out of him but he was talking right up to the time we got him in here, then he passed out cold," Scott added.

"Is my papa going to be okay?" Annabelle asked in a watery voice.

Seeing Wade's chest rise and fall in a smooth rhythm, his left boot already off, Jillian knelt next to Annabelle. "See this," she said, pointing out the steady rhythm of his breathing. "If your papa was really hurt, his breathing wouldn't be that steady."

"But he's not waking up!" Annabelle whimpered.

"Well, sometimes that's the body's way of dealing with an injury. As long as your papa's sleeping, he's not feeling any pain."

The girl nodded, but she didn't release her grip on her father's hand.

"Head wounds always bleed a lot. He may look worse than he is. We'll know once I get him cleaned up."

"I was just warming water when you knocked. I'll fetch it now," Eileen said.

"What can I do?" Scott asked.

With Eileen fetching water and James keeping pressure on Wade's head wound, there wasn't anything Scott could do.

"You can see to Hope. I hadn't planned on staying long, so I just tied her to the porch."

"I'll see she's taken care of." After a worried glance in Wade's direction, Scott disappeared outside.

Tears ran down Annabelle's freckled cheeks and her sniffles seemed loud as a herd of horses in the otherwise still room. Jillian knew that kind of pain, had felt its searing burn as she'd sat beside her own father's unmoving form. But Wade was going to be fine and since it appeared as though everyone had been too busy to reassure Annabelle, Jillian took the time to do so now.

But when she opened her mouth, Jillian realized she had no idea how to do so. She'd never dealt with children other than answering their questions regarding her work. Usually if an animal couldn't be saved, it was the parent left to do the explaining. Jillian thought to her own experience not so long ago when her father lay dying and what had brought her comfort. Jillian placed her hand on the girl's shoulder.

"Annabelle, your father is going to be fine, but it's important that I examine him to be certain."

"But I don't want to leave him!"

"I'd never ask that. I know you want to be near him, that you need to see for yourself that he'll be all right. But I need to wash him and have a closer look at that gash on his forehead."

Though Annabelle nodded her agreement, she didn't let go of her father's hand.

"I can't help him, Annabelle, if you're in the way." She reminded her gently.

"Do you promise I can stay?"

"I promise. All I need is some room. Maybe you could stand by his feet. If you're careful, you can pull off his sock.

I'll want to look at his ankle once I'm done with his head."

"Won't that hurt him?" she asked.

She wiped her cheeks dry and Jillian was glad to see the tears had stopped.

"You'll be careful, won't you?"

The answering nod came very quickly.

Jillian smiled. "Then I don't see why you can't do that."

Content to have some task to make her feel useful, Annabelle released her father's hand and shuffled to the end of the couch.

Jillian turned to James, reached for the handkerchief. "I'll need to examine the wound."

He nodded, stepped aside. She looked at his bloody hands and her stomach clenched at the thought that that was Wade's blood. She reminded herself as she had Annabelle that Wade had a strong and steady heartbeat. He was going to be fine. Seeing the worry etched on James's face she reiterated the fact to him as well.

"Why don't you go wash up while I see how bad this is?"

After James strode out of the room, Jillian turned to Annabelle, watched as the child slowly rolled the sock off Wade's foot. Already the ankle was badly swollen.

"I didn't wake him. That means I didn't hurt him, right?"

"Right. That was a good job, Annabelle."

With his daughter calm and reassured, Jillian focused on Wade. Though not schooled in human medicine, she knew the basics of what to do. With her fingertips holding down the handkerchief, she turned Wade's head toward her. His cheek was bristly in her palm but it wasn't an unpleasant feeling. In fact, there was something unexpectedly pleasant about the abrasive scrape of his beard.

Eileen came back and placed a bowl of water at her feet, handed Jillian a clean cloth. "Is there anything else I can do?"

Jillian reached out and squeezed her friend's hand. It was cold as ice. "He really will be fine. Why don't you go for a walk? I won't be too long."

Though she nodded, she didn't move. James stepped back into the room and placed a lit lantern on the small table beside the couch. Though it was daylight yet, the extra brightness would be useful in seeing how bad the gash was.

"I figured you might need it." He shrugged when Jillian smiled at him.

"I do, thank you. I could also use a chair."

After he'd brought her one, she said, "Now, really, why you don't you two get some fresh air."

"We won't wander far," James said.

"Truly, I don't think it's more than a cut and some bruises."

James, at least, seemed to believe her. "Come on, Button, let's give Miz Matthews room to work."

"No! I don't wanna go!"

"Annabelle, it won't be for long and—"

"But Miss Matthews promised I could stay!" Fresh tears

threatened to fall.

"She's right, I did." Jillian assured them before they could argue. "And she's fine where she's at."

"Then we'll leave you to it. Come on, Eileen." James took her hand and they stepped outside.

Once the door clicked shut, Jillian removed her hand from the handkerchief, leaving the stained cloth on Wade's brow for now. She took her seat and dipped the clean cloth Eileen had brought in the bowl. Warm water washed over her hand. Gently she lifted the kerchief off, then brought the clean cloth to his face. In tender strokes, she washed the blood from his temple and cheek.

He didn't stir and for that Jillian was thankful. Bathing his face was far more intimate than anything she'd done and her inexperience in this area had her flushing. She felt the burn of it as she slid the cloth over his cheek. He had strong cheekbones and an equally firm jawline and both intrigued her. She liked the way his skin darkened where his beard grew. Enjoyed the way the cloth scraped the stubble.

Jillian was lingering at the task more than she should but it was like she'd told everyone else, his coloring and breathing were good and she wasn't worried. She'd never had such an opportunity and though her heart hammered, she was enjoying herself. And it wasn't as though bathing his face would lead to anything. She was in Marietta to work. Only work, she repeated as she brushed his face once more.

"Do you think he likes you washing him?" Annabelle

asked.

Jillian's hand jerked. Annabelle had been so quiet Jillian had forgotten she was there. Hoping Annabelle hadn't realized how much she'd been enjoying herself, Jillian reminded herself she was here in the role as physician and nothing else. Absolutely nothing.

"I know when I wash an animal who's been hurt, they seem to enjoy it. I think the warm water and a gentle hand reassures them, lets them know I'm not going to hurt them."

"And you wouldn't hurt my papa either."

"No, Annabelle," Jillian answered with absolute certainty, "I'd never hurt your papa."

When the rest of his face was clean, Jillian moved to the gash that cut across his temple. He flinched, hissed in a breath. Opened his eyes.

"Jillian?" His voice was low and confused.

"Papa!" Annabelle cried.

He moved his head, grimaced when he did. "Hi, Button."

"Are you all better now?"

"Better?" His brows creased and then smoothed out as he remembered. "I'm sure I'll be fine. I'm sorry if I scared you."

"Grandma and James wanted me to go outside but Jillian said I could stay. Is it okay that I stayed?"

"I'm glad you did, Button." He rolled his head Jillian's way.

Jillian took the curve of his mouth to be his thanks. "She

needed to be with you," she said simply.

The room had been warm before but suddenly it was stifling. Since distraction had worked on Annabelle, she decided to use the same trick with the girl's father.

"You have a nasty cut above your temple. I was about to have a closer look when you woke up." She leaned closer, much too aware of his moist breath on her neck. She wiped away more blood. The wound wasn't deep but the blood kept coming. "You're going to need a few stitches." She clutched the cloth in her hands and sat back. "I'm not sure about your ankle, though, as I haven't had a chance to look at it yet."

His eyes continued to hold Jillian's for a few long beats then he shifted them back to his daughter. "See, Button, I'm going to be okay."

Despite the words, his daughter's chin trembled. "Can I give you a hug now?" she asked, her small voice cracking.

Tears stung Jillian's eyes. In that moment she missed her father desperately. She dropped the cloth in the bowl.

"I'll go get some clean water. Here, Annabelle, you can sit in my place."

She gave them plenty of time, even taking a moment to step outside where she found James, Eileen, and Scott lingering on the porch. After reassuring them Wade was awake and talking, James and Scott thanked her, then went back to work. Eileen, being a mother, rushed inside to see for herself.

"Ma, quit hovering!"

She hadn't stopped touching him since she'd run into the parlor. First his hair, then his cheek. At the moment she held his hand in a vise.

"I was worried. I'm your mother; I'm allowed to be worried."

He sighed. Why argue? "Well, as you can see, I'm fine now."

"But, Papa, you're still bleeding." Annabelle pointed out.

Though the wound was bleeding, it was a slow, sticky trickle. He wiped it away with his hand.

"It's just a cut, it'll heal. Remember how your knees healed after you fell in the yard that time you were racing Jacob?"

"But I had to beat him!"

Wade chuckled. Annabelle and Jacob were always racing. At the rate they were going, neither one would have any skin on their knees by the time they turned ten.

"And you would have, if you hadn't fallen. But even though you scraped them up good, they healed didn't they?"

"Yes, Papa."

"And I will, too. Now how about if you help Grandma with some oatmeal cookies? I'm sure they'll help me get better much faster."

Her blue eyes sparkled like sunshine off the Yellowstone River. "Come, Grandma, let's make Papa some cookies!"

His mother poked her index finger into his chest. "Don't you ever scare me like that again."

He grinned. "I love you too, Ma."

"Oh, go on!" She swatted him lightly on the shoulder, sniffled, and left the room.

Jillian came in as his mother and daughter were walking out. He heard her ask for sewing supplies, since she hadn't brought her bag along. She also promised Annabelle, after some rather determined begging on his daughter's part, that she'd stay afterward for a cookie. Hearing his daughter squeal with excitement after having seen the fear and sadness in her eyes eased his mind. Poor thing must have been so scared, thinking she'd lose her father.

When he'd first felt the warm cloth and gentle strokes, he'd been content to relax under the gentle ministrations, to savor the soothing caress. It wasn't until the touch brushed the wound that he'd felt pain and realized he wasn't dreaming.

Still, he'd expected to see his mother upon opening his eyes and it had taken him a moment to comprehend that Jillian was there. When had she gotten there? How long had he been out cold? But then fully understanding that it had been her hands on him—if only his face—he'd wished he could have gone back and enjoyed her touch all over again. Which, considering he'd already vowed not only to his mother but also to himself that he wasn't interested in Jillian, made him wonder just how hard he'd smacked his head.

Jillian placed the bowl at her feet and soon afterward his mother returned with a bottle of whiskey, needle, thread, and scissors. He watched silently as Jillian cut a length of thread, then soaked both it and needle in whiskey. Just as he'd noticed the night of the surgery, he saw that she had delicate hands, hands more suitable to another profession than the one she'd chosen.

"Did you ever consider being a nurse?"

"No."

"Because you wanted to follow in your father's footsteps?"

"Because animals don't talk," she answered with a twinkle in her eye.

Then, with a soft laugh that hit him square in the gut, she proceeded to thread her needle. Wade eyed the needle. This wasn't the first time he'd needed to be sewn up, but he hated needles almost as much as he hated heights.

"Where did you put the whiskey?"

Jillian handed him the bottle and he raised it to his lips, took a long swallow.

"I'm ready when you are," he said, passing her the bottle.

Being poked with a needle wasn't what Wade would call pleasant. It sure as heck wasn't as nice as having her bathe him with a warm cloth. Yet he couldn't think of a place he'd rather be. Lying on his side, with Jillian leaning over him to stitch, left him in the very enviable position of having her breast inches from his face. His eyes fixated on it like a moth to a lantern. The generous, soft curve of it tempted him until he figured he'd surely go to hell for the thoughts he was having.

What if he leaned forward, brushed his mouth against her breast? What if he opened his lips and drew the hard tip into his mouth despite the layers of fabric? Want coiled through him, harder and faster than he'd felt in years. He could almost feel the hard nub of her nipple rolling over his tongue.

"Ow!" he yelled when he jerked and the thread pulled his wound.

"Don't move!" Jillian scolded.

Then she leaned a little closer and Wade had to close his eyes. He couldn't keep looking at her without having such thoughts, without smelling her warm skin and wondering what it would taste like.

Sweat beaded his forehead. Why was it so blasted hot in here?

"Are you almost finished?" Even to his own ears, his voice sounded strained.

"I was about to cut the thread when you moved," she said, the admonishment in her voice was unmistakable.

A few more tortured seconds passed as she snipped the thread. Then—finally—the sweet, tempting smell of her eased and he was able to breathe again.

"Sorry, this will hurt."

She took the whiskey and poured a little over the sutures.

He flinched at the burn but was grateful it gave him something else to think about besides her body and what thinking about it was doing to his own.

She dabbed at the liquid that ran from the sutures. "I'm done."

He opened his eyes, took a deep breath.

"I'm sorry, I know that hurt."

While he was still battling to control himself, he felt the much cooler cloth once again sweep over his face. It felt too good to do anything but lie there and let her wash him. Of course it also prevented his body from forgetting what it had been two years without.

He caught her wrist. Her gaze reflected everything he was feeling: surprise, uncertainty. Desire.

Hellfire.

"I'm fine now, Jillian."

Wade felt less vulnerable sitting up. But as the blood rushed down, his ankle started throbbing. He tried to move it, grimaced as a stab of pain ricocheted up his calf.

"Do you want me to have a look?"

Not a hope in hell. He was barely keeping himself tethered as it was. If she put those hands on him once more he wasn't going to be able to fight it any longer.

"Nah. I've wasted enough of your time. Besides, I don't think it's broken."

"Be sure to keep it wrapped, then. And keep it up as much as you can."

Wade met those deep green eyes. Keeping it up certainly wasn't proving to be a problem so far. Even the pans clanging from the kitchen reminding him there were others nearby didn't ease his need.

"I know that's difficult with the work you do, but it really will heal faster if you can."

His lips curved. "All I'll have to do is tell Ma your orders and I'll be lucky to walk to the outhouse without help."

She folded her hands into her lap. Wade was intrigued by the blush that rode underneath her creamy skin.

"You look like you have something on your mind."

"I didn't happen by, though it turns out that was a stroke of luck. I actually came to thank you."

"For?"

"For coming to the meeting and speaking on my behalf. I don't know if it will help, but I appreciate the gesture."

He shrugged and struggled to stand, keeping his injured foot off the ground. Jillian pushed her chair back, rushed to help him but he held up his hand.

"I don't think you should be up yet. Are you dizzy?"

He held onto the couch until he wasn't. He managed to hop a few steps, but the pain was like a red-hot poker and it was jabbing him in both the head and the foot. Feeling like he'd just run up the steepest hill, he leaned heavily against the wall.

"It hurts like a son-of-a-bitch."

"I heard that!" His mother's voice came from the kitchen, but Wade didn't bother apologizing. He was too busy gritting his teeth.

"I really think you need to lie back down," Jillian said.

"I'll be all right. Just give me a minute."

She crossed her arms, which only served to push her breasts higher. Wade groaned, shut his eyes. The next thing he knew she was at his side, her arm sliding between him and the wall.

"If you're so determined to move, then at least accept some help. Clearly, you're not up to doing this on your own yet."

It was the same authoritative voice she'd used the night of the surgery and he grinned.

"What's so funny?" she asked.

"You can be very bossy."

"I'm not bossy."

His grin spread. "You most certainly can be. You've already bossed me around a time or two." The flush he so enjoyed seeing on her cheeks deepened.

"Well, you deserved it," she answered with as much starch as one of Shane's shirts.

She had her arm wrapped around his waist. Her head barely reached his shoulder. But her chin jutted defiantly and her eyes dared him to argue the point. He didn't bother. First, she was right, he had deserved it. And second, with her tucked in tight next to his body, there were much better things he could think to do than argue.

Before her eyes had more than a moment to widen at the realization of what was about to happen, Wade bent his head and touched his lips to hers. He'd felt the scorching heat of a grass fire. Hell, there'd been one, back when he wasn't more than Annabelle's age that had burned through the back edge of their pasture. Folks had seen the smoke and come running and it had been a long day of fighting the blaze, eating smoke and feeling the fine hairs on his arms burn off before they had it out.

But even that was nothing compared to the flames rising around him as he took Jillian's mouth with his own. She didn't resist, but rather leaned into him, sighed, and opened her mouth under his.

It was a burning the likes of which he'd never known. It came from his chest and pushed its way out, engulfing him until he heard the roar of it in his ears. He wrapped his arms around her, pulled her tightly against him. The movement nearly toppled them over. Before he lost his balance and took them both down, he swiveled on his good foot until he once again had the support of the wall at his back.

She felt delicate and small in his arms. She felt good. He held her pressed against him, all soft curves to his angles. He rubbed his tongue against hers, shuddered at the same time she did. Body burning, Wade slanted his mouth and took the kiss deeper. The roar intensified. Her scent enveloped him as much as her arms. He ran his hand up her back, clutched her braid in his fist, wished he could untie it and feel the satin of her hair pour through his fingers. He wished—

"Oh, my!"

"Papa!"

Jillian tensed and jerked free. He closed his eyes, let his head fall back and hit the wall. The small thud was the only sound save his and Jillian's labored breathing.

"Papa, you were kissing!"

Hellfire. He rubbed a hand down his face before he dared open his eyes. What he saw when he opened them was exactly what he figured he'd see. His mother looked like she'd just struck gold. Hell, she could've eaten it the way her face glowed. Annabelle's eyes were wider than a harvest moon. Jillian, on the other hand, was red as a beet.

"Cookies are baking, shouldn't be more than a few minutes. We thought we'd come see how the stitches were coming but"—his ma grinned—"I can see everything is coming along just fine."

"I'll just clean up," Jillian said as she moved to gather everything.

"Are you going to kiss my papa some more?"

Jillian wobbled the bowl and water poured over the rim and down her skirt.

"Annabelle! You've embarrassed Miss Matthews. Here, Jillian, let me take that," his ma said, taking the bowl. "There's a towel in the kitchen. Come and we'll dry you off."

Following his mother, Jillian didn't look back, but then

that was just as well since Annabelle was heading his way. She stopped before him, crossed her arms. Then, with one foot tapping, looked up into his eyes and asked, "Well, Papa, are you going to kiss her again?"

★

JILLIAN JOLTED AWAKE. Heart slamming against her ribs, she sat up, clutched the blanket to her chest, and tried to ascertain what had yanked her from sleep. A sleep that had been hard to come by since she couldn't stop thinking of Wade's kiss.

A pounding on the door, loud and insistent, carried into her bedroom, which was tucked behind the parlor. Knowing what woke her didn't help her erratic heartbeat. There was nothing but darkness behind her curtains and while she hoped whoever was at her door was there because they needed her medical skills, the truth of the matter was, after the town meeting, she couldn't be sure.

Tying her wrapper around her waist, she slid her loaded rifle out from under her bed. She tiptoed to the door, deliberately not bothering to turn on a lantern, not wanting her shadow to announce her presence. Pulling back the thin curtains she jumped when another thump beat on her door.

"Miss Matthews, it's Jacob Garvey. My dog is sick and I need your help!"

Releasing her death grip on the rifle, she placed it against the wall. The door opened with a slight creak and the loud sigh of Jacob Garvey. Damp night air wafted through the opening, its long, cool fingers swirling around her bare ankles.

Jacob didn't waste any time, words poured from his mouth before she could even get him in the door. "My dog, Fred, is hurtin' real bad." He sniffled, wiped his nose on the sleeve of his dark jacket. "You need to come quick."

"What happened?"

He took a shaky breath. "A rattlesnake bit him." His chin quivered. "Pa says he's gonna die."

Jillian seethed. Rattlesnake bites weren't normally lethal and she figured if his father didn't know for sure, he shouldn't have jumped to the worst conclusion and scared his son half to death.

"Jacob, is Fred an old dog?"

"No, he's only four years old."

"Is he a sickly dog?"

The boy sniffled. "He's healthy, ain't never been sick before."

Jillian placed a hand on Jacob's shoulder. Fred was going to be just fine.

"Come into the kitchen, Jacob. I'll make Fred a poultice. That will help draw out the venom."

She lit a lantern, opened her stove and poked at the now dead fire. After arranging kindling, she started another. It wouldn't take much to get the flaxseed boiling for the poultice. When the pot was set on the stove, Jillian turned to the boy.

He wasn't crying but his cheeks bore the tracks that he had. "Does your father know you're here?" Jillian asked.

Fear gave way to anger and small hands fisted at his side. "He said he'd rather see Fred die than ask for your help."

Her fury came fast and hard and it took a mighty effort to keep it contained. What kind of father would hurt his child so needlessly? Would let his son's heart break rather than get help, especially when it was so easily gotten? A shortsighted, pompous one like Steven Garvey.

"I hope you won't get into trouble for this, Jacob, but I can promise you Fred will be fine. Let me go change. When I'm done, the flaxseed should be ready. Then I'll show you how to do this, so if Fred ever gets bit again, you'll be able to help him yourself."

His large brown eyes met hers and the hope and gratitude in them gave her heart a squeeze.

"He'll really be all right?"

She smiled. "He really will."

Once dressed, she showed him how to make the poultice. When it was wrapped in a clean cloth, Jillian put it in her medicine bag and drew on her slicker.

Shadows danced on the plank walls of her barn and Rascal chattered a blue streak as Jillian tacked Hope. Once the bag was tied behind the saddle she led her horse outside.

"Ready," she said once she was astride.

"You're not gonna use that on Fred, are you?" he asked,

pointing at the rifle she had across her lap.

"No, Jacob. But I'm not familiar with this area and I want to be careful. Besides, I'll be riding back on my own."

He nodded in understanding and then kicked his own horse into a gallop. Hoping his father was a sound sleeper, Jillian followed Jacob.

They kept a steady pace despite the darkness and soon arrived at the Garvey farm. Jacob leapt from his animal, which knowing it was home, ambled for the fence. Jillian secured Hope, untied her bag and followed the boy into the barn.

Fred was in one of the stalls. The boy set a lantern on a peg and rushed in. Jillian followed into the straw-laden stall. Fred, a lean and healthy-looking golden dog, was licking his wound.

"Jacob, can you get me some clean water? Snake bites are usually dirty and we need to clean it."

He nodded and slipped outside. Water sloshed inside the bucket when he came back a few minutes later.

She washed the area clean of dirt and motioned for the boy to come closer. "See here." She lifted Fred's paw so Jacob could see the two holes that marked the snakebite. "There are two more on the bottom of his paw. All we have to do is—"

Suddenly another light shone from the doorway. Beside her Jacob froze. The thump of footsteps on the hard dirt floor accompanied the heavy breathing that pounded closer.

Jillian stood, prepared for the worst.

"Dammit, Jacob, I said no!" Steven shouted.

"Pa, I'm sorry—"

"Get out!" Steven's words she knew were for her, not his son. "Get off my land. Now!"

The whole ride over Jillian had prepared arguments in her head in case they were discovered. She used them now.

"And then what? You'll let the dog suffer?"

"No, I'd shoot it first."

"No, Pa. Don't shoot him!" Jacob wailed as he threw himself over the dog.

She pointed to his son's teary face. "Look at him! He loves that dog! What's to gain by letting Fred die and watching your boy pine over him? Is your dislike of me really worth having your son resent you for not letting him get help? This is easily fixed and if you weren't so stubborn you'd see that!"

Garvey swallowed and looked to his son. He seemed to lose some of his bluster. She pressed the advantage, small as it was.

"If you run me off, I'm taking Fred with me."

Both males faced her, one with terror, the other with hatred.

"You said yourself you're willing to let him die," she said to Garvey. "If you don't care enough to help the poor animal, why should you care if I take him?"

Jacob stood. "Please, Pa, let her help Fred. I don't want her to take him."

Garvey jammed a hand through hair in desperate need of a brush then fixed his resentful gaze on her. "I will not pay you, not one red cent. Nothing!"

Knowing that was as much acceptance as she was going to get, Jillian set down to her task. Behind her, she heard Steven's mumbled curses and then the curt order for his son to get back inside the moment they were finished. Jillian took a steadying breath as his boots thumped back down the aisle.

"Now then," she said as though they hadn't been interrupted, "there are two holes on the bottom of the paw, as well on the top. First"—she opened her bag—"we apply the poultice. That will draw out the venom." She tied it in place with a piece of string and gently nudged Fred's head onto her lap so he'd leave the poultice in place.

Stroking the dog's golden head, Jillian continued. "He won't like it, Jacob, but try to keep it on him. Make another one, just like I showed you, tomorrow morning. If you can, keep the poultice on Fred for most of the day. Tomorrow night you can take it off. Just make sure the wound stays clean. It has to stay open to drain."

Jacob didn't look convinced. "Is that really all there is to it?"

She patted Fred's head, praised him for being a good boy, and eased away. "I wouldn't lie to you, Jacob. His paw is a bit swollen, so it looks worse than it is. But I cleaned it good and, as I said, the poultice will work if you can keep it on."

"I will, I promise!" The boy threw himself at Fred's side and buried his face in the fur. The dog leaned into him and tears stung Jillian's eyes when the boy broke into sobs. This was why she'd become a veterinarian. It was amazing how much an animal could enrich a life.

"Remember to keep that poultice on and make another in the morning." She handed him a small bag of flaxseed. "You'll need this. If you get worried, you come see me again." At the doubtful look in his eyes she added, "Or get word to Mrs. Daniels at the mercantile. She'll let me know you need help."

He nodded, and for the first time since he arrived on her porch, he smiled. "Thanks, Miss Matthews."

"You're welcome, Jacob."

She let herself outside. A lantern burned on the front porch and a man's shape moved in the shadows. She stilled, wondered if there would be another argument. Darkness engulfed her, and even with her rifle she felt vulnerable standing there. Especially with the resentment that seemed to burn a swath from the porch to her feet. Jillian held her ground. He didn't have to like her but, by God, he'd better get used to her.

It was a few charged minutes, but then the front door opened and Garvey disappeared inside, slamming the door behind him.

Riding home, Jillian kept one hand on her weapon. She didn't really think Garvey would follow and harm her, but since she couldn't seem to rid herself of the lurking power of his hatred, she decided it wouldn't hurt to be careful.

★

STEVEN STEPPED BACK onto the porch. The moist air did nothing to calm him. Neither did knowing that woman was finally off his property.

Hell, he'd known it was just a matter of time until someone called on her. Much as he hated that it was his own son who'd done it, Steven was nonetheless smart enough to realize it was a good thing it had been Jacob and not someone else. Another farmer could be more easily swayed by her. He knew snakebites weren't normally lethal; it was why he'd told Jacob not to go fetch her. Still, he had seen a few die on occasion and he'd figured he'd rather see Fred succumb to venom than have Jillian here.

He should have just told Jacob the dog would be fine.

Steven crossed his arms, looked out in the night. He took small comfort in the fact she'd gotten nothing for coming. Other than Wade—though why in God's name he paid her after she killed his cow Steven couldn't understand—she hadn't earned a cent since arriving. And he knew she had expenses. He'd seen her loaded wagon the day she'd come into his feed mill, knew she had animals to care for. A person couldn't live without income for long, not with expenses like that.

Smiling, he went back inside.

Chapter Nine

WITH DAWN YET to color the sky, his ma padded to the stove and raised the lid on the coffee pot. "Mercy!" Clucking about how his insides must be made of steel, she went through the covered porch and tossed the black sludge out the back door. After refilling the pot with fresh water James had brought in last night, she put it on the stove to boil.

"What's got you up before the birds this morning?" she asked, as she smoothed imaginary crumbs aside and folded her arms onto the table.

"Just thinking."

"About Jillian or the ranch?" she asked, grinning.

He'd had a hell of a time avoiding talk of Jillian since she'd left yesterday. Annabelle was like a pesky mosquito, coming at him from all sides no matter how much he sidestepped it. And if it wasn't his daughter, his mother snuck in a question or comment hoping he'd trip and give himself away. And because his mother had told James, who, of course told Scott, he hadn't gotten any relief over supper last night either.

They were all on it like a pack of dogs fighting over the same bone.

"Isn't it a little early in the day for an interrogation?"

"Nope."

God help him. "Water's boiling," he said.

She was back at the table before he'd had a chance to think of something to tell her. He was certain she'd never ground beans faster in her life.

"When are you going to see her again?"

"When are you going to ask me a different question?"

"When you answer me," she answered with a smile.

He crossed his arms over his chest. He could be as stubborn as she was. Her fingers tapped the table as she waited. In the silence the house creaked, as though stretching for a new day. Sighing, his mother shoved from the table, poured the coffee.

Inside the stove, logs rolled and shifted as they burned. Outside the window, the sky was lightening with dawn.

He should have known the silence wasn't going to last very long. What he hadn't expected, however, were the words she used to break it.

"I know we haven't talked about it, and I know the wedding is in another few short weeks, but I was hoping, now that the barn is almost done, that we could have a dance.

"Now I know," she added before he could do more than take a breath, "it seems silly to have them so close together, but the barn will be full come the wedding, and it's tradition,

Wade, to have a barn dance once a new one is built."

Her eyes glowed with excitement and in them he saw the same exuberance and energy that poured from his daughter every day. *Hellfire.* How could his ma, at forty-nine, have more energy than he did at twenty-eight?

He finished his coffee, hobbled up, and poured them each more.

"Ma, this is going to slow me down," he said of the foot he propped on a chair. "Which will put me even further behind in my work."

She hesitated only a minute. "Life can't be all about work; losing your father brought that fact home. And everyone always brings something anyway, so it's hardly any expense at all. Please."

One word. One damn word that, coupled with the longing he saw in her brown eyes, undid him. He wasn't the only one who'd struggled since his father's death; she'd had a hell of a time, too. Yes, now she had James, and he was thankful for that, but their relationship had come about recently. For months she'd mourned and he'd been helpless to ease her pain.

He took a deep breath. The table smelled of oil and soap. She oiled it every week. She cooked on a small stove, smaller than most women owned. The checkered drapes she'd sewn herself had been washed so often they were threadbare and faded. He was pretty sure they'd been red at one time; they were mostly pink now.

Everything she had she tended well, but it didn't hide the fact that the floors were scratched and worn, the pots were blackened from use and the cupboards—the few the small kitchen had—were too small to hold all her dishes. What couldn't fit was stacked neatly in the corner, taking up counter space she couldn't spare. How could he possibly refuse her this one bit of excitement?

"Fine, let me know if you need anything and I'll settle up with Letty later."

She clapped her hands and squealed just as Annabelle came down the stairs. His daughter, much like his mother, was an early riser. She rushed over, threw herself in his arms.

"Why is Grandma excited?"

He wrapped his arms around Annabelle, kissed her forehead. "It seems we're going to be having a barn dance."

His daughter's squeal was even louder than his mother's and Wade cringed as it blasted right into his ear, added to the dull headache he'd woken with thanks to his fall yesterday.

"Will my friends come? Can I stay up past my bedtime? When will it be?"

"I should be ready by Saturday." And with any luck he'd be walking without limping by then.

"Are you inviting Jillian?" Annabelle asked.

"Of course he is."

His ma tugged Annabelle onto her lap and they sat before him, four eyes piercing him, two smiles all but blinding him.

Hellfire.

"I suppose she'll be invited same as most folks." He conceded.

His mother glowed. "Of course, you'll have to ask her. I'll be too busy to get out there myself," she said.

"I'll go ask her!"

"No, Annabelle. Not by yourself. You know I don't like you riding off the ranch alone. I'll go."

He didn't have to see his mother's sly grin to know she'd gotten exactly what she'd hoped for. Was that the reason for the dance, to get him and Jillian together? He shook his head.

Of course it was.

★

JILLIAN RODE INTO Marietta as though the hounds of hell were nipping at Hope's hooves. Her hair flew wildly around her face, her eyes burned with fury. She knew she looked half-crazed, a fact confirmed as she sped down the street and, from the corner of her eye, saw several mouths gape open.

She yanked on the reins and was out of the saddle the moment Hope's hooves skittered to a stop. With a quick knot she secured her animal to the rail and marched into the feed mill.

The place was empty, but rather than taking some of the billow from her sails, it simply filled them with more anger.

"Mr. Garvey!" she yelled, her voice ricocheting off the wooden walls. "You can't hide, I won't leave until I've spoken to you."

Surrounded by bags of feed and the smell of dust dancing on the air, Jillian jammed her hands on her hips and prepared to wait him out. She didn't have to wait long.

Smacking the dust from his trousers, Steven came round the corner.

"What's all the commotion?"

"Commotion? You haven't seen a commotion yet." She warned as those imaginary sails threatened to rip under pressure. "How dare you! How dare you come onto my property and destroy what's mine."

Rolling his eyes, he strolled to the counter, leaned back against it, and crossed his arms and legs. "I've been here all morning, Miss Matthews. I have no idea what you're blathering about."

Smug. He looked so smug standing there, a small half-smile on his lips, his blue eyes mocking. Her hands curled into fists. How she'd love to smack that smile right off his face!

She moved until they were toe to toe. "Then you did it last night, but I know it was you. Who else but you would have to gain by ripping all my feedbags open? By having most of it wasted?"

It had stolen her breath, seeing the bags ripped open, their contents spread wide like dirty bathwater. Zeke hadn't minded. He'd folded to his knees, twisted and craned his neck until his tongue could scoop whatever it could reach between the slats of his stall. Hope's gaze as she'd looked upon all that spilled food had been much like Jillian's—hopeless.

Jillian had salvaged what she could, but it had been smeared deliberately thin, then stomped on so she'd had to leave much of it. Those bags should have lasted her at least a few months. She'd be lucky to stretch what was left two weeks. And on top of everything else, the hay Mr. Fletcher had left her, which should have lasted her at least another week, was missing.

After leaving the meeting, she knew she'd made some progress, had managed to convince a few families to consider seeking her help when the need arose. But like people, an animal could go weeks, months, without needing help. She'd thought if she were frugal with her money, if she were careful, she could hold out until such a time when those folks needed her.

That had all changed when she'd seen the wasted feed, the missing hay. More than ever, time was becoming her enemy.

"Well, now, that's a might sorry tale, Miss Matthews, but I don't see how it has anything to do with me."

"Oh, it has everything to do with you and if you think I'll come back here now, buy from you again, you're dead wrong. I'd rather walk to the closest feed mill than ever give you another cent."

His eyebrow rose. "Not having you in my store will hardly be a hardship."

"You did this because I helped Jacob."

That, finally, knocked the smugness from his face. "I don't want you near my son ever again."

"I don't see how you can stop me. I may just have to time my trips into town to coincide with the end of the school day. You know," she said, tapping her finger onto her chin, "I should stop by the school today, see if I can't talk to Jacob and ask him how Fred's doing."

Steven's face went hard. "Stay away from my son."

"Then stay away from me," Jillian countered. "I'm not going anywhere, so you'd best get used to it."

Spinning on her heel, her skirt arcing wide around her ankles, Jillian strode for the door.

"Sure is a shame about all that feed wasted, though," Steven called after her. "I don't imagine you can spare the expense, what with nobody calling on you."

Jillian's hand hovered on the door. His chuckle was meant to irritate, meant to scrape at her pride. She wouldn't give Steven the satisfaction of responding. He hadn't won. She was still in Marietta; he still had to deal with her.

Flinging the door open, she called back over her shoulder, "School's out about two, isn't it?"

★

"I HOPE YOU don't mind me stopping in like this."

"Of course not. Why would I mind having a friend pay me a visit? Come in, I'll get us some tea."

As they had the last time, Jillian and Silver took their seats at the long bar in the saloon. The doors were locked but a few passers-by looked twice to see who Silver was entertaining.

"I'd meant to come earlier but, unfortunately, I had some unpleasantness to deal with at home and by the time I got it sorted out and cleaned up, I was later coming in than I'd planned."

"It's no problem, Jillian. I don't open the doors until two o'clock. That allows me to clean the saloon from the night before and do any errands I may have. Or, on rare days like today, it allows me to enjoy the company of a friend." Silver took a dainty sip of her tea. "Did you want to talk about this 'unpleasantness'?"

Jillian expelled a deep breath. It was tempting, so much so that the words crawled up the back of her throat. But she hadn't come to lay her problems at Silver's feet.

Instead, she smiled. "It's nothing important."

"Is that why your cheeks are pink? Why, when I opened the door, you were blowing more vapors than a steam engine?"

Too late, Jillian realized she hadn't taken the time to straighten her appearance. She'd been so angry; she'd raced to the feed mill, feeling her hair yanking from its braid the whole way. But she'd been too furious to worry about her appearance. Her fingers caught in the tangles and she dropped her hands, knowing it was pointless.

"I'm surprised you let me in." And no doubt it had given Steven extreme pleasure to see her so agitated.

Silver laughed. "And miss the reason for your dishevelment? Not a chance!"

Jillian's cheeks warmed further, and it had nothing to do with the tea she drank.

"I'll respect your privacy if you don't want to tell me, but I'd really hoped we were becoming the kind of friends who would confide in each other."

"I'd hoped that as well." Jillian set the cup onto the saucer. "I haven't had close women friends. Even my sister and I weren't very close. As to the other women back home"—Jillian scoffed—"none of them understood my desire to be a veterinarian. While they were sleeping or attending parties, I was with my father, learning about animals and getting unfashionably dirty."

"Which doesn't make for polite conversations over afternoon tea?"

Her gaze met Silver's and a burden slipped off her shoulders as she realized Silver would understand. She didn't imagine most women would want to know about the goings on in a saloon either. If they were to confide in each other, there was no time like the present.

"Steven was in my barn," she said. "Either late last night

or early this morning." Jillian shook her head. "Doesn't matter which. Anyhow, he ripped open all my feedbags and wasted over half of my oats. And my hay's missing."

"Are you sure it was Steven?"

"I didn't see him do it, if that's what you're asking. But he owns a feed mill. If he destroys what feed I have, then who but him stands to gain? Besides, you saw him at the meeting. It's no secret he hates me."

She told Silver about Fred and how Steven had reacted to Jacob's fetching her to help.

Silver slapped her palms on the bar. "Why I have a mind to refuse him when he comes in on Friday. If that pompous—"

Jillian grabbed Silver's hand. "No, don't. Don't get involved. Besides," she added when Silver tried to protest, "knowing that his money is going to you when he comes in here…" She shrugged. "It makes me glad."

Smiling, Silver shook her head. "All right. But if I hear one word out of his mouth about you…"

"Then you do whatever you want," Jillian answered.

"Agreed." Silver poured more tea, took her seat next to Jillian. "Now, you said you were coming anyway. What was the other reason for your visit other than my great company?" she asked with a twinkle in her eye.

"Oh, well." It seemed like days not hours ago that she'd been excited to visit Silver. "If you're sure you have time."

"Other than having to open the saloon in"—she took

out a pocket watch, checked the time and dropped it back into her pocket-"twenty minutes or so, I am at your disposal."

Jillian dropped her gaze to her lap, twisted her fingers together. When she'd envisioned coming earlier, she'd hoped to discreetly learn more about Wade. She hadn't been able to stop thinking of his kiss and wondering what it had meant to him. Surely he wasn't courting anyone else to kiss her in such a way, but she had no way of knowing. She'd thought perhaps she could weave him into a conversation. She'd never imagined that Silver would outright ask the reason for Jillian's call.

"It's about Wade, isn't it?"

Jillian's head came up so fast the room spun. "What makes you ask that?"

"Oh, I don't know. Perhaps it's the look you get in your eyes when you talk about him. Or the way your cheeks flushed when he came into the town meeting. Or," she added, tongue in cheek, "the fact that he was so grateful to you for fixing up his head after he fell that he kissed you."

"How do you know?" Jillian gasped.

"It's all right; you're hardly the subject of town gossip." Silver grinned, tossed her blonde hair over shoulder. "Well, you are, but not because you kissed Wade. Eileen was in town and I happened to be at the mercantile when she was telling Letty about your…doctoring skills," she added with a giggle.

If the tea had been cold, she would have pressed the cup against her heated cheeks.

"Wade is an attractive man."

Jillian thought of Wade, shirtless and sweaty. Of the texture of his face as she'd bathed him. Of his lips expertly caressing hers.

"Apparently you agree as your face is redder than a tomato."

Silver grinned, all the while watching Jillian as though she were a pot of water set on to boil.

"Yes." Jillian conceded. "Wade is a handsome man and I enjoy being around him."

"And just how many times have you 'been around him'?" Silver asked.

Despite her embarrassment, Jillian couldn't help but laugh. Silver was right, having a friend to discuss such matters with was indeed special.

"That was our first kiss."

"The first of many?"

If it were only a matter of the rush of emotion she'd felt in Wade's arms, the answer would be simple. But there was more to consider. Frowning, Jillian pushed her empty teacup aside.

"What is it? Clearly it isn't a lack of attraction. And I know Wade; he's a good man, so it can't be that."

"No, it isn't that. I've already seen the kind of man he is and there's no faulting him there. It's me." Her gaze met

Silver's. "I was engaged back home. Clint and I courted for months; he was from a good family, treated me well. He didn't seem to mind that I was a veterinarian."

"But…"

"But as the wedding day drew nearer he made it very clear that I was expected to give up 'the foolishness of being a doctor and become a proper wife'."

"Then he was an idiot. Who says you couldn't do both?"

Lord, but it was a balm to her soul to have another woman understand. "It's what I told him as well, but he was adamant. It was all about his reputation, you see. So when he said it was him or being a doctor…"

Silver laughed. "Good for you, Jillian. You'd have never been happy otherwise."

"I know. As did my father. And, funnily enough, it was the only time I could remember agreeing with Katie on anything. She's my sister," Jillian added when Silver looked confused.

Someone tapped on the door. Silver glanced at her pocket watch, signaled to the patron she'd be five minutes.

"Jillian, we're going to have to finish this another time, but let me say this, if you're worried Wade would do the same, don't be. Amy was a midwife, much to her mother's dismay."

"Her mother didn't approve?"

"Mrs. Hollingsworth approve? I think not."

Jillian nearly fell off her stool. "Wade's wife was Mrs.

Hollingsworth's daughter?"

"Indeed. She wasn't happy her daughter had chosen a rancher, and then when she became a midwife? Poor woman had the vapors for weeks. Anyhow, that wasn't my point. The point is that Amy didn't become a midwife until after she'd had Annabelle. So if you're worried Wade wouldn't want a woman who has work outside her family, don't."

Hope, bright as the sun beaming onto the saloon floors, spread within Jillian's chest. Was it truly possible she could have a man *and* be a doctor?

The knocking returned, louder and more insistent.

"I'll be right there," Silver hollered.

Jillian helped Silver carry their cups and saucers to the back kitchen.

"I'm so glad you stopped by. I hope you'll do it again."

"I will. As I hope you'll ride over sometime so I can return the favor. After all, I've yet to find out if there is a man you have your eye on."

Silver sighed. "That, Jillian," Silver said, opening the back door to the breeze and the birdsong, "is a long story and a conversation for another day. Now, not to push you out but it is time I open this saloon. I'll see you Saturday."

"Saturday?"

"Eileen said they were having a barn dance at the ranch on Saturday. And since most folks will be there, there's no sense in me being here." Silver grinned. "You'll be wanting to get home; she mentioned Wade would be riding over to ask you."

Jillian's hands once again flew to her hair. "Oh, dear, I have to go!"

Then, with Silver chuckling behind her, Jillian rode out of Marietta as fast as she'd ridden in.

★

SHE'D THOUGHT HIM handsome at first sight, but never more so than she did when he rode into her yard. He wore a worn, soft-looking chambray shirt with the sleeves rolled to the elbows. Pants that clung to his long, muscled legs. His hat cast a shadow over his eyes, which only added to his appeal. He rode closer and the sun caught the gold hair on his muscled forearms. Swallowing became impossible.

With little more than the move of his lips and a gentle pull on the reins his horse came to a stop. Jillian dropped the curtain and came to her feet. She shook her legs to get the blood flowing, cast a quick glance in the mirror. Then, as though she hadn't rushed home to change clothes, brush out her hair until it shone, and sat at the window for the last forty-two minutes, she slipped on a mask of surprise when she opened the door.

Wade paused at the bottom of the porch. He tipped his hat back revealing the golden eyes she'd come to dream about. She'd spent hours reliving their kiss, reliving and wondering if it had meant as much to him as it had to her. Did he close his eyes and remember the way their mouths had touched? The way they'd clutched each other when the kiss had deepened? Did he yearn for another the way she did?

Feeling a wave of heat rush up her neck, Jillian cleared her throat. Then, mortified to realize she was still standing in the doorway, closed the door behind her and stepped to the edge of the porch.

Her porch wasn't high off the ground and stepping to the edge of brought her eye-level with the open vee at his neck. Remembering how his chest had looked, naked and sweaty, Jillian couldn't help but wonder what it would feel like to run her hands over his golden skin, to feel his heartbeat under her touch. She'd never touched Clint's chest, hadn't really she just now realized, felt a desire to. But Wade's?

She was doing it again, standing there like a ninny. She yanked her gaze up, nearly faltered at the heat she saw reflected in his eyes.

"I—" Her voice squeaked. Her cheeks flamed. She worked in a man's world for goodness sake but the whole of her life her voice had never squeaked as it had just then.

His lips twitched into a smile and there was nothing to do but smile in return.

"I'm sorry; I'm not usually so ungracious. Did you want to come in? I have sun tea or I can make coffee if you'd prefer."

He shook his head. "I can't stay. I told James and Scott I wouldn't be long."

She licked her lips. "All right."

His gaze fell to her mouth and the pulse in his neck throbbed faster. Since Clint had asked her father permission's to court her before he ever talked to her on it, she'd always known Clint's feelings. She'd never had to wonder, never had to gauge what a man was thinking. But surely if she got a man's blood pumping faster, he was interested, wasn't he?

Wade coughed, met her gaze once more.

"Ma talked me into having a barn dance before we fill the new barn. Most of the town will be there, so I'd understand if you didn't want to come."

The excitement that had driven her from Silver's and chased her as she'd anticipated his invitation withered. Was he warning her because he cared about her feelings or because he hoped she wouldn't go?

"Well, I wouldn't want to ruin the evening. It's probably best if I—"

"Having you there won't ruin anything. I just wanted you to be prepared, is all. I'm having this dance to make Ma happy and it would make her happy if you were there."

Despite fearing his answer, she asked it anyway because it wasn't in her nature not to go after what she wanted.

"And you, Wade? Would it make you happy if I went?"

His eyes darkened. There wasn't a soul around but the two of them yet he whispered when he answered.

"Yes, Jillian. It would make me very happy if you came."

Chapter Ten

WADE LOVED THIS part of the day. The chores were done; he was clean and could unwind. There wasn't anything calling to him, weren't a million things he needed to get to. He could concentrate on his daughter and enjoy some quiet time with her.

Washed and in her nightgown, Annabelle snuggled as they enjoyed this time before she went to sleep. They were sitting on her bed; the light from the lamp was as soft as the little hand that held his.

"Papa? When do you think you'll want to get married?"

Wade grimaced, glad Annabelle's head was against his shoulder so she couldn't see his face. Yet he wasn't surprised at her question. He'd evaded most of the ones she'd asked about kissing Jillian by telling her it wasn't appropriate for little girls to talk about kissing. He knew it was only a matter of time until Annabelle got around to forming her question in such a manner that her father would run out of excuses and have to answer.

"I'm not sure I want to marry again."

Annabelle sighed. "It sure would be nice to have a mama

like everybody else."

He couldn't help but smile. She was clever, his Annabelle.

"You have me, Grandma, James, and Scott. Even Grandma Hollingsworth. I know you're not lonely."

Another sigh. "It's not the same."

"I know it's not, Button. But we have a family and we need to be thankful for what we have."

She pushed herself back and looked into his eyes. "I wouldn't mind if you married Miss Matthews."

Had he been standing his knees would have buckled. Where had that come from? Granted, he'd been caught kissing Jillian, but marrying her? Sweat beaded his upper lip and his heart gave a solid thump against his ribs. Yes, she was beautiful. And soft. And the way her mouth moved with his, the way she'd leaned into him—

He shook his head. Desirable or not, he couldn't go down that road again. Not after where the last one had taken him. Heartbroken, widowed. Ashamed. But he couldn't tell his daughter any of that.

"I'm glad you like her, Annabelle, but I don't plan on marrying her."

"But you asked her to the dance, right, Papa?"

The gleam in her blue eyes and the curve of her mouth warned him if he thought he had his hands full now, it would be nothing compared to what she'd be like once she got older.

"Grandma wanted me to," he said. No way was he going to admit he wanted Jillian there as well. His daughter had enough ideas without planting more in her head.

"But you like her, don't you? You'll dance with her, won't you?"

"Yes, Button, I'll dance with her."

"A lot?"

He shook his head. "At least once," he said.

With another deep sigh, she resettled against him. He placed his cheek against her head, inhaled the innocence and sweetness of her. He didn't blame her for wanting a mother. And since Jillian was the first woman he'd kissed since Amy, he wasn't surprised she'd come to the conclusion she had. Still, despite his undeniable attraction to her, Jillian wasn't a woman he'd consider marrying.

She'd never give up being a doctor and he would never settle for being second best again.

★

WADE COULDN'T HAVE heard Liam right. Goddammit, he couldn't have heard right.

"You can't be serious," Wade said.

He and Scott had headed out after morning chores, each with a rope around the bull's neck, the big animal plodding along between the horses. Since it wasn't far to Liam's ranch, the air was still moist and cool when they rode onto his land. Liam had been waiting on the porch.

"Afraid so, Wade. I'm sorry."

"You're sorry?" Wade gaped. "We arranged this back in the winter. We agreed to trade bulls when it was time to breed the cows again. I won't have time to look for another one now, not if I want them bred soon."

He shoved his hat up his forehead so he could see Liam better. "What the hell happened?"

The tall, bow-legged cowboy shrugged. "Change of plans, is all."

It didn't take a whole lot of smarts to figure out what was going on.

"This is because of the town meeting, isn't it? Because I stood behind my decision to hire Miss Matthews."

Liam kicked some dirt aside with his boot, looked out over his pastures. "Look, Wade. You do whatever you need to, whatever you feel is right, but the rest of us have got to do the same."

"What do you mean by that?" Scott asked.

Unlike Wade, Scott remained astride, his gloved hands holding tight to the bull's rope.

Liam squinted as he raised his eyes to Scott. "I have a ranch to run, too, and I can't afford to be sentimental." He turned back to Wade. "I had a better offer. Look, I'm sorry, I know you were counting on me, but I can't afford to pass it up."

The fields and pastures were green around Wade but all he saw was red. He'd counted on this. He'd planned on the new blood line, needed it, as some of his heifers wouldn't be able to be bred now, not when they were the same blood as the bull. It would mean yet more money lost if he couldn't breed all his heifers.

"Wade, there's nothing more I can say. I gotta get to work."

Ambling to the barn, Liam left Scott and Wade in stunned silence.

"That was a dirty, bloody trick," Scott said.

Wade ran his hand down his face, struggled to hang on to the last threads of his temper. Though there wasn't anything to be gained by it, he wanted nothing more than to charge after Liam and get in one good punch. Did the man not realize the damage he'd done?

"I'm sorry, Wade. But it's not too late, I can check around, Liam can't be the only one—"

"He is. We checked back in the winter, remember? Nobody else was willing to trade straight across." And he didn't have any money to throw in to sweeten a deal, which is clearly what had changed Liam's mind. And whoever made the deal would have known Wade had no way to counter offer.

Once he was back in the saddle, Scott tossed him his rope. "Any idea who might've given Liam the better offer?" he asked.

"Seems suspect, don't you think? Liam doesn't breathe a word about backing out of our arrangement and within a day of me defending Jillian suddenly he has a better offer?"

"Steven, then?"

"If not directly, I'm sure he was part of it."

They rode in silence back onto the Triple P. Despite his plans, he'd have to cull the herd, keep those heifers that couldn't be bred from going up into the high country with the rest of the herd. Then come fall, whether he liked it or not as he couldn't afford to feed them all winter, he'd have to sell them. And with less calves next year…

"You going to rest that foot for an hour or so?" Scott asked.

"Nah, it hardly hurts at all," Wade lied as his ankle throbbed and his boot fisted around it like a vise. "Let's get James. We have some heifers to move."

★

JILLIAN HEATED WATER, washed and rinsed her hair. She soaked in a rose-scented bath until the water was tepid and her fingers and toes looked like prunes. Though it was neither practical nor needed to fuss with her hair on a daily basis, she nonetheless knew how and she drew upon that skill as she curled and pinned her hair. Knowing she'd have little use for fancy dresses in Montana, she'd left all but two of them back in Pennsylvania, opting to bring the ones best suited to a simpler way of life.

Taking the pale blue silk—which would match the ribbon she'd woven through the complicated tangle of curls—

she laid it gently on her bed. She wasn't putting it on until the animals were fed for the night, she'd eaten her supper and Hope was saddled. It was silly to be this excited considering the reception she'd received at both the church picnic and the town meeting. But then it wasn't those people she was anxious to see.

Silver would be there, as would Letty and Eileen. They'd come to mean a great deal to her and she was looking forward to spending an evening with them. As she ate a cold meal of bread, ham, and cheese, she acknowledged she wasn't fooling anyone, least of all herself. She hadn't taken hours to ensure she looked her best for Silver's benefit. It had been done with Wade in mind. He'd said it would make him happy if she came to his dance. In the hours and days since then, she'd clung to those words, along with how they made her feel.

Like her feet couldn't quite touch the ground. Like she couldn't quite catch her breath. Like she'd never once felt before.

With her supper taken care of, though she'd barely done more than nibble at it, Jillian tidied the kitchen and headed for the barn.

The evening was perfect for a dance. The air was calm and warm. Green and silver leaves spread wide, caught the sun's heat and shone. Wildflowers staked their claim at the edge of the trees and filled the air with perfume.

As Jillian neared the barn, the smell of hay, grain, and

soiled bedding competed with the blooms but she wouldn't be a veterinarian if she couldn't tolerate and accept all aspects of animals, and the ripe smell coming from the barn meant they were healthy.

She stopped. She cleaned her stalls every morning and that morning hadn't been an exception. Her barn never smelled this strong in the evening. Knowing something was wrong, she grabbed her skirts and ran into the barn.

"Oh!"

Even with her hand covering her nose and mouth the stench burned her eyes. Which wasn't a surprise considering the amount of manure spread in the narrow aisle. Gagging, Jillian backed away until she was standing outside looking in. The stench wasn't as bad in the open air and she was able to lower her hand.

Like the spilled feed, this too was designed to irritate and poke at her. It needed to be cleaned, and it couldn't wait until morning. Which meant she'd get dirty and be late for the dance.

"They don't want me to go at all," she whispered, knowing that was the real reason for this mess.

Jillian looked toward her house, thought of the dress she'd laid out on her bed. Her head fell forward a moment as she acknowledged just how late this would make her.

Damn them.

She allowed herself a moment to wallow and then she set to work. She'd be late, there was no question about that now but, by God, they wouldn't keep her from going. Bracing for the stench, Jillian stormed in and grabbed some shovels, which, naturally, were clean at the other end of the barn.

Angry and irritated, she used that energy to scoop out the mess. As she tossed shovelfuls into her wheelbarrow she couldn't help but take some solace in the fact that whoever had done this—and she knew it was likely Steven—had to have ridden over with it in a wagon of some sort. Which meant they would have had to put up with the stench the whole way. She hoped they smelled as awful as she knew she did.

When the barn was scraped clean and her animals were fed and secured for the night, she grabbed her saddle, leaving the barn door open to clear out the lingering smell. She'd have to hurry, but she could still get to the dance. It would mean washing in cold water as she didn't have time to heat it but—

The world shifted sideways. The door of her house gaped open and she knew she hadn't left it that way.

Jillian swallowed the fear that bubbled in her throat. She held her breath, strained to hear. There wasn't a sound. Yet someone was there. She could feel it. And her rifle was in her house.

"You'd better get your sorry self outside! I'm armed and I'm coming in!" she yelled for good measure. Setting the saddle on the porch, Jillian pushed the door further open.

Her home was as it had been when she'd gone to the

barn. There was nothing amiss, nothing out of place. Still, she grabbed the rifle, put it to her shoulder and closed the door firmly. Armed, she headed for her bedroom.

There was no missing it.

Jillian's arm went limp and she brought the gun down weakly to her side. She blinked but what she saw didn't change. From the open window—the one she knew she'd closed—came the racing sound of a wagon rattling away. They must have hidden it in the trees. She didn't bother looking out. Couldn't. Not when her gaze was stuck on the shredded scraps of blue silk that an hour ago had been her best dress.

★

IT WASN'T THE first barn dance Marietta had seen since Silver had arrived. It was, however, the first she'd been invited to and she'd been looking forward to it since Eileen had stopped by for a quick tea and visit. Eileen had made no bones about the fact that she was hoping it would bring Wade and Jillian together. Silver hoped so as well, but it wasn't Wade and Jillian she was thinking about when she pinched her cheeks for color before stepping into the barn.

She'd made a point of not coming too early and already a fair-sized crowd was gathered in the barn. A small platform had been made at one end to accommodate the musicians. Two fiddlers tapped their toes while their bows skated over the strings. John Daniels was on the banjo and Scott's lips moved expertly over his harmonica. Her mouth curved when she saw Reverend Donnelly's red face and full smile as he squeezed perfect notes out of an accordion.

Many couples spun and twirled on the dance floor and, on the opposite end of the barn, women and children gathered around the refreshment tables. As with any social event, folks gravitated to those they knew best and there were clusters of people laughing and talking along the walls of the barn. Silver's gaze raked over them as she looked for Letty, Eileen, or Jillian. Or Shane. Her stomach clutched at the thought.

"Silver, glad you could make it."

"Wade. Looks like your mother was right to suggest this. Folks seem to be having a good time."

"Don't tell her she's right; I'll never hear the end of it."

"Well, that's not much reason not to tell her, is it?" She teased.

Wade shook his head. "Women. You'll be the death of me."

"Just wait until Annabelle starts catching the boys' attention."

He looked pained. "I tell you, Silver, I have nightmares about just that."

She laughed, touched his arm. "You'll do just fine."

The fiddle faded on the last notes of a waltz and John announced they were going to liven things up with a series of polkas before they took a break.

"May I?" Wade asked.

She gladly accepted Wade's offer and while she enjoyed the thump of heels on the ground and the music flowing through her limbs, she kept her gaze over Wade's shoulder and sought out another.

★

Wade liked to dance. Maybe because his parents had, or maybe because opportunity didn't present itself often, but he enjoyed moving to music and it was never a hardship to have a pretty girl in his arms. Tonight was no exception. Though he enjoyed dancing with Silver, his mother, Letty, and his current partner, Annabelle, it wasn't those women he'd been anticipating dancing with.

But then, knowing things couldn't go any further with him and Jillian, he shouldn't keep looking over bobbing heads hoping to see her step into the barn. He shouldn't feel disappointment that she wasn't there yet. But he did.

"Right, Papa?"

Wade blinked, looked down at his daughter. They were dancing, if Annabelle's feet over his own constituted such a thing. He didn't mind, though, since he knew she wouldn't be able to dance on his feet forever. One day she'd be doing it on her own. With boys. The thought scared the hell out of him.

"What, Button?"

She gave him a patient look, sighed and said, "Jacob says

boys don't like to dance, that they just do it to keep their wives happy. I told him he was wrong. I'm right, aren't I, Papa?"

"Depends on the man, I expect. I don't mind dancing and I know James doesn't either."

"Scott loves to dance, he told me so."

"There, see? But I'm sure Jacob is also right in that there are men out there who do it to keep the women they love happy."

"Jacob says it's to keep them from nagging."

Also likely true, but not something his daughter needed to know just yet.

"How would Jacob know? You two didn't go off and get married did you?" He teased.

"Eww!" Annabelle grimaced.

Wade laughed. "Just making sure."

"I'm too young to get married. Besides, I wouldn't marry Jacob anyway. His papa's too mean."

That grabbed Wade's attention. There was no love lost between him and Steven but as far as Wade knew Steven had never mistreated Annabelle. If that had changed…

"Mean, how?"

"He got mad at Jacob for fetching Miss Matthews when his dog was bit by a snake. Then he said some mean things to her, but Jacob said Miss Matthews was real brave and didn't cower. Jacob said his pa was so mad he wouldn't pay her, even after she saved Fred."

Wade hadn't heard anything about that but, knowing Steven, it didn't surprise him.

"And he says mean things about Miss Matthews when she isn't around either."

Not that Wade doubted it, but hearsay was known to make things worse than they were and he was quick to remind Annabelle of that.

"But I heard him, Papa. I heard him talking." Her little face went fierce. "He used bad words."

The bastard. Jillian hadn't done anything to Steven other than help his son's dog and for that she was punished? Wade looked around the room. It was hard to pinpoint anybody with the crowd constantly shifting, but he didn't spot Steven. Still, Steven had better watch himself because if Wade heard him malign Jillian, he'd do something about it.

★

WITH SEVERAL MEN having brought their instruments, the musicians switched as breaks were needed. Silver was pouring herself a glass of punch when Scott sidled to her side.

"I never knew you played." Silver nodded to the harmonica he put in his pocket. "You're very good."

He shrugged as he accepted the glass she'd poured. "It passed the time when I was younger."

"No boys you could have gotten into trouble with?" Silver took another glass, filled it.

"Not a lot of kids where I grew up," he answered.

Silver wondered at the shadows that darkened his eyes but decided not to push. She liked Scott. He was quiet, a gentleman. He'd been a good friend to her and she could repay that kindness by not prying.

"I haven't seen Jillian yet," she said. The dance floor was doing a brisk business and there was more than one face with a sheen of sweat on it. "Or Shane."

Scott poured himself another glass, grabbed a handful of cookies. "Shane's here. I saw him outside with Melissa."

The bottom fell out of Silver's stomach. Melissa. Perfectly respectable Melissa. Why was Silver surprised? Suddenly, the evening lost its charm. The lanterns hanging on the walls weren't soft and romantic. They were cruel and mocking. The music didn't fill her until she couldn't help tapping her toes; it pulsed in her head until she felt the beginning of a headache. The smell of fresh wood turned her stomach.

She turned to put her full cup back onto the table.

"Finally decided to come in, did you?" Scott badgered.

"Scott, I said I wouldn't dance with you and I meant it," Shane answered, laughter in his voice.

Silver's hand stilled and her traitorous heart squeezed. Shane was here. Which meant Melissa was, too. She pushed the smile onto her face, forced the easiness into her voice.

"Hello, Shane. Melissa."

Melissa wore a pale pink dress with ivory lace at the collar and cuffs. Unlike Silver who'd chosen to pull back the sides of her hair and leave the rest down and unfettered,

Melissa's tresses were a complicated concoction of twists and braids that circled her head like a crown. If only there were thorns in it.

Shane nodded. His gaze swooped down to the hem of Silver's sunny yellow gown and up to her unbound hair. It lingered there a moment. "Silver."

"Isn't it nice that Shane escorted me tonight? Ma wasn't feeling well and Pa decided to stay with her. Why, if it wasn't for Shane's invitation I might not have come at all." She wrapped her hand around Shane's arm like an eagle's talon holding onto its supper.

"Well, that would have been a shame."

Over Shane's shoulder she saw Scott smile before tucking another cookie into his mouth.

Just then the music ended. Over the applause and the conversation, John Daniels told everyone to get a partner for an upcoming square dance.

"Yee haw." Scott cheered.

Before Silver knew his intention he'd grabbed her hand.

"Come on you two."

With one hand in Silver's, Scott used the other to push Shane into the crowd. Since Melissa had yet to release her claws on Shane, she went along as well.

Eileen, James, Wade, and Letty ran forward and joined them just as the music began and John started calling the dance. To Silver's mind, the best part of a square dance was that you danced with everyone in the square and so she found herself quite often touching Shane.

For their do-si-do, Silver swore the music seemed to stop. Shane's eyes locked on hers as he circled around her. His shoulder brushed hers and though it wasn't more than a blink of an eye, she felt the burn of his touch. He stepped back and it was her turn. Brushing her hair off her shoulder, Silver moved toward him, angled her head so she could watch Shane as she circled him. Their shoulders didn't touch, but she made a point of brushing her hand over his. Shane's eyes darkened briefly but then John instructed them to promenade and the mood was broken.

Scott twirled her; James told her she looked pretty. Wade laughed when she got distracted and accidentally stepped on his foot. She hoped he hadn't noticed it was because Shane had smiled at her as he'd passed that she'd faltered her step.

Too soon the dance ended. She was up for another but John announced he was done for the night. He took the groans and boos in stride and stepped off the platform. Soon his wife had him by the hand and announced she wasn't letting go.

"Wade," Eileen said. "Perhaps you should go outside and see if Jillian's arrived yet."

James shook his head. Silver bit her cheek.

"Ma…" Wade groaned.

"Oh, go on. The lady may need your help." Shane urged.

"Speaking of a lady that needs help." Melissa purred as she turned to Shane. "I sure am thirsty."

It took all of Silver's restraint not to tell her to get her own.

"A lawman's job is never done." Wade teased. "Better get to it, Sheriff. I think I'll go get some fresh air after all."

★

THE SKY WAS a spill of purples, pinks, and indigos by the time Jillian rode up to the Parker ranch. The barn doors were thrown open. Music drifted in the warm air. Light glowed from within. There were children running about, squealing in delight. Men circled to smoke and, just as likely, to avoid having to dance.

Dozens of horses and wagons were tied to the fence. The animals greeted her arrival with a mixture of snuffles and bored glances. Despite her tardiness and the residual anger that threatened to boil over if she dwelled on what had taken place earlier, Jillian was glad and relieved to have finally arrived.

She was securing Hope when footsteps crunched behind her. If whoever had been on her property had the nerve, the gall, to come up to her then he'd better be prepared for her wrath. She wouldn't back down. Jerking the knot tight, Jillian spun round.

"Whoa!" Wade took a step back, held his hands in surrender. "It's only me."

Jillian took a deep, calming breath and released it slowly. "I'm sorry. I'm later than I'd hoped to be and I'm a bit out of sorts."

He tipped his head—she liked the look of him without his hat—and reclaimed the step he'd taken. "Everything all right?"

She loved that he was concerned. It was nice knowing someone cared. "Yes. Just irritated."

"Can't say I've ever seen a woman look as pretty irritated."

It wasn't the lovely blue she'd hoped to wear but suddenly the forest green dress didn't feel like second best any more.

He smiled and his eyes crinkled at the sides. It drew her attention to the healing sutures.

"How is that feeling?" she asked, pointing to the stitches.

"Itches something fierce."

"Means it's healing. Another few days and they can come out."

"Can't be soon enough for me."

"And the ankle?"

His gaze was hot on hers. "Good enough to dance on, if you care to join me."

Her breath fluttered. She couldn't have withheld her smile if she tried. "I'd love to."

They strolled to the barn, Wade's broad hand warm on the small of her back. She'd have been just as happy to keep right on walking.

"Looks like you've drawn a big crowd."

"Yeah. Folks 'round here work hard and occasions like

these can be few and far between. They tend to take advantage of them when they arise."

Most people worked hard. She had a nasty feeling she'd be spending her summer watching the grass grow.

"Annabelle, wait! I'm sorry! Wait!"

Jacob sped around the corner of the barn, chasing a crying Annabelle. Wade stiffened.

"I'm sorry; I have to see what's wrong."

His long legs ate up ground. Then he dropped to one knee and caught his daughter as she flew into his arms. Jillian wasn't sure what she should do. On the one hand, she wanted to see if the little girl was all right, but on the other she realized it really wasn't her place. Her decision was made when Silver stepped outside.

"Jillian. I thought you'd changed your mind. Have you only gotten here now?" Silver asked as she stepped closer.

"Yes. Wade and I were on our way in when Annabelle came running from behind the barn." Jillian gestured to where the little girl, her father, and Jacob clustered together. "I'm not sure what's happened but she's quite upset."

Silver didn't seem the least worried.

Instead she turned to Jillian, a twist on her lips. "You and Wade? Just how long have you been here?"

Jillian shook her head. "I only arrived a few minutes ago. Wade must have seen me as he came to the fence as I was securing Hope."

"Did it ever occur to you that perhaps he was waiting on

you?"

"I-Well, no, it didn't."

Had he? She had no idea. But the thought was intriguing.

"Come on." Silver laughed as she took Jillian's arm. "Let's go see what the fuss is about."

She wasn't sure they should intrude but Silver left her little choice. Jillian's skirt flapped around her ankles as she hurried to keep her friend's pace.

"I'm sorry, Mr. Parker," Jacob was saying as they approached. "I shouldn't have made it worse." Jacob hung his head. "I shouldn't have said nothin'."

Wade placed a hand on the boy's shoulder. "Jacob, there's no shame in what you did. You were trying to defend your friends and I appreciate what you did for Annabelle. As I'm sure Miss Matthews would appreciate what you did for her."

"For me?" Jillian questioned.

Three sets of eyes, two of them wet with tears, met hers. Since he seemed so little standing there alone while Annabelle was safe in her father's arms and since Jillian was already fond of the boy, she crouched at his side.

"What happened, Jacob?"

But it was Annabelle who spoke.

"We were playing outside. I heard Mr. Garvey and his friends talking. They weren't saying nice things about you. When I told Jacob what his pa said, he got mad. I tried to stop him." The look she gave Jacob was almost the exact same look her father had given Jillian when she'd first met him.

"But Jacob wouldn't listen," Annabelle continued. "He ran up to his pa, told him what he was saying about you was lies, that you *are* smart and you *do* know what you're doing. But the more Jacob talked, the madder his pa got. I got scared from all the shouting so I ran."

Jillian's eyes smarted. She turned to Jacob. It wasn't difficult to picture him standing up to his father. But she feared, knowing what she'd seen of Steven to date, the man would take his anger out on his son.

"I appreciate what you did, Jacob. It was very brave. And you, Annabelle." She looked at the girl, smiled. "I think it's wonderful that you both wanted to defend me but I'd hate to think you got in trouble on my behalf." She took Jacob's hand. "Especially you. You already know your father doesn't like me."

Jacob's little jaw jutted out. "He's wrong!"

"He's entitled to his opinion, whatever it is."

"Not sure I could be so generous," Silver mumbled.

"Next time, just walk away, Jacob. Words can't hurt me."

The problem was, she feared it wasn't only words Steven was capable of. He'd already gone to her house three times now to scare her and each time had escalated into something worse. It scared her to think what might be next.

Jacob bobbed his head. "All right."

Touched, Jillian pressed a palm to his cheek. "You're a wonderful boy, Jacob, and one day you'll make an even better man."

"Get your hand off my boy!"

Steven's voice snapped like a whip and had the desired effect. Jillian yanked her hand back, lost her balance and promptly landed on her behind.

"I'll get Shane, just in case," Silver whispered and fled toward the barn.

Jillian scrambled to her feet. Wade rose to his. "Button, go inside. Take Jacob with you."

"But, Papa!"

It was hard not to like a man who'd take the time to reassure his daughter. Wade gave Annabelle a quick embrace, kissed her head.

"There's nothing to worry about. I'll be in before long."

"Go with her, Jacob," Jillian said.

The little boy looked torn; his eyes darted from Jillian to his tight-lipped father to a simmering Wade.

"If you don't go she'll only worry about you."

Jacob cast a furtive look at his father, swallowed hard at his father's cold glare, and ran to join his friend. In a sign of solidarity, Wade stepped to Jillian's side. It didn't stop Garvey from stepping nearly toe-to-toe with her.

"You leave my son alone." Garvey warned.

His breath was as hot as his words, only his words didn't

smell of whiskey. Jillian knew he was trying to intimidate her and though her legs trembled, she held her ground. Beside her Wade tensed, but she spoke before he could.

"All I did was talk to Jacob."

"I saw your hand on him, don't you ever touch him again, you hear me?"

"I didn't hurt him and you know it." Jillian raised her chin when Steven's face went red. "He was defending me and I was thanking him."

Steven's eyes narrowed to slivers. "I don't want him defending you."

"Then stop telling everyone how awful I am and maybe your son won't feel the need to."

Garvey's chest swelled. He pointed a thick finger at her, barely missing her face. "You shut your mouth."

"That's enough." Wade pushed between them.

Dusk was upon them. Only the thinnest wisps of clouds stretched across the horizon. The air crackled with tension. Hearing people running toward her, Jillian turned. Shane led the group, followed by Scott and Silver. Jillian stepped from behind Wade as Scott and Shane flanked him. She took her place next to Silver.

"Come on, Parker, you can't possibly defend her, she killed your cow."

"No, she didn't. She saved my calf."

"That's the biggest cock and bull story I've ever heard! What the hell did she do to make you believe that?" Steven sneered as his eyes crept over Jillian.

The result left her feeling soiled.

"Never mind, I bet I know. You only have to look at who she keeps company with"—he jerked his head toward Silver—"to know what she did for you. Or to you."

All three men moved as one but it was Wade who wound up chest to chest with Garvey. Fear flooded Jillian. This wasn't good. Not good at all. Every man standing had their hands coiled into fists. Violence was in the air. She tasted it with each inhale.

"You son of a bitch." Wade growled. "Get off my land."

But Garvey didn't seem intimidated in the least. He simply smiled, crossed his arms over his chest in a stance of superiority.

"Did I hit a nerve, Parker? You been so lonely since that wife of yours died that you're willing to dip your pecker in just about anything?"

Jillian recoiled as though slapped. Silver grabbed her hand.

"Ignore him," she whispered.

But that was impossible. She was used to not being respected for her skills but she'd never been called a whore before.

"Get your family together and get off my land or I'll do it for you."

Garvey's body went rigid and his arms came down. "I'll leave when I'm good and ready."

"You're ready now," Shane said. His voice was cold as the six-gun he carried in his holster.

"You need the sheriff to fight your battles, Wade?"

Wade threw his arms out, effectively holding back Scott and Shane. "Nope, I surely don't. Either you leave of your own accord or I'll be more than happy to toss you off myself."

"She must really be something." Garvey leered. "To have you so hot and bothered."

"Don't hit him, Wade!" Jillian cried when Wade's fist came up.

She couldn't believe what she was seeing. Wade was poised for a fight; Steven had blood in his eye. Nothing good was going to come of this.

"Yeah, don't hit me, Wade." Steven mocked.

"It would hardly be a fair fight," Wade answered in a calm voice that belied his stance. "Taking on a man who hides in the dark disparaging women? Hardly seems right to take on a coward such as that."

"Though I can't see it taking more than one punch," Scott added.

"Bastards." Steven snarled.

Wade leaned forward, his eyes locked on Steven's. "But at least we're manly bastards."

The fist came fast and hard and the crack of it against Wade's jaw had his head whipping to the side.

"Wade!" Jillian screamed.

"Did you see that, Sheriff?" Wade asked, wiping his mouth on his sleeve. "He threw the first punch."

Shane rolled back on his heels. His palm rested softly on his revolver. "I saw it."

"Good," Wade said, then he barreled into Steven and the two went down in a blur of fists.

Chapter Eleven

By the time everyone had left, Wade's face had been wiped of blood and Annabelle lay sleeping. It was late and he was exhausted. His jaw throbbed, his knuckles were raw and his fingers hurt when he flexed them. There were more bumps and bruises but nothing he couldn't live with. At least his sutures hadn't ripped open.

Goddamn Steven. The man just couldn't keep his mouth shut. Wade might not be able to prove it, but he suspected Steven was behind Liam's change of heart. And then to attack Jillian tonight…

What Steven had said was vile, and worse, a pack of lies. Jillian didn't deserve what had happened tonight. And since it had taken place on his land, he felt responsible. Wade shook his head. His argument didn't ring completely true in his own mind so it was no wonder James and Scott had given him knowing looks when he'd said where he was going and why.

At first he thought she was asleep. No lights shone from her windows. Both the barn and house looked tucked in for the night. But then movement on the porch caught his eye and he realized she was sitting outside in the dark. As he rode in closer he saw she was holding a rifle.

Damn, she'd been more afraid than he'd realized.

"Jillian, it's Wade," he called out, not wanting to scare her more than that jerk Steven had already done.

She set the rifle aside, tucked her legs in close. He tied Whiskey to the post and climbed the porch.

"You're going to catch a chill. I can go inside and fetch your shawl."

"I'm not cold." She sat with her hands firmly clasped around her bent knees, her cheek resting on them. She looked as exhausted as he felt. "Has everyone left?"

"All but the usual miscreants." He smiled because her mood seemed as dark as the shadows that darkened her yard.

"I'm sorry. Had I known…"

"Then you wouldn't have come, and I'm not sorry you did." He took off his jacket, placed it around her shoulders then sat next to her.

"Jillian there's only one person to blame for tonight and that's Steven."

"It's not how everyone else will see it," she said, sitting upright and drawing his jacket closer.

Seeing her in his clothes, looking pretty and vulnerable, knocked him speechless.

It took a moment to find his tongue. "I don't care about everyone else. I care about you."

He hadn't meant to say the words but realized they were

true nonetheless. Maybe he'd tried not to, but he did care about her. He remembered how she'd looked after her wagon had lost its wheel. How his gut had clenched, how he'd been afraid she'd been hurt or violated. It had been the same feeling that had grabbed him by the throat tonight when Steven had gotten too close to her. He'd have done anything to keep her safe.

He flexed his hand again, felt the stiffness from the fight. He hadn't gone out of his head for a woman since Amy. Hell, he didn't think he'd ever gone so out of control for her. Being with Amy, if not her mother, had been easy. There'd been no obstacles, no hardships, just an easy slide into love and then marriage.

Not that he was thinking either of those about Jillian.

He swallowed back something that tasted like denial. No, he wasn't thinking that way about Jillian, he simply realized he'd never been this…volatile around Amy.

"Why?" she whispered.

Why what? But then he remembered what he'd said before his mind had veered off course.

"Because you're smart and pretty. Because you're tough. Not many women would have stood up to Steven the way you did."

"My legs were shaking so badly, I could almost hear my knees rattling."

"I'd never have guessed."

"Comes from living in a man's world, I suppose. I don't

dare show weakness, it's only one more thing they can use against me."

"Must get tiring."

She sighed. "You have no idea."

He touched her cheek, let his hand linger over the softness. "You don't have to pretend around me."

Slender fingers wrapped around his, held him there against the warmth of her face. Something shifted in her eyes. The sadness melted away. What replaced it shot straight through Wade.

"Jillian…"

Her grip tightened. "I'm sorry for everything that happened tonight, I truly am. But is it wrong that one of the things I'm most sorry for is that we never got the opportunity to dance?"

Dance. He took a relieved breath. That he could manage.

Wade stepped off the porch, held out his hand. "Miss Matthews. Would you do me the honor?"

Her eyes widened. "Here? Now?"

"Come on, Jillian. You've faced worse. I'm actually a decent dancer." He teased.

A thousand stars lit up her face when she smiled. He might have been standing in a dirt yard, dressed in simple pants and plain blue cotton shirt, but he suddenly felt like a king.

She placed his jacket on the porch. Her hand fit perfectly

in his as he moved them away from the house. Her body felt even better when she stepped into his embrace. The warmth of her, the feel of her, all the wonderful, mysterious scents of a woman encircled him, blurred the edges of reason. Want. Need. Wade felt as though he were on top of a mountain, about to lose his footing.

How bad could the fall be?

★

It was even better here. There were no judging stares to worry about, no need to keep to propriety to keep tongues from wagging. If she wanted to step a little closer to Wade who was there to condemn her? To start gossip about her in town? Here there was only the moon, the damp air, and the man who held her firmly yet tenderly in his arms.

She'd always thought him rugged, but with shadows darkening his face, with the moon playing in his hair, he seemed mysterious. And appealing. Very, very, appealing.

His fingers flexed around hers almost as if he'd read her thoughts. Dark eyes fell to her mouth. Her hand had been resting comfortably on his shoulder but she moved it now as a recklessness she'd never experienced before drove her to seek what she most wanted.

What she wanted most was to kiss him.

Her fingers slid up the back of his neck, delved into the cool silkiness of his hair. She stopped moving, pressed her body to his. Her heart raced as he watched her intensely, as his own hands wrapped around her back.

He leaned down, pressed his lips to hers and held there for a few seconds. For a moment, a terrible moment, she thought that was all he was going to do, kiss her chastely then tell her goodnight. But his tongue stroked her lips, teased until they trembled open on a sigh.

He sank into her. Claimed her. Hot and hungry, his mouth took hers until she was deaf to everything but the blood surging through her veins, blind to everything but what her body ached for.

Her hands dropped to his shoulders where she clung. Underneath her palms, wide, strong shoulders kept her anchored. Yearning pooled in her breasts and lower still, surprising her. His kiss continued to take, his tongue left no part of her mouth untouched. Aching, restless, she shifted against him. His chest rubbed against hers and her nipples reacted immediately. The sensation was delicious, forbidden. Jillian did it again.

Wade pulled her hard against him. Jillian was a doctor. She knew what pressed against her. But she was also a woman, a woman with desires. Her breasts were heavy, weighted with need. Where his arousal pushed against her, she was wet and throbbing.

"Jillian." He panted, pulling his mouth away. He rested his forehead on hers. "We have to stop."

"No, we don't," she whispered. "Come inside."

His eyes were dark and tortured when he looked at her.

"I know exactly what I'm asking, Wade."

He shook his head, though he continued to hold her firmly against him. "Don't tempt me, Jillian. I'm trying real hard to be a gentleman. I don't want you to think—"

"I know what I want, Wade." She cupped his face. "What is it you want?"

★

More than he deserved. More than he had a right to. It would be easy to take her. And damned if his body wasn't primed to make love to her. Her eyes searched his, challenged him to take what was being offered.

Her thumb rubbed his bottom lip. Her breath tickled his throat. She was more intoxicating than Silver's best whiskey and he already knew her taste was unequaled. He throbbed for her. Throbbed to sink into her, to hear his name on her lips as he drove her over the edge. But he couldn't. She'd never be content to be a rancher's wife, she'd always want more. He'd never be enough.

"I want you, Jillian," he admitted because he respected her enough to give her the truth. "I want to make love to you, but I can't make promises. The ranch is in dire straits, I have Annabelle to consider and—"

"I don't need promises," she whispered.

"You do. You should. You deserve them."

"I deserve to be held, to be cherished. I'm not asking for more than tonight, Wade. I have my own problems right now as well and I can't make promises either."

Her hand slipped down his arm, took his. She stepped away until, if she moved any further, their connection would be broken. Then she looked him in the eye and said, "Come inside?"

Hellfire.

He'd never seen anything more seductive in his life than Jillian in the moonlight, her eyes challenging him, her voice wrapping around him. There was no denying he wanted her. Hell, he was hard and ready and his heart was pounding as though it was his first time. But he wasn't fifteen anymore and despite his straining erection he could control his desires.

Even if it meant a dip in the river to cool off.

"If we did this, Jillian, you'd regret it come morning."

She tipped her head. "Are you sure about that? Because right now my body's aching for you, Wade. And *not* having you, *that's* what I'd regret come morning."

Oh, Jesus, he was losing the battle.

"Are you not attracted to me?" she asked, managing to look both vulnerable and seductive.

He wiped his brow. "You know I am."

"Then, come." She tugged his hand. "Lie with me."

With all the blood shooting to his loins it was hard to think. Hell, it was just hard and he couldn't think of any more arguments. Not with her looking at him that way, with him already envisioning undressing her, feeling the heat of her skin next to his.

Without a word, Wade followed her inside.

★

HE COULDN'T GIVE her promises, but he could give her romance. Two lanterns glowed in her small room, one from the dresser and one from the small table next to her bed. He pulled back the covers, met her gaze.

His first thought, and he was sure he'd go to hell for it, was that she didn't look scared or timid the way Amy had on their wedding night. Instead, she looked him in the eye and came to him. She reached within her curls for a pin but he stopped her. He'd been dying to get his fingers in her hair for too long.

"Let me."

He wasn't careful with the pins; they pinged on the floor as he released them of their duty. Auburn strands fell in silken ribbons over his hands. His fingers plowed through them, tangled in them. Using them as leverage, he tilted her head back. Her mouth was open and ready for his and he took what she willingly offered, sipping then gulping. Her taste was a flavor he couldn't get enough of.

But it wasn't only her taste he was after. He was desperate for her touch. With two hands on the material, he yanked his shirt from his pants. He reached for the buttons—he'd already left two open—but her hand stilled his.

"Let me," she said, mirroring his words.

Her eyes were on her task and he hungered as he watched

her face, as he felt her hands brush his chest. There were only four buttons on his shirt so it didn't take her long. With her eyes rising to his, she grabbed his shirt and drew it over up over his chest. Her breath whispered against his nakedness as she reached to draw the garment over his head.

The moment the shirt was free, his hands were at her waist, not to hold her, but to hold on as her splayed fingers explored his chest, from his collarbone to his belly. His mouth went bone dry when she followed the trail of hair down to the waist of his pants.

The day she'd come to him for help she'd stared at his chest. He'd pictured this exact moment ever since. Not a damn thing compared to the feathery touch tracing over his muscles, discovering the differences that made them man and woman.

★

IF SHE WAS dreaming she never wanted to wake up. She'd wondered what the ridges of his abdomen would feel like. Would the hair sprinkling his chest be soft or coarse? She'd never imagined his belly would twitch when her hands skimmed over it. That the hair would be a combination of soft and coarse that drew her attention over and over again. Or that a man's nipples could get as hard as hers. Intrigued, she scraped her nails over them.

His breath hitched. He shackled her wrists with his hands and held her arms at her sides. His mouth came down hard on hers; his tongue seduced hers until she could barely catch her breath.

"I need to see you." He rasped when he came up for air.

Heart pounding, Jillian held her breath as his hands reached for her. Button by button, he moved down her blouse until the garment fell open and there was nothing between him and her breasts but her thin chemise. He cupped her through the fabric, circled and squeezed. The cotton rubbed at her nipples, creating a sweet ache in her breasts.

His eyes found hers, held. Everything fell away but the man before her. The commotion at the dance, the regret, the hopelessness of ever being accepted in Marietta, it all slipped away like a dissipating fog until there was only this man, this beautiful man, before her.

He captured her mouth again, and she rose to her toes to give him everything. To take everything in return. His hands moved to her hips and soon her skirt pooled at her feet.

Her heart skipped then thudded. Clint had never done more than kiss her and hold her hand. In truth, she hadn't minded. She realized now as Wade grabbed her chemise and began to tug it up, she'd never wanted him to. She'd never *needed* him to.

It was different with Wade. In that very moment it was as though her soul needed him in order to survive.

His lips moved from her mouth to her temple, from her jaw to her neck where he burrowed, his mouth hot and wet.

Jillian clung to him as desire rippled through her, and all the ugly things Steven had said to her were swept away. She let everything fall away but Wade and the all-encompassing need she had for him.

"Wade." She moaned when his teeth bit down gently on her earlobe. "Touch me."

★

HE WAS GOING as slow as he could but his body shook with the effort. Her response was fire in his blood and it licked at him. He felt as though he were burning from the inside out.

He rubbed against her, nearly dying when her softness enveloped him. Ending the kiss, he pulled her chemise over her head then watched as she stepped from her drawers until she stood before him in only her stockings.

It was tempting to leave them on as she was a picture standing there wearing nothing else, but he wanted to feel every inch of her. Nothing would do but to have her completely naked, all for him. Sitting on the bed, he urged her forward, lifted her foot and propped it on his thigh.

Concentrating only on her legs—an endeavor he deserved a medal for accomplishing—Wade eased a stocking down, inch by glorious inch, while his fingertips skimmed the exposed skin.

He looked at her, felt the punch of satisfaction at the desire clouding her eyes. But then he felt another kind of punch just looking at her. Naked but for one stocking, her auburn hair loose and seductive around her shoulders, her mouth swollen from mating with his. Wade struggled for breath.

"You're stunning," he whispered.

He hurried more with her other stocking because, hell, he just needed her naked. When finally she was, he swooped in and claimed a breast with his mouth.

★

Jillian gasped. The feel of his wet mouth on her flesh hit her like lightning. Her body jolted. His hands clamped on her, held her as his tongue laved her breast. She grasped his head, held on lest she melt right then and there.

His mouth was everywhere. It opened over her throat, licked its way to her ear. It feasted on hers until every part of her trembled, yearned. A burning heat rose within her and the room was suddenly too hot, the air too thick to breathe.

His thumbs brushed her nipples, one then the other until they hardened into over-sensitized peaks. When she didn't think she could take the assault of sensations, he dipped his head, enfolded the hard nub into the heat of his mouth and fondled it with his tongue.

Her back arched. "Wade." She pleaded because her legs were turning to water and she couldn't stand.

He scooped her up, placed her on the bed, and followed her down. Soft breasts met hard planes. His chest hair tickled her, teased her nipples, and kept them hard. It was glorious.

But it didn't do anything to lessen the need building lower. She was damp and achy, restless. Like a cat, she moved against him.

★

Wade couldn't remember ever being this hard, this desperate. He knew he should wait, should draw out her passion, but Jillian was making it impossible. When she ground against him, the last of his control snapped.

He captured her mouth, slipped a hand between them and claimed a breast. Her answering groan drove him, increased his pace. He took the kiss deeper, ravishing her mouth while his hand stroked her.

Long auburn hair fanned the pillow, her full, aroused breasts showed the marks of his stubble on her sensitive skin. His pride relished the thought he'd left his mark, even temporarily, on her. He looked lower and his loins thickened.

He shucked the rest of his clothes and finally, finally, they were both naked.

★

Jillian knew what mating entailed physically. But she'd never realized just how special being this way with a man could be. Her skin hummed as his hands moved over her body but it was more, so much more than that. The kisses he left on her temple, the whispers he spoke in her ear. The heat, the power of his body as he positioned himself over her, the way his heart beat against hers. It was all embracing, all part of a beautiful whole.

And so, when his hand moved between her legs, when he played with her as though she were the rarest of instruments, she thought nothing of letting him, of glorying in the way her body responded to him. His fingers stroked, delved into her.

"Jillian." He moaned and she felt the hard length of him press against her leg. "I have to have you."

He shifted and she felt him at her center. A flash of uncertainty, like lightning across an inky sky, flew through her mind and she had a moment of panic. Once she gave herself to him there was no going back, no pretending she was innocent.

He kissed her. "I don't want you to regret anything."

What was there to regret? Her heart filled to bursting. She knew what she wanted. Wade. Only Wade. The man who cared for her despite her being a doctor.

Smiling, she cupped his face. "I want to be with you."

With a searing kiss that stole her breath, he plunged into her. Her body froze at the intrusion, her muscles stretched to accommodate. Sensing it, Wade stilled, eased the kiss until it was light as a breeze, soft as silk. As her body began to surrender, he began to stroke, long and leisurely. She raised her hips, he went deeper, and the sensations made her gasp, made her reach for them again and again.

Jillian wrapped her arms tightly around him as a storm built within her. She reached higher. For what, she didn't know but her body seemed to as it matched Wade thrust for thrust.

★

WADE COULDN'T STOP. Her nails scraped down his back, her moans filled his ear. He pumped his hips, driving harder and harder. He claimed her mouth, plucked her nipples. She was tight, so tight. And wet and hot and—

"Wade!"

She clamped around him like a fist. Liquid fire poured over him. Feeling his own release coming, Wade buried his face in her neck, filled his hand with her breast, and shot to heaven right alongside her.

Chapter Twelve

The wind had picked up overnight and it blew through the leaves. Despite the grey sky that seemed capable of letting loose a sprinkle or two; there was no smell of rain in the air. It was almost as if the clouds couldn't decide what they should do. Jillian stepped off her porch. It was a feeling she could relate to.

She was still in awe of it all. How Wade had touched her body, how she'd responded. How they'd touched, kissed, and made love until he'd left in the deep, dark of night so he could be home before his mother or daughter awoke. Though she certainly wouldn't have minded if he'd stayed, she understood why he hadn't. And truth be told, she'd needed a little time to think as well.

While her body hummed like a well-played violin, her mind and heart were like tumbleweeds turning from one thought to another. She hadn't come out west to find love or get married. Between the way most men treated her and Clint's betrayal when he'd told her she'd have to choose either him or being a doctor, Jillian had given up hope of ever finding love. She wanted to work at what her father had taught her, what she knew. What she loved.

Yet how she could turn away from what she'd found with Wade? After last night, she couldn't imagine ever letting another man touch her. The thought alone made her shudder. She only wanted Wade.

She crossed the dusty yard and tucked back the hair that the wind kept tossing into her face. She was getting too far ahead of herself. It wasn't as though Wade had professed his love and proposed. In truth, Jillian had no idea what he was he thinking or feeling as he'd simply kissed her goodnight and slipped out the door.

On awakening this morning, she'd decided to go see Silver. Jillian knew the woman didn't go to church, as she'd never seen her there, and she herself wasn't up to seeing Wade and his family just yet. Especially at church. Not until she settled a few things, if only in her mind.

Hopefully talking things over with Silver would help. Of course that would mean telling her about last night. Jillian's face warmed. Well, perhaps she wouldn't tell Silver everything.

First things first, however, she had chores to do. Jillian walked through the barn door she'd left open last night. Hopefully by the time she got her work done and washed up she'd have a few things settled in her mind.

She sniffed, but most of the stench from last night's manure was gone. Mostly all she smelled was what usually greeted her in the morning. Jillian stepped into Whiskers' stall. He didn't thump. He always thumped when she came in.

"Oh, Whiskers," she whispered when she saw his still form lying in the cage.

She'd no idea how old he was but he was always active and alert, always eager to get to his food once she closed the cage. Certainly she wouldn't have expected him to die anytime soon.

Sadness swept over her. She'd so hoped to earn his trust, to get him to stop thumping his foot when she came near. Now she'd never get the chance. It might not have been more than a few weeks since she'd taken over his care, but she'd come to love his ever-twitching nose and his cautious little eyes.

It wasn't possible to be a veterinarian and not love animals and she considered Whiskers worthy of the tears that hovered in her eyes. Grabbing the shovel from the tack room, Jillian absently patted the other animals that had edged over their stalls for a morning greeting.

"I'll get your breakfasts soon," she said and went outside to find the perfect place to bury Whiskers.

She chose a spot at the edge of the trees next to a bright pink rose bush and dug deep enough that other animals wouldn't smell what was there and unearth it. Her heart was heavy when she opened the cage and lifted him out.

She knew immediately Whiskers hadn't died a natural death. His head lolled unnaturally. His neck had been broken. Feeling sick, she laid him back into his cage.

Spilled feed, spread manure, and a torn dress were simple things. Annoyances, mean pranks. But Steven had crossed the line this time and she was done keeping these incidents to herself.

It was time to get the sheriff involved.

★

WITHOUT BEING PHYSICALLY sick, there was no way to talk his way out of going to church without rousing his mother's suspicions. But after last night, the last thing he wanted was to go to town. He wasn't worried about running into Steven. Shane likely still had Garvey locked up but Jillian would be there and he wasn't ready to face her. Had no idea what he'd say to her when he did.

He scraped a hand over his freshly-shaven face and let out a deep breath. On second thought, maybe it was a good thing he was going to church. He could pray for wisdom, a solution to his conflicting emotions.

Because he sure as heck didn't know what the hell to do next. All he knew was last night had been so damn perfect and yet it didn't change what Jillian did, who she was.

"Papa, will Mr. Garvey be at church?"

Wade was driving the wagon, his daughter bouncing along between him and his mother while James rode alongside on his gelding. Scott, the lucky bastard, was never expected to go. Since he'd first come to work at the Triple P,

Scott made it clear he didn't go to church and Eileen had never had pushed him. Because Scott wasn't her son. She had no such reservations about pushing Wade.

"I'm not sure. That depends on Shane."

"Does your hand still hurt?"

"A little," he admitted.

"Will I be able to play with Jacob after church?"

"Not for long, I have a lot of work to do today."

"I wonder why Mr. Garvey is so mean. Mrs. Garvey isn't, she's always real nice to me."

"Annabelle." His mother warned. "If you can't say anything nice…"

"I know." Annabelle huffed and crossed her arms. "But you grown-ups do it all the time. I hear you."

From Wade's right, James chuckled then tried to hide it behind a cough. It wasn't even ten and Wade had a headache. Lack of sleep could only be blamed for a part of it. Since breakfast, his daughter hadn't stopped talking, asking questions about last night. She wanted to know everything that had happened after she'd gone to bed. Since it was the first time she'd ever seen him hit anybody, it wasn't unusual for her to be curious. Still he longed for one single moment where he could think in silence.

"Do you think Miss Matthews will be there?" Annabelle turned wide eyes on her father. "Will you get into another fight?"

"No, he won't," his mother replied with a pointed look

at her son.

Annabelle looked almost disappointed at the news.

More wagons than usual filled the grassy area around the church. The gossipers were out in full force.

"Great, just great," Wade murmured as he set the brake, jumped down, and lifted Annabelle out.

On the other side, James helped his ma.

"Uncle Shane!"

Annabelle ran to Shane, threw her arms around his waist.

"Hey, Button," he said, using the name they'd all adopted for her.

"Is Mr. Garvey still in jail?"

"Annabelle!" Wade reprimanded at the same as his mother.

"I'll get us a seat inside," his mother said, taking Annabelle's hand. She smiled at Shane, patted his arm. "Good morning."

He tipped his hat. "Morning, Mrs. Parker."

"Do you need me?" James asked, looking from Wade to Shane.

"Nah, just need a minute of Wade's time."

James nodded. "Then I'll see you later."

They waited until James was inside. The doors to the little church were open, letting in the breeze, but they were far enough away that their voices wouldn't be heard. Nothing else moved around them but the grass bending in the wind.

"You were waiting for me?"

"Just thought I'd let you know that I'll keep Garvey until church service is over. He's not happy about it but I figured it would be best."

It would allow Wade to get away from town before Steven was released. He felt some of the strain on his shoulders ease.

"Thanks."

"Any time." He studied Wade for a moment. "Anything else I need to worry about? You look like you didn't sleep."

"Had a hard time settling down after last night." Which was true, but it wasn't due to his fisticuffs with Garvey.

"Don't blame you, but at least you got to hit him. I didn't have that satisfaction."

Wade smiled. "Next time."

"Speaking of that," Shane said and his grey eyes got a little darker. "I don't think it's only Steven we need to worry about."

"You're talking about Justin and that bunch."

"I think they're harmless, for the most part, but I was watching them at the picnic and at the town meeting. They don't look too happy about having Jillian here either. Luckily, everything happened so fast last night they didn't have a chance to get involved."

Wade remembered how they'd glared at him as they'd left, which was right after Shane had hauled Steven away.

"I'll keep my eyes open but I'm hoping last night was an

isolated event."

"Yeah," Shane said as he thumped Wade on the shoulder. "Let's hope."

★

JILLIAN BREATHED A sigh of relief when she rode Hope into town and saw all the wagons around the church. With any luck at all Shane wasn't among those inside, although she had seen him in church before. But if he was, she knew he kept a room over the jail; she could always wait for him there. She tied Hope to Shane's back stairway and, on the chance he was at his desk, slipped around front and went inside.

"Get out!" Steven seethed from the cell at the back.

Shane wasn't anywhere to be seen.

Steven looked awful. Stubble darkened his face, his eyes were red and narrowed, his shirt hung out of his pants, and everything he wore was wrinkled. Even from where she stood she smelled last night's whiskey on his breath. His hatred for her barreled across the floor and knocked her back a step.

"You don't belong here, bitch, and I won't rest until you're run out!"

Jillian was glad the bars were firmly between them. His loathing was thick and black as smoke and it curled around her neck, making it hard to breathe. Well, he might yet succeed in running her out, but for the moment she was still there.

Swallowing her fear, knowing there wasn't anything she could do about her racing heart or her damp hands, Jillian moved closer to the cell. His eyes went cold. His nostrils flared. Jillian ignored the rancid breath that flooded from his mouth.

"Get out of here." He snarled.

"Stay away from me." Jillian warned. "If you so much as think about hurting another of my animals, I'll shoot you."

"What the hell are you blathering about?"

"I'm not scared of you, Steven."

He pounced on the bars and roared.

Jillian screamed and jumped back.

Steven laughed. "Looks like you're plenty scared to me."

Shane burst through the door. "What the hell is going on?"

"Your friend's whore stopped by for a little visit."

Shane glowered. "Apologize right now or you can spend another night in here."

"Hell, no, I won't apologize. I was minding my own damn business until she came in."

Shane shrugged. "Suit yourself. Don't matter one way or the other to me." His eyes were still hard when he met Jillian's. "Let's go outside."

"Where are you goin'? Let me out!" Steven yelled.

"I don't remember hearing any apology," Shane answered as he steered Jillian toward the door.

"I goddamn apologize!" Steven cursed.

Shane opened the door, looked back at Garvey. "I'll consider it," he said then shut the door on Garvey's cussing.

"Why would you do that?" Shane asked the moment they were on the boardwalk. "You had to know that wasn't going to help anything," he said gesturing to the jail.

"I needed to talk to you; it's important. I didn't think Steven would still be here."

Shane let out a breath. "Well, you found me. What was so all fired important?"

"If you're angry about last night I didn't mean—"

He held up his hand. "I'm not stupid, Jillian. I know last night wasn't your fault and I don't hold you accountable. Hell, Steven's had it coming for a while. You're not the first woman he's disrespected."

"You're talking about Silver."

He nodded, looked down the street toward the saloon. "Yeah." He pulled his gaze back. "Anyhow, as I said, he's had it coming. Doesn't mean I have to be happy about the fallout. There was a steady stream of folks come by this morning who were more than happy to tell me what a bad decision I made locking up Garvey." Shane regarded her closely. "You were the last person I expected to see in my jailhouse this morning."

"I had better things to do myself, but my plans changed when I went into my barn." There wasn't anybody about but she didn't want to get into details on the boardwalk. "Can we go somewhere more private to talk?"

"There's my room upstairs but, truthfully, Jillian, that's not going to help either of our reputations about now. How about Silver's? Saloon's not open so we'd have privacy there."

Jillian nodded. He was right; it was a better solution than upstairs. "I'll get Hope."

He waited for her and they walked the street together, Hope clomping along behind them. Silver let them in through the back door.

"You're in luck. Had the saloon been open last night, I would still be asleep, but as it happens I was in bed earlier than usual," she said with a smile. "So you two can talk all you want, I'll go upstairs and give you some privacy."

"Silver, wait." Jillian grabbed her friend's arm before she could leave. "I was planning on telling you anyhow, this will save me the trouble of repeating myself."

"All right. We'll just sit here then, if that's to everyone's liking."

They sat around the table, tension high in the air as both Shane and Silver waited for Jillian.

She started from the beginning. She told them about the saddle, the spilled feed, the manure, the shredded dress, and the rider she heard riding away.

"That's why you were late coming to the dance." Silver surmised.

"I wish you'd have looked, Jillian. Then it would be easy. Now, it could be any one of Steven's friends."

"I'm sorry. I was so upset about the dress and I felt so

violated..." She sighed. "Anyhow, it didn't seem that important at the time. Until then all they'd done was scare me, wasted some feed, and ruined a dress."

Shane didn't look happy. "What do you mean, 'until then'?"

With sorrow in her heart, Jillian told them about Whiskers.

"Why didn't you come to me before this?" Shane asked.

"And say what? That my saddle was moved? That some feed was spilled in my barn? I think you have more important things to deal with than that. Besides, it seemed innocent enough until..."

"You saw the dress," Silver finished.

"That felt personal." Jillian clasped her hands on the table. "I suppose I should have heeded the warning and not gone to the dance but"—she looked pointedly at Shane—"I haven't done anything wrong and I wasn't going to be scared into staying home."

"I'll talk to Steven."

"What makes you think he'll give you the truth?" Silver asked.

"Because I hold the keys to his cell."

Jillian twisted her fingers together. "But he's the only one in jail. The others won't have the same reason to cooperate."

"I know."

"It could have been Hope," Jillian whispered feeling sick at the thought. "He could have killed Hope instead of

Whiskers." Not that she didn't love the rabbit, but she relied on Hope for more than just companionship. Silence filled the room. Jillian felt Shane's stare and met it. "Is there anything I can do?"

"Yeah," he answered soberly, "until we know for sure who did this, keep your gun handy."

★

SHANE WAITED FOR church to let out and everyone to head home for lunch before he grabbed his chair and plunked it in front of Steven's cell. The man had a head full of resentment but his eyes latched onto the key ring that dangled from Shane's fingers.

"Before I let you out, Garvey, I have a few questions for you."

"Who says I have to answer them?"

Shane merely shrugged, swung the keys from side to side.

"Fine." Garvey relented after a few heated minutes of staring. "What do you want to know?"

"Ever been to Jillian Matthews' property?"

The flicker in Steven's blackened eye gave him away.

"When?" Shane demanded.

"About a week or so ago," Steven admitted. "I didn't hurt nothing, just dumped some feed bags."

"It wasn't 'just'. You were sending her a message."

Garvey wet his chapped, split bottom lip. "I was just"— he swallowed at Shane's scowl, started again—"I was trying to scare her enough that she'd reconsider settling in Marietta."

"It must have really burned your ass when she showed up at the dance."

"She should have stayed the hell at home. If she hadn't gone, I wouldn't be in this stupid cell." Steven contended.

"Wrong. If you'd kept your damn mouth shut you wouldn't be in this cell."

Beneath the yellowing of his bruises Steven's jaw clenched. Shane simply raised a brow. *Go ahead; give me a reason to keep you in here another night.*

"Who did you get to go to her place last night?"

"Last night? How the hell do I know what happened last night? I was here!"

"You don't know what happened at Jillian's after the dance? You didn't arrange to have someone go there, go into her barn?"

"When would I have had the time? When I was rolling around in the dirt with Wade or when I was being tied and dragged back here?"

Well, he had a point. "You have friends, Steven. Friends who agree with you that Jillian shouldn't be here. Do you have any idea which one of them is capable of killing one of Jillian's animals?"

Steven looked legitimately shocked. "Someone killed her animal?"

"Yeah." Shane searched Garvey's face.

Considering how much the man disliked Jillian, he appeared honestly taken aback by the news. And more than a little afraid that this might keep him in jail for a while yet.

"Look, I don't like her, I've never made any bones about that, but whatever went on last night, I wasn't a part of it. I'm not a killer."

"Funny. Jillian tells me you were more than willing to let your boy's dog die."

"I didn't want to pay her. Besides, it was just a dog." He shrugged.

"Well, maybe to you it was 'just a rabbit'."

Steven shook his head as though he hadn't heard properly. "Someone killed her rabbit and you're interrogating me for that? Shit, we eat the damn things, what's the big deal about a rabbit?"

Shane crossed his arms over his chest.

Sweat beaded Steven's lip. He wiped it with his palm. "I'm telling you I had nothing to do with her rabbit. I swear it."

Shane leaned forward. "You can swear to it all you want. But I'll be checking with all your friends, asking them where they were last night. You'd better be telling the truth that you had nothing to do with this or you'll be seeing a lot more of this cell."

★

WADE PROPPED HIS elbows on the top rail of the corral and

wondered how in hell his life had gotten so damn complicated. When he'd married Amy he'd envisioned a long marriage, a handful of kids, and eventually a ranch known for quality horse breeding. Instead, he was widowed, most of the time had no idea if he was doing right by Annabelle, the dreams of his horse ranch were fading by the day, and now he'd gone and made love to a woman who not only wasn't his wife, but never would be either.

He buried his face in his hands. Wouldn't it all be so much easier if she could be?

"Church go that bad?" Scott asked as he sidled up beside him.

Wade lowered his arms, extended them over the rail. "The reverend took it upon himself to preach about acceptance and loving thy neighbor."

"Makes me glad I wasn't there."

"Yeah, made me wish I hadn't gone. Especially when over half the congregation converged on me afterward. I should tell you you're talking to a 'jackass', a 'moron' and 'a goddamn idiot'."

Scott propped a booted foot on the fence, the leather of his chaps creaking with the movement. "The town's opinion has never mattered to you before, so I know you're not out here gnawing on that bone. Is it the ranch?"

"It's everything." Wade sighed.

In the corrals, horses twitched their tails in an effort to escape the flies. Beyond them, the valley stretched wide and green before it rose to meet the mountains. Through the open windows in the house he heard the sound of pots clanging and his daughter's chatter. Scott didn't say anything else, but Wade had a feeling his friend had more yet on his mind.

"May as well spit it all out, Scott."

Scott's lips twitched. "Okay, but remember you asked for it. That horse ranch we've talked about? I'm willing to do more than talk about it. I live simply and I've tucked money aside. Let me help with the starting costs."

Wade was already shaking his head. "No, out of the question. As it is, I'm not paying you anything close to what you're worth. I'm not taking your money on top of that."

"I'm not giving it to you. It's not a loan, Wade, it's my future, too. I'd like to be your partner in this."

Partner? They'd never talked about a partnership before. Dreams danced in Wade's eyes. He could see it. And it was tempting. It really was, but there was debt yet and Wade couldn't see to starting anything new until that was paid off.

"Scott, I can't. Not now. Maybe in the future but I have no idea how long it'll take to get this ranch out of debt."

"Then we'll wait," Scott said. "In the meantime, I won't quit trying to convince you otherwise."

Wade shook his head. "You could be foreman anywhere else, hell you'd make a lot more money. Not that I'm complaining, but why do you hang around?"

The smell of fried meat carried from the house. Dinner

would be ready soon.

"I may have only been here for five years, but it's the only home I've ever known." Scott clapped Wade on the back. "Now let's go eat. I'm starving."

★

"I FEEL LIKE I'm wasting your time," Jillian said.

Yet she wasn't sorry Silver was there. Whiskers was still in the barn and Jillian felt less rattled with her friend around. At Shane's suggestion, Silver had accompanied Jillian home from town. Since Jillian had raced to Marietta without a weapon and considering what had already happened to her things, both Silver and Shane thought it best Jillian not go anywhere unarmed.

And so, with Silver tucking a derringer in her dress pocket and tying a shotgun to her saddle, they'd headed out of town. Shane didn't want Jillian touching anything in the barn until he got there, but first he was going to talk to Steven. While they waited on Shane, they sat on the porch where they were mostly sheltered from the wind.

"Saloon's closed today; I didn't have much else to do." Silver turned to her, her smile coy. "Besides, it'll mean riding back with Shane."

Jillian's eyes went wide. "Shane? Are you two—"

"Only in my dreams, Jillian," Silver said and her laugh held a shadow of sadness.

"Does he know?"

"I don't think so. At least I've tried not to let it show."

"Why?"

"I haven't seen any sign that he feels the same way." Silver had braided her hair today. It fell over her shoulder in a golden rope. "He seems smitten with Melissa."

Jillian had seen them together at the picnic when Shane had won Melissa's basket.

"That's why you didn't stay long at the picnic. I'd wondered."

"I don't know why I bother, Jillian. I've done this since moving to Marietta and he never bids on my basket. I guess I have a hard head."

Jillian took her hand. "No, a soft heart. Are you so sure he wouldn't change his mind about Melissa if he knew your feelings?"

"I'm scared, Jillian. I'm scared I'll give him my heart and he won't want it."

"Then he'd be a fool, Silver."

"Thank you." She took a deep breath. "Now that you know how I feel about Shane, are you going to tell me how you feel about Wade?"

"I was planning to, this morning. I was going to come see you after chores." She tugged at the sleeves of her blouse. "Wade came by last night, after the dance."

Silver scooted closer. "He kissed you, didn't he?"

"Several times." Despite feeling very self-conscious, Jillian looked at Silver. "Last night wasn't the first time we kissed, but it was the first time…"

It didn't take long for Silver to understand what Jillian meant.

"Oh!" Silver's hand flew to her mouth.

Her golden-brown eyes held no judgment and Jillian let out a breath, realizing she'd feared her friend would think less of her.

"Really?" she whispered. "You'd never been with your fiancé?"

"No!"

"Despite what everyone thinks, I've never been with a man either." She smiled. "Was it beautiful?"

Jillian had been flooded with many conflicting emotions since Wade had left last night. Happiness, confusion, uncertainty. But at no time had she regretted it. Remembering the tender way he'd kissed her, stroked her, the way he'd brought her body to life, she sighed.

"It really was."

"I've always imagined it would be with the right man. I'm so excited for you both. Wade's such a great father and I know he was a good husband to Amy." Her eyes widened. "Do you think he'll propose?"

Jillian held up her hand, shook her head. "We didn't talk about the future, other than he can't make any promises."

Silver looked taken aback. "But that doesn't make sense. Between Wade, Scott, and Shane, Wade was the only one who married, had a child. That's who he is."

"Well, maybe he's changed. At any rate, it's just as well. I'm not sure what I would have answered."

Silver looked appalled. "Why ever not?"

"I moved away from my family and left a fiancé to pursue being a vet. What if Marietta never accepts me as a doctor? Silver, I couldn't stay here. Following in my father's footsteps is all I've ever wanted."

Jillian shook her head. "But after being with Wade, I can't imagine being without him either. He makes me feel beautiful, desirable. I want to be part of his life, his family." She smiled. "I've never spent much time around children, but Annabelle makes it easy. She's curious and bright. I think I could be a good mother to her."

Silver squeezed her hand. "Of course you would be."

"Do you suppose if Wade and I were to be together, that eventually I'd win the town's favor? That they'd actually come to accept my skills?"

"I wish I could say yes, Jillian. But the truth is, this town is stubborn. Look at me; they've yet to accept what I do." Silver looked at her closely. "What if they couldn't? What if you married Wade and they never changed their minds? Is that a chance you're willing to take?"

Jillian pressed a hand to her heart.

"I guess that's what I need to find out."

Chapter Thirteen

After seeing Whiskers and the mutilated dress she hadn't thrown out yet, Shane helped Jillian bury the rabbit while Silver wandered the woods nearby for a handful of wildflowers. She stuck them in the fresh mound of dirt, lest the wind toss them away, while Shane put the shovel back in the barn.

The wind billowed the sleeves of his white shirt when he stepped outside. His hand flew to his hat just as the wind tossed it off his head. Grabbing it, he gestured to the porch. Away from the brunt of the wind, Shane put his hat on and addressed Jillian.

"I talked to Steven. It wasn't him."

"You're sure?" Silver asked.

Shane turned his head, looked at her. Now that Jillian knew how her friend felt about the sheriff she couldn't help but will him to see it as well.

"He was already at the dance long before you got there and, as you know, he left with me."

"What about his friends?"

"I don't know yet. All I can tell you, Jillian, is to be careful. And don't go anywhere unarmed. Even if it's just to go to the outhouse or the barn."

Chilled at the thought of not being safe on her own property, Jillian hugged herself. "I won't."

"I really hate the idea of you being alone out here."

"Steven's trying to scare me, Silver. He'll tire of the game soon."

At least that was her hope. But clearly she didn't only have Steven to worry about and apparently they weren't above acting without him.

"I'll let you know if I find anything. I have a few things I'm working on. In the meantime, since most of those men work in town, I should also be able to keep an eye on them, at least to some extent."

"I appreciate that, Shane. Thank you."

"You won't reconsider Silver's offer to stay at the saloon?"

"First of all, I don't want to put Silver in harm's way."

"You wouldn't. We'd be perfectly safe and Shane would be just down the street."

Jillian smiled her thanks but shook her head. "What if they leave me alone while I'm at your place but the moment I'm back here it starts again? I can't live at the saloon indefinitely."

"I know." Silver acknowledged, though her eyes remained troubled.

Shane rested his hands on his hips. Though the mood

couldn't be more serious, Jillian had to fight a smile when the movement drew Silver's undivided attention.

"I don't want to scare you, Jillian, but I can't stay awake all night and neither can you."

"I'll keep the rifle handy."

"And your doors locked."

"I'll see they are."

Shane blew out a frustrated breath. "I wish there was more I could do, but there just isn't."

"I'll be fine. I won't let my guard down."

"All right then. I'll check in when I can." He turned to Silver. "Ready?"

He helped Silver mount then, side by side, Shane dark and handsome and Silver fair and beautiful, Jillian watched them ride out of the yard. They made a stunning couple.

If only Shane could see it and Silver wasn't afraid to tell him how she felt.

★

THE THICK BLANKET of grey clouds blocked the sun and the gusty wind tugged at his hat. Wade ducked his head to keep the dust from his eyes. A small whirlwind spiraled across the yard. His shirt flapped against his chest and he put his weight into the gate to close it. He slipped the rope over the post and sighed.

Taking the saddle off the fence, Wade spit out the dust the wind was determined he eat and headed for the barn. He nearly bumped into Shane on the way out.

"Twice in one day. You must be lonely." Wade chided.

"Anyone else in there?" Shane nodded toward the barn.

"No, why?"

"Good. I'm tired of eating dirt." Shane brushed past Wade and made himself at home on a bench.

"Did Steven give you more trouble?" Wade asked, taking a seat next to Shane.

"Not yet. But I let him out, just before dinner."

"You worried he might come after me?"

Shane shook his head. "Not you, so much, but I do recommend you keep an eye open. He's not real pleased with you at the moment. Also wouldn't hurt to carry a weapon."

Wade scowled. "He threatened me, didn't he?"

"No. Actually, when I spoke to him he was almost cooperative." He took a deep breath, let it out. "It's Jillian I'm worried about."

It took everything Wade had to sit and listen as Shane recounted the trouble Jillian had been having. By the time Shane was done, Wade's jaw throbbed from clenching it.

It hadn't occurred to Wade when the bull deal with Liam had gone bad that Steven was also hurting Jillian. Goddammit, it should have.

"Look, I'm not telling you this for you to go tear into Steven. I'm just warning you. Who knows? Maybe now that I'm involved, things will settle down."

"Or get worse. Whoever wants her gone bad enough to

do this isn't going to be happy the sheriff's on her side."

Shane nodded. Wade figured it was just habit for him to set his palm on the gun that rode in the holster.

"We all need to be careful. Silver was at Jillian's this afternoon. She's in with your ma now, but I'll be riding with her back to town.

"Wade, don't make this worse. Stay away from Garvey and his cohorts." The men came to their feet. "I have a real bad feeling about this; that it's going to get ugly. But in case I'm wrong, you going after Steven or anyone else associated with him just might push things further than anybody wants."

The thought of Jillian hurt turned Wade's blood to ice. "What if we do nothing and he takes it further anyway? What if he goes after her next time, instead of her property?"

"I'm going to do everything I can so that doesn't happen."

"But you can't guarantee it, can you?"

Shane held up his hands. "Wade, I—"

"You can't, can you?"

"No," Shane admitted, looking about as happy about that as Wade felt. "I can't."

★

JILLIAN PICKED AT the food on her plate, created a pile of mashed potatoes, and then flattened it down again. She'd cut the ham into bite-sized pieces but after stacking them until they toppled over, gave up on her supper. She hadn't been hungry to begin with but she'd prepared her small meal because she'd needed to do something.

"Maybe I should get a dog," she said, looking at her plate of uneaten food.

She'd said it in jest, thinking of being able to give her leftovers to an animal rather than throwing them away, but now that she thought about it, she realized it wasn't a bad idea. She was alone; she couldn't stay awake indefinitely. A dog would alert her if someone or something came into her yard.

After the day she'd had, it was a relief to feel something other than dread. A dog! She smiled, threw her leftovers in a pail she'd toss outside later when she did her evening chores. Tomorrow, she'd go into town. Surely Letty, as the owner of the mercantile, would know if anyone had puppies to give away.

Until she found a dog, though, she was sleeping in the barn. With her rifle. Nobody was going to kill another of her animals. Jillian dug into the chest at the foot of her bed for extra blankets. The sound of hoofbeats approaching carried through the bedroom window she'd left open for just that purpose. Jillian flung the blankets on the bed and ran to grab her gun. Once it was firmly in hand, she braced herself and looked out the kitchen window.

She wilted like a flower in the heat of July. It was only Annabelle. Not wanting to scare the girl, Jillian placed the weapon behind the door.

"Miss Matthews!" Annabelle called the moment Jillian stepped outside.

Jillian waved, but waited for the girl and her horse to get closer before talking. Annabelle's shadow was taller than she was when she jumped from the saddle. As always the little girl's eyes glittered with life and energy.

"Hello, Annabelle. What a nice surprise." Jillian looked down the road and beyond. Her stomach jittered, thinking Wade may be coming along. Though she'd had a busy day, she'd secretly been hoping he'd come see her. To talk. To…

"You didn't come alone, did you?" The thought left Jillian nauseous.

She didn't know Steven well enough to truly know what the man was capable of, but Annabelle was Wade's daughter and if he was mad enough at Wade…

The little girl clutched her horse's reins. "I heard Papa talking to Uncle Shane today. Uncle Shane says you might be in danger."

Jillian scowled. She might not be a mother but she knew enough not to say such things around a child. Why scare the poor child for something she couldn't control?

"I'm not, really. Your Uncle Shane just wants me to be careful."

"Is this because of me? Because of what I said to Papa last night?"

Jillian held her hand out for the pony to smell, and then

patted the warm hide along its neck. "Let's get your pony some water, then we'll talk."

They walked to Hope's enclosure where Hope came to make her introductions. The horses snuffled each other over the fence rail while Jillian let herself in and brought Hope's water bucket out. With Annabelle's horse tied and drinking, Jillian turned her attention back to the little girl.

"Why would you think this is your fault?"

"Because after I told Papa what I heard Mr. Garvey say about you, he got into a fight. I've never seen Papa in a fight before."

It was clear the girl was both frightened and awed by what she'd seen.

"Adults can do stupid things sometimes, Annabelle. And it's of their own doing. You're not to blame."

The little girl slipped her hand in Jillian's as she fixed trusting eyes on her. Warmth spread through Jillian's chest and she squeezed Annabelle's hand.

"Now, you haven't answered my question. Does your father or anyone else know where you are?"

She looked down, shuffled dirt with her boot. "No, ma'am," she answered.

Clearly, she expected to be sent right back. Though the sun was sliding toward the horizon, dusk wouldn't be upon them for at least another hour. There'd be plenty of time to get Annabelle home before then.

"I have a goat and a raccoon in the barn; would you like

to see them?"

Annabelle's gaze flew to Jillian's. Her excitement was tangible. "Yes'm, I would!"

Before Jillian could say anything else she found herself being tugged toward the barn.

★

WADE'S HEART POUNDED in his throat as he ripped up the stairs, flung the door open.

"Annabelle!"

He smelled his own sweat, his own fear. His voice echoed off the empty log walls. He'd already checked the house once when he'd come to fetch her to go fishing. She hadn't been there. But he'd checked the barns, too, and by the river. She hadn't been at either place. He'd thought maybe they'd somehow missed each other and tried her room again but it was as empty as it had been the first time.

"Annabelle!"

He raced down the steps and out the front door.

"Annabelle!"

Scott came running from his bunkhouse. Shirtless, with boots hastily yanked over his pants and a rifle in his left hand, he sped around the corrals toward Wade.

"What's happened?"

"When was the last time you saw Annabelle?"

"At supper. No, wait! I went back in about an hour ago, had a piece of cake. She was heading outside. You said you two were going fishing so I figured she was going to meet you."

Wade's mouth was so dry it made talking difficult. "No. I told her I had a few things to finish first. I can't find her anywhere."

"Could she be with your ma and James? If they went on a walk maybe she went along? She's done it before."

His ma. Wade heaved a breath, wiped the sweat off his upper lip with the sleeve of his shirt. He hadn't thought of that and yet he should have, since he hadn't seen either James or his ma as he'd searched for his daughter.

"Yeah, that makes sense," Wade took another breath. "It's this business with Steven. I thought maybe…"

Scott placed a reassuring hand on Wade's shoulder. "I'm no friend of Steven's, either; I barely know the man, but I can't see him going after a little girl to settle a score with you."

"I'm sure you're right." Well, pretty sure. Still, Wade wouldn't breathe easy until he saw his daughter. "I'll saddle Whiskey. It'll be faster to catch up to them that way."

His hands were steady as he tacked his horse. He'd panicked, but now reason took over. His daughter was fine; she was with her grandma. He'd assumed the worst because his talk with Shane was still fresh in his mind. The more he thought about it, the better he felt. That didn't mean, however, that she wasn't going to be scolded for scaring ten years off her father's life.

The air outside the barn was beginning to dampen. He could hear the frogs singing in the long grass as he led Whiskey out. The corral pen slammed to his left. Scott had his horse—the only thing he had come with five years ago other than a bag over his shoulder—by the halter. He'd put on a shirt, though he hadn't bothered tucking it into his pants.

"Forget your saddle?"

"Don't have time." He gestured over Wade's shoulder.

Wade knew even before he looked, before Scott's words confirmed it. James and his ma had indeed gone for a walk and, hand in hand, were walking into the yard. Annabelle wasn't with them. The bottom fell out of Wade's stomach.

"Peanut's gone as well," Scott said of Annabelle's pony.

How had he not noticed the pony was gone? *Because I was blinded by panic.* And because they had a rule about her riding alone.

"Maybe they saw her," Wade said, leaping into the saddle.

His mother looked as scared as he felt when he told her Annabelle wasn't to be found. "We didn't see her."

"When was the last time you did?"

"She helped me with the supper dishes and then she went upstairs."

Wade's heart was pounding. He stood in the stirrups, looked around. Nothing moved but grass and leaves.

"Scott saw her about an hour ago."

"She's on Peanut," Scott said. He was riding bareback, the only one of them who could do it and still retain absolute control of his horse.

"I was around the yard the whole time," Wade said. "I don't know how she could have slipped past me."

"You did it all the time," his ma said, placing her hand on his leg. "It's amazing how fast you could disappear when you had a place in mind."

"Yeah, but where would Annabelle want to-Jillian!" Wade exclaimed though the thought of possibly knowing his daughter's whereabouts didn't ease his fear. Not with what Shane had told him earlier.

"Stay here in case we're wrong. Scott and I will go to Jillian's."

"Take this," James said, handing over his Colt.

Wade still hadn't come to terms with the idea of needing to carry a weapon everywhere he went but in this case he didn't argue. If his daughter were in danger, he wouldn't hesitate to use it. Besides, there were rifles in the house so James wouldn't be unarmed. Wade jammed the revolver in his waistband and tore out of the yard.

Beside him, with his hands in the horse's mane as he bent over it, Scott kept pace. Now that the wind had died, dust hung in the air behind them. The road to Jillian's contained several small knolls and it was as they crested the third that they saw two riders approaching. One was on a pony.

Wade eased on the reins and slowed Whiskey to a walk. The horse's heavy breathing matched his own. As the distance between the animals closed, his daughter had the good sense to look contrite.

"Annabelle, what were you thinking riding away like that without telling anyone?" He demanded. Though he didn't yell, there was no masking his irritation either. "You scared us all."

Annabelle wouldn't meet her father's eyes. "I'm sorry, Papa. Everyone was busy and I just wanted to talk to Miss Matthews for a bit."

"You could have asked, Annabelle, and if we were busy it could have waited until tomorrow."

She nodded, kept her head down.

"Scott, you mind taking her home? I won't be long."

"No problem. Come on, Button. Nice to see you again, Jillian."

"And you," Jillian replied.

"Annabelle." Wade caught her reins as she moved by. He waited until his daughter finally met his gaze. "After you take care of Peanut, clean up and get ready for bed. I'll be home soon."

Her shoulders sagged. "We're not going fishing, are we?"

He leaned over, kissed her forehead. "Not tonight. We'll talk about what you did and how you scared everyone when I get back."

She sighed, turned to Jillian. "Thanks, Miss Matthews.

Goodnight."

"Goodnight, Annabelle," Jillian answered.

Wade waited until Scott and Annabelle had disappeared over the hill. He hadn't planned on anything but finding his daughter. Now that he had, however, and he knew she was safe, his mind shifted to the woman before him.

She wore no bonnet to protect her face and Wade had come to realize he liked that about her. He liked seeing her hair. His loins swelled as he thought about what it had felt like to touch that hair, to have it draped over him as she'd kissed him. Before he truly realized his intent, he'd swung off Whiskey and was at Hope's side.

Jillian's cheeks turned a lovely shade of pink that had nothing to do with the sun's setting rays. She leaned into him. His hands clasped her around the waist. He deliberately eased her slowly down the length of his body, feeling her breasts slide down his chest. She smelled of fresh air and her own subtle scent that wrapped around him the same way it had last night.

Her green eyes searched his, her soft hands rested on his shoulders.

"I'm sorry you were worried."

He'd been terrified, but now that his daughter was safe and Jillian was in his arms, his attention was easily diverted. Since walking away last night, he'd relived every touch, every kiss. Her mouth lifted to his and damned if he was going to waste the invitation.

The moment her soft lips opened under his, his grip tightened and he pulled her hard against him. The same satisfied moan he'd heard several times last night escaped her as their tongues danced, explored. She set him on fire until he either had to step away or he'd take her right there on the road. The thought wasn't without merit, but the location was wrong. And he'd meant what he'd said last night; he couldn't make her promises.

With a last gentle nip on her mouth, he ended the kiss.

"How are you?"

She smiled, wound her arms around his neck. "Better now."

Oh, hell, he was in trouble. Before he gave in to temptation and ravaged her again, he gently pulled her hands from his neck and stepped back.

"It would be easy, Jillian," he said when he saw the disappointment on her face, "to kiss you again. To make love with you. But—"

"But you can't make promises. I remember."

"I think we both have enough complications in our lives, don't you?"

She clasped her hands together. "Shane told you about Steven?"

"This afternoon."

"I know what he wants. He's trying to scare me out of town." Her chin rose defiantly. "He won't succeed."

"It's not you personally he has a problem with, it's what

you do."

Jillian threw up her hands. "Why is what I do so hard to accept? I'm not a whore! I don't steal. I help animals and for that I'm being punished? Why?"

Here was a chance to try to explain where folks were coming from, why they thought the way they did. Why he thought the way he did. If he could get her to understand, if he could get her to reconsider being a vet then maybe…

"It's a man's job to take care of his family, Jillian. From the beginning of time that's the way it's been. Men work, provide for their families while the women tend the home and the children."

"Women teach in schools. Letty works the mercantile; Mrs. Hollingsworth runs a boarding house. Why is that all right but what I do so wrong?"

"It's different. You do a man's work, Jillian, and it's hard and dangerous. You could get hurt. You can be called upon any time of day, in any kind of weather, making it even more inappropriate for a woman. And," he said, warming to his argument, "Letty and Mrs. Hollingsworth's work doesn't put them in harm's way."

"Since neither Steven nor his friends even like me, why would they care if I got hurt? And the same argument stands for the time of day I could be called upon to tend an animal. What I do would never affect them personally." Her eyes widened and her jaw dropped. "You're not talking about them. You're talking about yourself, aren't you?"

The steel in her gaze didn't bode well for him.

"Jillian—"

Her fists jammed onto her hips. "You lied. You told me the reason you couldn't make promises was because you had too much to deal with at the moment. But it's because of what I do, isn't it?"

Hell, there wasn't a good to answer that.

"Jillian—"

"Don't 'Jillian' me!" Hope shied at the shout and Jillian grabbed the reins before Hope could bolt.

Wade took in her narrowed eyes, her small fisted hands. He had a bad feeling he'd already dug himself too deep a hole. It shouldn't matter, given the fact she was right, that it was his thoughts he'd been discussing. But suddenly it mattered very much.

"All right, yes, it's how I feel." He raised his palms. "But I'd never hurt you over it."

Jillian's gaze could cut glass. "Does that make everything all right to you? You kissed me, made love to me."

"I didn't lie to you."

Her eyes narrowed. "Well, you weren't honest either."

"I'm in debt up to here." He slashed his throat with his finger. "I can't possibly think about bringing a wife into that. And I do have a daughter to consider. And a ranch to run and—"

"Tell me this, then. If I had come to town as the schoolteacher, or if I were a seamstress, would we be having this discussion? Would you be refusing to be with me? Refusing to make promises?"

Wade ran a hand around the back of his neck. He was sweating again and his palm came away damp.

"That's what I thought." Jillian stuck her foot in the stirrup, lifted herself into the saddle, and adjusted her skirts.

Wade grabbed Hope's reins. "You make it sound simple, that it's black or white. It's not. Look at this." He gestured to the rifle she had tied to the saddle. "Your home, your possessions have been attacked because of what you do. You can't go anywhere anymore without carrying a rifle."

"That's because of Steven and his friends!"

"It's because of what you do!" He took a deep breath, tried again. "I've never feared for Annabelle the way I did tonight."

★

JILLIAN TRIED TO wrestle away the reins but Wade held fast. They weren't done yet. He wanted her to understand.

"Annabelle was never in any danger." Hurt darkened her eyes. "I've come to care for her. I'd never let anything happen to her."

"Not on purpose, no. But she rode to your place alone. Anything could have befallen her. Don't you see?" He pleaded.

"I'll tell you what I see," Jillian said. "You didn't know about any of what's happened at my house until today. And it was last night when you told me you couldn't make promises, so your mind was already set. The rest is just excuses."

"It's not an excuse! It's—"

"I've already lived through this once!" she shouted. "I thought you were different, that you were a better man than Clint."

Wade felt as though he'd been punched. "Who the hell is Clint?"

"The man I was engaged to before he decided that what I did wasn't proper. Before he told me that once we were married he wouldn't allow me to be a doctor."

Wade reeled. She'd been engaged?

But Jillian was like a freight train full of steam and before he could speak she was charging ahead. "From the time I decided to follow in my father's footsteps, I've never wavered from my goal. And despite it being what I wanted most, I sacrificed a lot to pursue my dream. Because it was all I wanted. I never thought that would change."

Her voice cracked and Wade felt its effects as though he were being horsewhipped.

"But after last night, I questioned whether it would be enough. I thought maybe there was more to life than what I had." Her hands fisted over her breasts. Her eyes shone with pain. "And I considered sacrificing all of that for a chance to have a life with you and Annabelle, because I was stupid enough to think you believed in me. That maybe you loved me as much as I was coming to love you."

The earth shifted beneath his feet. She loved him? "If you were thinking of giving it up, then why are we arguing?"

Jillian's jaw dropped. "Why? Because when I considered giving it up it was because of the town. Because *it* wouldn't accept me, not because *you* wouldn't. If I stayed, it would be with the hope that one day they'd change their minds, that one day I'd get to work at what I love. But now I see that you would never accept that. You're just like Clint."

He felt like he was on the edge on the hill and his boots were losing purchase. Any minute now he'd tumble down.

"Jillian, you're not the only one who's gone through this once already. Amy, my wife, decided after she had Annabelle that she wanted to be a midwife. I wasn't happy about it, but I thought if it made her happy, what was the harm? She died, Jillian, riding out to deliver a baby. It was dark and something spooked her horse. She was thrown."

He shut his eyes and saw Amy lying there, broken and bleeding. By the time they'd found her, it had been hours since she'd fallen. They'd been too late to help her.

"Annabelle lost her ma and I lost my wife. For what? If she'd been home that wouldn't have happened."

"It could have. Did she never ride around the ranch?"

His teeth set. "That's different."

"No, it's not. You're just too narrow-minded to see it and you're blaming Amy's midwifery as the reason she died."

"She'd be alive if she hadn't gone that night!"

Jillian flinched. Wade heaved a breath. "I can't put myself and Annabelle through that again."

"I'm not Amy, Wade."

He could see she was fighting tears and he wasn't proud of it. But he needed to be clear, needed her to understand.

"I know that. But in some ways you're the same. A man, a family, will never be enough for you. You'll always want more."

"Is that what you think? That you weren't enough? That by Amy deciding to be a midwife, it somehow made you less of a man?"

It wounded his pride to say it, but they'd made love and now he was telling her they couldn't be together. She deserved the truth.

"Yes," he admitted with a hitch in his voice.

"Did it never occur to you that Amy's being a midwife didn't make you less? It made her more."

Wade shook his head. "What?"

"I'm sure she didn't love you or Annabelle less. But maybe there was a part of her that needed something else."

"And you don't think that makes me feel as though I wasn't enough for her?"

"You have a ranch, Wade. Could you give it up?"

His head snapped. "Absolutely not."

"Why? It's not making you rich."

Her words stung, because, dammit, they were true. "Because I love it. Because—"

"It's a part of you. It's no different for me. I'd never ask you to give up the ranch. It's your legacy, and it's who you are." A tear slipped out and she wiped it. "I'd work with you on the ranch. I'd stay no matter how little money it earned because, without it, you wouldn't be who you are." Her chin rose. "And I won't accept less than the same in return."

She pulled on the reins.

Knowing there was nothing more to be said, Wade opened his hand and let her go.

Chapter Fourteen

Jillian rode low and let Hope fly. The trees and grass were a large green blur as they raced toward home. Of course speed was only one reason for the blurry image. The other was the tears tumbling from her eyes.

What a fool she'd been! Until meeting Wade, she'd been single-minded in her thinking. She wanted to be a veterinarian. Everything she'd done from the time she'd made the decision as a young girl was toward that purpose. To think she'd considered compromising that for a man, a man who would never consider her worthy!

The tears flowed from the corner of her eyes into her ears. Hope's hooves pounded the ground. Jillian was indifferent to it all but the tearing sensation in her heart. When her little house came into view, Jillian didn't ease her speed, but she did pull the rifle out of the scabbard. If someone was there, he'd picked the wrong time to threaten what was hers.

But other than Zeke, the calf and its mother, the yard was empty. As Jillian finally reined Hope in, she couldn't help feeling disappointed. She might have been scared earlier. But, right then, she was more than ready to defend herself.

With the rifle within arm's reach, Jillian removed the saddle, bridle, and blanket. Then, with the fingers of one hand curled in the halter and her weapon in the other, she walked Hope around the small yard until they'd both cooled off.

In the barn, she brushed her horse, praised her, and fed her. Once the tack was put away, she grabbed the gun and went into the house. She wasn't hungry but she'd left the blankets and pillows on her bed. Her plan to sleep in the barn hadn't changed.

The house was unchanged; nothing had been disturbed. Jillian took the covers and made herself a bed in Whiskers' now empty stall. She didn't linger, simply moved his cage outside, lit and hung a lantern, and made herself a pallet. She did her evening chores, availed herself of the outhouse.

Keeping everything on but her shoes, Jillian crawled underneath her covers. The barn door was closed and secured. Her gun was beside her bed. The lantern filled her stall with soft light. Around her the animals shuffled in their pens, crunched their food.

Animals had always been a refuge for her. They didn't judge, didn't criticize. She could be around them and be herself and for the most part they welcomed her.

"Unlike this stupid town," she muttered.

From the first they'd heard of her, before most of them had even met her, they'd judged. Judged and, like Wade, found her lacking. She'd been polite and tried to win them over. And what had it gotten her?

Nothing. She had no work. Her property had been damaged. She was worried enough about her animals to sleep in a barn. The man she'd given her body to couldn't accept her for who she was. And her money was drying up faster than a drought-ridden prairie.

She couldn't afford to stay much longer. While she'd made good friends, and she knew how hard true friends were to find, she couldn't stay for them. After Eileen and James's wedding, if she hadn't had work, she'd need to move on. If Marietta couldn't find a way to accept her, then she needed to find a place that would.

★

BY THE TIME Wade left Annabelle's room he was exhausted and had a thumping headache. He'd explained about Steven, how they had to be careful for a while. How she couldn't wander off without telling anyone again.

She'd apologized, explained why she'd gone to Jillian's to begin with, and how they'd spent time in the barn before heading back to the ranch. Wade had been furious to hear this. Knowing Jillian had kept Annabelle in her barn for nearly an hour when she had to know he'd be worried sick, and knowing Steven or one of his friends was crazy enough to come after her, reinforced his decision.

His daughter was better distanced from Jillian.

He poked his head in the kitchen. All was quiet. It wasn't completely dark outside yet but his ma had left a lantern burning low on the table. It cast flickering shadows on the log walls. His mind full, Wade turned down the light and stepped outside. The swing creaked and Scott came to his feet.

He grabbed a couple fishing poles he'd set against the railing. "Thought you could use a little distraction."

What Wade could use was a whiskey but, since Scott didn't drink, Wade accepted the pole and followed his friend to the river. Scott had dug up worms and he settled the jar of crawly creatures between them.

Wade baited the hook, tossed the line in the gently flowing water. Scott was a bit more selective with his worms but his line plopped in not long after.

"I haven't changed my mind about the horse ranch," Wade said after a few minutes.

"I knew you wouldn't have." Scott pulled in his line then calmly let it out again. "But, out of curiosity, have you noticed Jillian's filly?" Scott whistled. "I bet a colt out of that one, especially if we bred her with Whiskey, would be a hell of an animal. Likely bring in a nice profit."

"Dammit, Scott." He could see it. It was so clear it made his heart yearn. "I told you I can't."

Scott looked over his shoulder. "And having a wife with Jillian's skills would come in real handy."

"I'm not marrying Jillian to save money on vet bills!"

"Of course not, you'll marry her because you love her. The vet bills are just gravy."

"Jesus." Wade pinched the bridge of his nose.

He wished... hell, he didn't even know what to wish for anymore but it seemed there wasn't much point in praying for peace and quiet since it seemed in damn limited supply these days.

"Jillian and I won't be seeing any more of each other."

"Why? You hit your head on a rock and lost all good sense?"

"Look, I already had this argument once today with Jillian. We aren't suited and that's all there is to it."

"Who says you aren't suited? You or her?"

"Scott—"

"It's not a hard question, Wade. You or her?"

He dropped his hand. "Me. All right?"

"Tell me you don't agree with Steven."

"I'd never hurt her!" Wade exclaimed.

Around them the crickets went silent.

"But you don't think she should be doctorin' either? Why, when she's clearly remarkable at it?"

"Ma was always there for me," he said after a while. "I never had to worry that she wouldn't be there at the end of the day, that she wouldn't come home."

"What happened to Amy was an accident, Wade. It doesn't mean the same thing would happen to Jillian."

Wade gave up the illusion of fishing and tossed his pole

aside. "But it could and I can't take that chance. I've got my hands full with the ranch. I give Annabelle what time I can, make more when I need to, but it's not the same as having a ma she can count on."

"Annabelle has you, me, your ma, James. Even if Jillian had to leave to tend an animal, your daughter would hardly be abandoned."

Maybe not. But he'd been helpless to keep Annabelle from losing her mother at such a young age. The least he owed her, when he did decide to remarry, was to give her a mother who would be there for her. Who wasn't in danger—not only from the town but also by the very profession she'd chosen.

"She deserves a mother who'll be with her."

"Oh, for the love of God." Scott threw his pole next to Wade's. "There are things more important in life than who will cook her damn breakfast!"

Wade gaped as his usually affable friend went hot under the collar.

"Let me tell you what Annabelle needs. She needs love, respect, and to know that she's safe."

When Wade had accepted the fishing pole he'd expected a little quiet camaraderie by the river, he hadn't expected to get torn into. It turned his already foul mood rancid.

"And how would you know this?" Wade demanded. "You have ample experience with children you've kept to yourself all these years?"

Scott's face went hard as the rocks that poked out of the river. "I'd have given anything for what Annabelle has. A real home. A family. A father she knows and adores. I'd have given anything for a mother who loved me enough to leave me the hell alone!"

Scott had never mentioned his past before and he looked as surprised to have said it as Wade was to have heard it. Scott wiped his mouth with his sleeve, took in great gulps of air. Wade wasn't sure what to say or do and Scott's silence didn't help.

Finally Scott nodded to the poles. "You mind taking those back?"

"Uh, no," Wade answered.

But it was too late; he was already talking to Scott's back.

★

WADE STAYED BY the river a little longer. With Scott gone, he was finally alone to dwell on everything that had gone on today. He lay back on the grass, watched the stars emerge, and tried to lasso his wandering thoughts.

Scott's words resonated in his ears. What did he mean by he wished his mother had loved him enough to leave him alone? Hell, since Scott was so tight-lipped about his past— the only thing he'd ever said was he was from Colorado— Wade figured he'd been orphaned or some such thing. Instead, it sounded like that might have been a better alternative.

Which brought Wade around to Scott's other words. That all a child needed was to be loved, to feel safe, and to have a home. Annabelle had all of those things, he'd seen to it. But unlike Scott who didn't seem to have happy memories of being a youngster, Wade did. He could look back and remember his ma kissing his scrapes, his ma helping him read, his ma kissing his forehead at night, long after he'd told her he was too big to be kissed by his ma.

Annabelle had had all that with Amy. Until Amy had decided to be a midwife. Then, there'd been checkups, long nights of delivering a baby, follow-up visits to ensure mother and child were doing fine. She'd missed meals. She hadn't always been back by Annabelle's bedtime. Then the accident happened and she hadn't been there at all.

He'd heard what Scott said but it didn't change Wade's mind.

He'd promised himself when Amy died that he'd always do his best by Annabelle. And no matter that he felt the same for Jillian as she'd professed to feel for him, the truth remained that she wasn't what was best for either him or his daughter.

★

IT WAS A simple plan, but that didn't make it easy. In the hours Jillian had lain awake, listening to her animals and mulling over her situation, she'd made some decisions. Firstly, while she could certainly keep her animals safe at night by sleeping in the barn, she couldn't always be home, nor she did she intend on sleeping in the barn indefinitely.

Hope, and the dog if she found one, would be as safe as Jillian could make them. She'd lock Hope in the barn at night and during the day if she left her property, she'd have both the horse and dog with her. That left Zeke and Rascal vulnerable.

And she wouldn't have them killed because of her.

So after folding her bedding and tossing it over the rail, Jillian went into Rascal's pen. His masked face peered at her. His little hands pressed on the bars.

"You want out? Well, you're about to get your wish."

She dragged his cage outside, unwound the wire that was holding the door closed. It was bittersweet, saying goodbye. On the one hand, she'd always felt he was a wild animal that shouldn't be caged, but on the other, she loved the way he looked at her. The chattering noises he made when she brought him food or talked to him.

"Now don't be coming in the house and making a mess or you'll be right back where you started." Or worse, if whoever bought Jillian's house once she moved on wasn't as forgiving as she was.

Maybe he'd learned his lesson; time would tell. But he looked from the cage to the house, house to cage as though he understood one would lead to the other. Then with a twitch of his pointed nose, he ambled for the trees.

Zeke wouldn't be as simple to deal with but Jillian had

little doubt that by the end of the day, he'd have a home. In the meantime, she stored Rascal's cage with Whiskers' empty one and, with the shotgun handy, went about her morning chores.

Within two hours, she was clean, dressed, and had saddled Hope. She'd fashioned a collar for Zeke and tied one end of a rope to it and the other end to Hope's saddle. It would take longer to walk to town that way, but it would guarantee the animal's safety.

As for the cow and calf, she just had to hope they'd be safe for a few hours. Since the cow had milk and the heifer could be sold come fall, Jillian could only pray that, if anything, they'd be stolen rather than hurt.

Apparently Monday mornings meant brisk business in Marietta. Several wagons rattled by. A stagecoach was loading in front of the post office. Already its roof was half-filled with trunks and bags. With school now through until fall, children of varying heights walked alongside their mothers while the younger ones toddled along the boardwalk, their little fists clasped in their mother's long skirts.

Jillian had always drawn stares but she drew more than usual when she rode in with Zeke. Usually, she smiled at everyone but she didn't have the heart to this morning. Shane stepped out of the sheriff's office as she rode by. For him, she fashioned a smile, pulled Hope to a stop.

Shane looked at Zeke. "A goat isn't much in the way of protection."

Jillian accepted his help down. "I can't protect him when I'm not home. I kept him because he was left to me but I don't want him hurt. I was hoping someone might take him."

He tipped his hat up. "Can't say I know anybody. Anyhow, I'm glad you're here." He glanced around but there were a lot of folks rambling the street. "Come inside for a minute, I have some news."

In the jailhouse, Shane perched on a corner of his desk. Jillian settled in a chair.

"Steven's friends deny killing your rabbit."

"I hardly expected them to admit it."

"Maybe not, but I'm a good judge of folks. Of them all, I'm most likely to believe it was Bill, the stable owner."

"But you said he denied it."

"He did, but I spoke to his wife. She claims she heard Bill leave the room that night. Of course he says he just went to the outhouse."

"Was he gone long? Maybe if he didn't come right back…"

Shane shook his head. "I thought of that. She said she fell back asleep and has no idea how long he was gone."

"Have you asked Harvey Black?" Jillian told Shane about her visit to his place and his comment about dealing with animals if he needed to.

"I went over there but he wasn't home. Steven didn't think he was back from Bozeman yet."

So he had gone to advertise for her replacement. Well, it seemed as though her future was set no matter what she wanted. Her time in Marietta was coming to an end. Still, if she was going to be forced out, she wanted to know the rest.

"It was all Steven then? I mean, other than killing Whiskers?"

"The lost feed and the dress were. He told me it was Justin who moved the saddle. He's claiming he has no idea about the rabbit and his friends deny any involvement."

"Well, Whiskers' neck didn't snap itself."

Shane held up a hand. "I'm not done with them, Jillian. I'll be talking to their wives when they're at work. I'll also be checking in on them here and there throughout the day. They're going to get good and sick of me with the amount of time I'll be spending watching them. Hopefully, that'll be enough to leave you alone.

"And I haven't forgotten about Harvey. He'll be back soon, so I'll keep checking on him as well." He paused. "It's all I can do, Jillian. Hopefully it will be enough."

It might make the attacks stop, but it wouldn't assure she'd get work. Yet she appreciated Shane's efforts and thanked him before stepping outside.

A little girl was crouched next to Zeke, and she giggled when he tried to nibble her skirt. Her mother watched, a warm smile of adoration on her face.

"His name is Zeke and don't let his handsome looks fool you, he'll eat that skirt until it's gone if you let him," Jillian said.

The mother grabbed her daughter's hand. "I'm sorry; she saw the goat and ran over."

"You think he's handsome?" the little girl asked.

Jillian knelt close. "Of course he is. Look at those big brown eyes of his, and the smart grey whiskers on his chin."

"And these things," the little girl said, touching the two loose furry growths that hung from each side of the neck.

"Those are called wattles," Jillian said.

"Really?" her mother asked, looking in closer. "I never knew that."

Jillian looked at her, smiled. "I didn't either until my father taught me. He was a veterinarian as well," she added.

The woman nodded, placed a hand on her daughter's bonnet. "You learned at his side?"

"I did." Jillian straightened then shifted to keep the sun from her eyes. "My fondest memories are of times we spent together."

"He's passed?"

"Yes," Jillian admitted. Her heart squeezed briefly. "Earlier this spring."

"I'm sorry for your loss. Come, Ruth," she said to her daughter. "It's time to go."

"But, Mama."

"Ruth," she said. "We've kept Miss Matthews long enough."

"Oh, well, I don't mind. I've enjoyed talking with you

both."

The woman looked startled for a moment then nodded her head. "I have as well. I'm Mary, by the way. My husband Justin is the blacksmith."

And a friend of Steven's. But she wouldn't judge Mary by her husband.

"Pleased to meet you. You know, Mary, I was on my way to the mercantile to ask Mrs. Daniels if she'd know of anyone who might like to have Zeke." She looked to Ruth, grinned. "You wouldn't know of anyone, would you?"

Ruth clasped Zeke around the neck. "Mama, we could keep him!"

Mary didn't seem sure. "Oh, but—"

"I'm not asking you to pay for him. I simply want him to go to a good home." She smiled at Ruth. "And to be given lots of love."

"Can we keep him, Mama? Please?"

"Really, Mary, you'd be doing me a favor. But," she added, since she didn't want Zeke to have the same fate as Whiskers, "only if this won't upset your… family."

Mary blinked. "No, he spoils Ruth." She looked from her daughter's smiling face to Jillian. "Well, if you're sure…"

Jillian untied Zeke and handed the rope to Ruth. "Mind that he doesn't eat too many of your dresses, it will give him a belly ache."

"Don't worry; I'll take good care of him." Then before Jillian knew what had hit her, the little girl was wrapped around her legs.

Laughing, Jillian patted her back, met Mary's smile. "You're very welcome."

Suddenly Jillian had the feeling she was being watched. She said her goodbyes to Mary and Ruth and looked around. The stagecoach had gone; a few wagons remained in front of the mercantile. She looked left. Two men were walking into the barber's, but she saw no sign of Steven or anybody else who seemed particularly interested in what she was doing.

Yet, as she made her way to Letty's store to ask about a puppy, she couldn't shed the feeling that someone was keeping an eye on her.

★

STEVEN LIFTED HIS head as they filed into his feed mill.

"What the hell are you doing?" He hissed.

"Ain't no law against coming in here," Harvey answered as he led the pack to the counter where Steven was standing.

Steven's stomach knotted. He came round the counter, strode across to the window, and saw his fear was warranted. The sheriff was heading their way.

"Goddammit, Shane's on his way!" His eyes snapped to Harvey's. "I told you the man hasn't left me alone in days. I told you to stay clear of me. I'm not spending any more time in jail."

"We ain't done nothin' wrong." Harvey placated.

"Well, tell him that," Steven muttered as Shane pushed

open the door.

Dust motes flittered on the breeze that Shane's entrance created. Though he knew he'd done nothing wrong, sweat dampened Steven's neck. He'd kept his nose clean since being let of jail but he still felt like a prisoner. Of course with Shane stopping in at least twice a day on top of making "neighborly" visits to Steven's house, was it any wonder he felt like a damn criminal?

Shane's pointed gaze fell over them all. "Good afternoon, gentlemen."

"We haven't done anything, Shane."

He raised a brow. "Did I say you did, Justin?"

"Then why are you treating us like we did?" he answered.

"I can't even go to the outhouse without worrying about you watching." Robert complained.

"Shoot, you've been to my house so often of late why don't you just bring yourself a bedroll and stay next time?" Bill grumbled.

Shane grinned. "Thanks for the invitation. I might just take you up on that."

"Shit." Bill groaned. "And won't that just make the missus' mood even brighter."

"What do you want?" Harvey asked.

The sheriff faced Harvey, but the damn fool didn't have the sense not to aggravate Shane. Harvey crossed his arms, sneered.

"You plannin' on playin' my nursemaid too now that I'm

back?"

Shane took a step toward Harvey. "I'll do whatever it takes to make this nonsense against Miss Matthews stop."

"My hands are clean," he said, raising them. "Seems to me Miss Matthews is just the victim of a series of unfortunate accidents."

"Cut feedbags, a butchered dress and a snapped rabbit's neck aren't accidents."

Steven's stomach rolled when Harvey laughed.

"Mishaps, then." Harvey grinned.

Shane and Harvey had themselves a staring match for a few charged moments before Shane shifted his attention to the rest of them. Steven wanted to punch the son-of-a-bitch but he wasn't that stupid. He'd kept his nose clean; Shane had nothing on him. All he could hope was that soon he'd tire of playing nursemaid and leave them the hell alone.

"Unless you want to get real friendly with my jail cell," Shane added with a hard look at Harvey, "you'd best steer clear of Miss Matthews, her house, and anything that's hers."

"You plannin' on arrestin' your friend, Wade, then? 'Cause he seems to have gotten real close to what's hers."

"Harvey, you dumb son-of-a-bitch." Steven growled.

Shane's hand settled on his six-shooter. He went toe-to-toe with Harvey. "Ask Steven how he enjoyed my cell."

Steven held his breath, but though Harvey's eyes glittered, for once he kept his big mouth shut.

At the door, Shane gave them a last warning. "Judges aren't too friendly toward men who abuse women. You might want to keep that in mind."

The mill remained quiet as they watched Shane walk down the street. The moment Shane entered his jailhouse, Steven rounded on Harvey.

"What the hell were you thinking? I don't need Shane riding my ass every time I turn around!"

"Well, we can't exactly discuss anything at Silver's. This seemed the best place."

Steven snarled. "Really? And you don't think coming to my house after work would be better? Or maybe not all coming in here at once like a damn herd."

Harvey snarled right back. The venom in his gaze shocked Steven.

"You think all of us skulking in the dark would look any less suspicious?" He scoffed.

"Fine." Steven conceded. "You have a point. Now can you get to the reason you're here?"

"Why is she still in Marietta? I thought we agreed while I was gone to Bozeman that you'd work at getting her out of here."

"It's not as though we haven't tried." Robert explained. "Steven dumped her feed and cut her dress. Justin spread the manure."

"And I killed her rabbit," Bill said.

Harvey rolled his eyes. "And you think those petty little

games are enough?"

Justin stepped closer. "Well, it's all I'm willing to do. I told you from the beginning I wasn't hurting her."

"And I'm not spending any more time in jail," Steven added.

Not to mention every time Shane came calling, his wife nagged him even harder. Shit, he'd do just about anything to make her shut up.

"What are you sayin'? That you're all through?"

Justin shrugged. "I've got more work than I can handle and a wife and daughter at home. You went to Bozeman, put out the advertisements. Let's just see what happens."

Harvey went red. His thick hands clenched at his sides. "Is that how you all feel?"

"We don't like her any more than you do," Bill said. "But Shane's breathing down our necks and we have businesses to run. We can't afford to lose them because of this and if we end up in jail, that's exactly what'll happen."

Harvey's nostrils flared. "She hasn't won."

"Won what? Nobody's seeking her help, that hasn't changed," Steven said.

"For now, but what if we don't get another vet, then what?"

Nobody answered him. The feed mill seemed to shrink in size as Harvey's hot, rapid breaths filled the room. Steven didn't like Jillian. Hell, he'd hoped she'd be packed up and gone by now but she wasn't and his life was enough of a mess because of her already. He wanted her gone, no question, but he had to weigh the costs of taking this any further.

"Goddamn bunch of worthless cowards you turned out to be." Harvey spat on Steven's floor then marched for the door.

"What are you going to do now?" Steven asked.

Harvey stopped, but he kept his back to them. "Whatever I have to do," he answered.

He flung the door open and though it was warm outside, it was an icy breeze that Harvey left in his wake.

Chapter Fifteen

Shane had made fresh coffee and cradled a cup of it as he sat at his desk, booted feet propped on its edge. Trouble was brewing. He smelled it as surely as the air changed right before a good thunderstorm. He was pretty sure Steven's time cooling his heels in jail had served its purpose. Besides, Shane had always known Steven to be more of a blowhard than an actual threat.

He didn't know the others as well, but they'd never given him trouble before and as he'd shadowed them for the last few days, hadn't gotten a sense that they were especially mean. Pranks, yes. He knew they were responsible for what had happened so far, even if nobody was owning up to the rabbit. He wasn't convinced, however, they'd take it further, not now that he was involved.

Harvey Black, however, was another matter. He seemed primed and ready for a fight.

Dropping his feet, Shane set his coffee down and moved to his files. He knew most everyone within a twenty-mile radius of Marietta and had small files on every family. Nothing sinister, just who lived where, who was married to whom. More to keep things straight in his own head. When anyone new moved in the vicinity he made a point of introducing himself. It served two purposes. One, it kept him abreast of the town and who was coming and going and, two, in case there were ever trouble, he'd have records to look back on. He'd done it with everyone, including Jillian and Harvey Black.

Sorting through his papers, Shane found what he was looking for.

He pulled the notes he'd written on Harvey Black and skimmed over them. It didn't take long, as there wasn't more than a paragraph or two, to find what he was looking for. Harvey claimed to come from Boise. Never married, he'd been bored and wanted a change. Montana, he'd said, seemed as good a place as any. Well, Shane would just have to see what Boise had to say about Mr. Black.

Shane finished his coffee and headed to the stable. He smiled when Bill looked up from his work and frowned at him. Taking his horse, Shane rode of town.

He couldn't do what needed to be done here but luckily it wasn't far to Chico. And, like Marietta, it had a telegraph office.

★

WADE CAUGHT HIS mother around the waist and pulled her into the house. "I need to borrow two dresses, quick."

"You what?"

"Don't look at me like that, I'll explain everything later. Can you fetch them? The brighter the better."

"Oh, but Letty's just riding in. We were going to do the last few stitches on my wedding dress."

The wedding. It was coming fast. Not that he didn't want his ma and James happy, but it still gave him a tug around the heart to think of her marrying someone other than his pa.

He kissed her cheek. "This won't take long; I promise." The rest of her words sank in and he smiled. "Mrs. Daniels is here?"

"Yes, I saw her riding in and was going out to greet her when you grabbed me."

Laughter bubbled in his chest. "Perfect!"

She eyed him curiously. "What are you up to?"

"You'll see, but you need to hurry." He nudged her toward the stairs.

"You're not going to ruin them are you?"

Since she wasn't moving fast enough, he skirted around her and took the steps two at a time. Then grinned as he heard her run to catch up.

He chose the brightest colored dresses she had.

"Thanks, Ma. Bring Mrs. Daniels and wait for me in front of the bunkhouses."

Leaving her sputtering, he all but leapt down the stairs.

He ran fast as he could to the river, switched the clothes and raced to the bunkhouses. His ma, Annabelle, and Mrs.

Daniels were just getting there.

"Oh dear," his ma said. "I know that look."

Annabelle giggled.

Wade tossed clothes in first James's then Scott's bunkhouse, taking chairs out as he left each one. Once they were all seated within a stone's throw of the bunkhouse doors Wade sagged with relief. He'd done it. He'd been tempted after falling face first into their practical joke to retaliate, but he'd forced himself to wait, to think of something even better rather than hastily seeking revenge. Stretching out his legs he chuckled. This was going to be worth the wait!

"What did you do?" Mrs. Daniels asked, though she looked as excited as he felt.

His ma had shared with her the jokes he, Scott, and James had played on each other over the years but this would be the first Letty would see firsthand.

"It's best I don't ruin the surprise." He chuckled.

It took longer than he figured. No doubt they'd sat at the river and considered their options before realizing they had none. Wade sat up as the riders approached then burst out laughing as they kept taking turns trying to hide behind the other.

Clothed—as much as the too-small garments allowed—in his ma's dresses, Scott and James had never looked so pretty. The bodices, clearly too tight to fit over their broad shoulders, hung around their waists. The full skirts barely reached past their knees. Wade grinned as all three ladies chortled. Scott, his face flaming red in embarrassment, tried to yank up the bodice to cover his chest.

"Pink is your color, James." Wade teased as his foreman pulled his horse to a stop and tried to dismount while keeping the material between his legs.

"You think you're pretty funny, don't you?" James glared at Wade.

"Hell, yeah. Best part was you hollering from the river when you realized I had no intention of taking a bath, only your clothes!"

His ma was laughing so hard tears rolled from her eyes. Annabelle's eyes were wide as her smile. Letty jammed two fingers in her mouth and whistled. Scott's face went scarlet. James looked capable of murder.

"Your legs are too scrawny to be wearing such a short skirt." Wade teased. "Next time find one that goes all the way to the ground."

Wade knew his grin took up his whole face.

Clearly trying to ignore them all, Scott made his way toward his bunkhouse. Unfortunately that meant passing Wade. As he moved past, Wade smacked him on his backside.

"You look mighty fine there, ma'am." Wade whistled before Scott escaped into his bunkhouse, slamming his door behind him.

James's gaze had yet to shift from Wade. "I take it you brought my clothes back?"

Wade pointed to James's cabin. "In there."

Muttering curses and vows of revenge, James disappeared inside wearing nothing more than a half-donned gown, a scowl, and worn cowboy boots.

Wade couldn't wait to tell Jillian about this, to see her face when—

His laughter died. He wouldn't be telling her. He wouldn't be sharing this moment, or any others, with her. The thought left him feeling empty and took away the joy he'd felt at getting his revenge on Scott and James.

Leaving the women giggling, Wade trudged back to work.

★

A FIRE COULDN'T be any hotter than her kitchen, Jillian decided as she pulled out the last of the golden-brown loaves from her oven. Flour covered her apron, sprinkled across her floor. As she'd wiped the sweat off her forehead with her forearm more than once, she imagined there was flour on it as well.

She'd begun baking bread in the morning while it was cool, but it hadn't taken long for her house to become unbearably hot. Perspiration trailed down her back and moisture gathered between and underneath her breasts.

Still, she'd had to do something. She had no work to occupy her time and with Zeke, Whiskers, and Rascal gone, her chores didn't take much time at all. And since Letty hadn't known of anyone with puppies to give away, she couldn't fill her time with a rambunctious dog either.

There was no way she could eat all the bread before it went to waste, but she'd talk to Letty, see if she could sell it in her mercantile. Or she'd give it to Eileen. Surely with three hungry men to feed, she could use extra bread. Jillian looked down, thought of Wade eating what she'd made and felt a yearning so deep, so strong, it brought tears to her eyes. Damn it, he shouldn't cause this reaction in her, not after what he'd said to her.

An unexpected knock on her door had Jillian grabbing her gun.

"Jillian, it's just me."

Recognizing the voice, Jillian set the gun down, ensured her eyes were dry, and opened the door.

"Hello, Letty."

Movement to the woman's right caught Jillian's attention and she found herself looking into Wade's indecipherable eyes.

Despite her residual anger her traitorous heart fluttered. "Wade." She acknowledged.

"Jillian."

"I hope I'm not interrupting anything," Letty said. "I was at the ranch helping Eileen with the last minute wedding preparations when I suddenly remembered I had something to ask you. Wade was kind enough to keep me company. For safety." Letty's smile showed more teeth than usual. She nodded to Jillian's apron. "I see you're hard at work."

"Actually, your timing is perfect. I just pulled out the last loaves."

"Oh, good!" She plunked herself on the porch, fanned herself. "It's so blessed hot out. I could use a nice tall glass of water."

Though Jillian had planned to sit outside once her bread was done, she hadn't expected Wade to be there when she did. Was he truly there for Letty's safety or was there another reason? Could he have changed his mind about her?

There was no way of knowing. His eyes watched her, but he didn't smile, didn't talk. She wished he'd say something. His silence was unnerving.

"Mrs. Daniels, I have to get back to the ranch. I thought you said you only had to ask Jillian a quick question?"

"Hmm? Oh, yes, I do. But now that we're here, we can spare a moment for a glass of water, can't we?"

Wade frowned. His gaze shifted down the road. Jillian's hopes fell. Clearly he couldn't get away fast enough.

"If you need to go, Wade, I can ride Letty back."

"No!" Letty said. She began fanning her face in earnest. "It's sure hot out here."

Something was amiss and Jillian knew she wasn't the only one who sensed it. Wade wasn't looking too happy either.

"I'll get the water." Jillian slipped inside, was pouring three glasses when Wade stepped into her small kitchen.

"She's asked for a wet cloth. Seems suddenly the heat's

gotten the best of her."

Even knowing Wade didn't want to be there, Jillian couldn't help the smile that pulled at her lips. "She's toying with us."

Wade nodded, accepted the glass Jillian passed him, and drank down half before he answered. "I know it. Just as I knew Ma was involved when Letty told me she needed to come over here right away."

"Didn't she ride alone to the ranch?"

"Yeah, but here it's…different."

Because, though nothing had happened since Whiskers' death, Jillian and her home remained targets. And she was only a target because of what she chose to do.

"If you'll excuse me, I'll get this to Letty."

"Jillian." Wade grabbed her arm. He didn't hurt her but his firm grip held her in place. "It's not that I don't enjoy seeing you."

"A pity then, isn't it," she said, yanking her arm free, "that I'm so unworthy of those feelings."

The sounds of galloping hooves coming from the open front door broke through the tension. They darted to the porch. Letty was already barreling down the road, a haze of dust hanging in her trail.

"Those two planned this," Wade muttered.

Jillian had no doubt who he was referring to—his mother and Letty. She also had no doubt why they'd done it. Clearly, though, they didn't know what had transpired between her and Wade or they would have known that any effort toward matchmaking was futile.

"Well, this way you're free to leave."

Jillian went back into the house, set the two full glasses of water onto the table. Wade was right there when she turned around. She smelled the salt on his skin, felt his heat add to her own until she thought she'd burn. Didn't he know what having him close did to her?

He brushed her forehead with his fingertips. Jillian felt the power of his touch clear to her toes. She forced herself not to show it. She'd already told him how she felt. She'd rather be struck mute than admit it again.

"Flour," he said.

Of course. He hadn't touched her because he needed to, because he felt as though his next breath depended on the contact.

"You need to leave."

Though he nodded agreement, he didn't step away. "I never meant to hurt you."

He didn't touch her, but he didn't need to. His gaze held her in place as strongly as any physical bond. When he looked at her that way, as though nothing else mattered but her, it was easy to dismiss what he thought of her being a vet. Her fingers twitched with a fierce desire to reach into his open collar and feel the heat of his skin, the ridges of his stomach. Instead, she steeled herself and backed away.

"Wade, you really need to go. I can't—" She tugged at

the collar of her dress. "I can't breathe." Now that the bread was done rising and baking, she opened the windows to let the heat out.

He was leaning against her counter when she'd finished. "Are you coming to the wedding?"

Did his steady gaze mean he wanted her there or he hoped she wouldn't go?

"I am. Your mother has asked me to stand with her and Letty."

"She did? I didn't know that."

"I was surprised when she asked. Surely she had more friends she could have asked."

"She's very fond of you."

Having him so near, so formal, was fraying her nerves. "I like her, too. And despite what's happened between you and me, I plan on remaining her friend." Even if she moved, Jillian had decided she wouldn't let go of the friendships she'd made here. They might have to keep those friendships by correspondence, but Jillian wouldn't lose them.

Wade stepped to her, cupped her cheek. "It's not that I don't wish it could be different between us."

At his touch, everything in Jillian sizzled. She wouldn't settle for less than love and respect. Marriage. But that didn't mean the time they'd spent together wasn't special to her. Pushing onto her toes, Jillian kissed his cheek.

His eyes were shadowed. "What was that for?"

"Despite how it ended, I don't regret anything."

He froze for the briefest second, then yanked her hard against his chest and opened his mouth over hers. It never occurred to Jillian to fight him. Clutching his shoulders, she allowed him into her mouth. In the silence, the sound of their mouths mating was sinful. Exciting.

How could this be wrong, when they fit so perfectly together? When his touch made her burn and his kiss melted her knees? Why couldn't he see that together they were better than they were apart?

A sound permeated the fog that swirled through Jillian's head.

"Letty's come back," she whispered as they stopped kissing long enough to gulp air.

Wade's eyes took a moment to focus. "What?"

Jillian smiled. "There's a rider coming in the yard. Don't you hear it?"

He ran a hand down his face, took deep breaths. "Yeah. I guess she figured she's given us enough time."

Only it wasn't Letty. It was Mary, the mother of the child she'd given the goat to. She didn't seem to notice Wade, or if she did, she didn't care. Her frantic eyes were fixed on Jillian.

"What is it, Mary?"

"Our mare foaled, but the birthing sac hasn't come out. We can see part of it, but we're afraid to pull on it." She wrung her hands. "This has never happened to us before."

"I'll get my bag."

Wade caught up with her in her bedroom. Jillian couldn't help pausing a moment as she remembered the last time he was in her room.

"I'm going with you."

Though nobody had called on her, she nonetheless opened her bag and checked she had everything. "That's not necessary," Jillian said, brushing past him to the kitchen cupboard she'd set aside for her medicines.

"I'm not leaving you to ride alone."

Jillian paused in her choices, knew by his set jaw he wasn't going to change his mind. "Fine. How fast can you saddle Hope?"

Wade loped outside and Jillian tossed some cloths over her bread to keep the flies off. Outside, she turned to the woman who'd come for her.

"Mary, I'll help you, but I need to be prepared. How angry will your husband be that you fetched me?"

"Justin won't be angry. He's the one who sent me."

★

"You don't have to stay."

Hell, after what he'd seen today, there wasn't any place else he'd rather be. She'd calmly examined the horse, soaped her hands and arms, and reached inside the animal. Since Wade knew firsthand just how tender her touch could be, he knew the mare was being well taken care of. Soon after, she'd pulled the placenta free.

As a precaution she'd then rinsed out the uterus with warm salted water, after which she'd examined the colt and its mother. While both were deemed healthy, Jillian had decided to stay the night in the barn, to be nearby in case the mare hemorrhaged. Though it wasn't said aloud, he knew she'd been thinking of his cow.

"I didn't like the idea of you sleeping out here by yourself. Besides, Ma and Annabelle know where I am so they won't worry and when I rode back I asked James to stay in my room for the night."

Jillian sat in a clean stall, on top of the pallet that had been made for her. For propriety's sake, he'd made his own across the aisle. But for now he sat with her. The heat was easing, but not enough to require blankets just yet. She rested her head tiredly against the wall.

"Coming back will only encourage your mother."

"I know." And at the moment, he couldn't say that bothered him.

He was still in awe of what Jillian had done earlier. When she'd done surgery on his cow, it had been his animal's life in the balance and he'd been too worried and later too devastated to fully appreciate what she had done.

Today, he'd been able to stand back and watch without all the emotions blocking his judgment and Lord, what he'd seen. She had a calmness about her that seeped into the animals she tended. She didn't rush, despite the worried owners who urged her to hurry. And she was skilled; there was no question. He'd heard of men being called to the church; that God spoke to them. Well, Wade had no doubt Jillian had felt the same calling, only hers was to animals. Did that make hers any less important?

"I know I said it before, but I really am sorry for what I said to you after my cow died. You're too skilled and too compassionate for it to have been anything but one of those things that was out of your control. I'm sorry I ever questioned your knowledge or your integrity."

Though he'd paid her a compliment, the words seemed to make her sad.

"Thank you."

"Your father must have been a great teacher."

"He was. But he was an even better vet. My skills don't compare to what his were."

"I doubt that."

Her chin wobbled. "I miss him. I wish I'd have had more time with him."

Wade thought of his own father, of the ache that never went away. "I know what you mean."

Her smile was full of understanding. "Yes, I imagine you do."

"Did he ever try to discourage you? About being a veterinarian?"

Love blossomed on her face. "Not once. He accepted that it was my choice, though he did warn me it would be a difficult road. However, once he knew I was committed to it, he helped me do everything I could to succeed." She peered at him. "You think he should have discouraged me, don't you?"

Wade stretched his legs, shifted when the straw poked through his pants. "I think it would take a hell of a man to not only accept that his daughter had chosen a difficult path but to help her with it as well."

She struggled not to cry, then with a tight smile said, "You're right, he was a hell of a man."

It was galling to realize the same couldn't be said for him.

He'd be furious with any man who didn't love Annabelle for the person she was. And yet, it was what he'd done to Jillian. What he'd done to Amy. He was glad there wasn't a mirror handy. He wasn't sure he could stomach his reflection.

Darkness fell outside. Inside, a single lantern lit the small stall they shared. The only noise was that of colt and mother breathing a few stalls down. Jillian hid her yawn behind her hand but there was no masking the shadows beneath her eyes.

Not even trying to resist, Wade shuffled to her side, put his arm around her shoulders.

"Don't—"

"Shh. Just lean on me." He guided her head to his shoulder. "I'll go to my own bedroll once you're asleep."

He held her while her breathing evened and her body

eased into sleep. Then he gently laid her down. Instead of going across the aisle, however, he lay next to her, watching, thinking.

Hoping.

★

WHEN SHANE HAD sent the telegram to Boise asking for information on Harvey, he'd also given the telegraph operator extra money so he could have someone deliver the response as soon as it came. In case anything incriminating was uncovered, Shane didn't want to alert Harvey's friend Robert, who ran the office in Marietta.

He hadn't expected an answer this quickly.

"It came in last night, Sheriff. I left as soon as dawn broke this morning."

"Thank you."

Leaning back in his chair, Shane waited until the door closed before unfolding the paper.

"Holy hell." Trepidation knocked up Shane's spine.

He opened his desk drawer, grabbed extra ammunition. He slid the six-shooter from the holster, ensured the chambers were loaded. Grabbing his hat off the rack, Shane ran to the stable to get his horse.

He was back in town within the hour and in that time, his unease had turned to dread. Behind the saloon he yanked on the horse's reins and was out of the saddle before his horse stopped. It was early yet and he figured she'd still be asleep.

"Silver!" He banged on the door. "Open up!" He pounded again, then stepped back. His gaze climbed the back wall of her saloon.

"Stairs."

He took them two at a time, knowing her rooms were there and she'd have a better chance of hearing him.

"Silver!"

The door flew open.

"There better be a fire, Shane McCall, or I'll toss you off those steps!"

Shane couldn't answer. He was struck dumb. She wore a wrapper of the palest blue. Her hair was tousled from sleep, her face still flushed with it. Underneath the hem of her nightclothes her pink toes captivated his attention until she once again demanded where the bloody fire was.

Snapping his gaze to hers he was ignited by her glower.

Finally he found his tongue. "There's no fire, Silver."

She pushed her hair off her shoulder. "Then what in Sam Hill are you doing waking me up?"

He pulled his eyes from the bare skin of her neck. "Has Harvey Black been in the saloon lately?"

"Haven't seen him since last week. He usually only comes in on Fridays, so I suppose I'll be seeing him tonight. Why? Are you looking for him?"

Because they were on the back stairs, and there was nothing behind the saloon but open field, Shane felt safe enough talking.

"I've been doing a little investigating on him. He told me he'd never been married but when I telegraphed Boise to see if they had any knowledge of him they had quite a bit to say. Apparently he had been married, for many years in fact. And his wife went missing unexpectedly not long before Harvey suddenly disappeared from the area."

Silver's hand went to her neck. "He killed her?"

"He claimed she just up and left one day while he was at work. She hasn't been seen since."

"You don't think it was that simple, do you?"

"According to what I learned, her whole family is from Boise. It doesn't make sense she'd leave, especially without saying goodbye."

"Did you ask him about it?"

"I can't. He's gone. I just got the telegram this morning and I rode out right away to talk to him. He wasn't there."

Silver frowned. "He's a trapper, isn't he? Maybe he was checking his line?"

"I thought so, too, but the place was abandoned. His clothes and personal effects were gone, too."

"You don't think he moved?"

Shane blew out a breath. "He was furious with me when I confronted him and his friends in the feed mill. He was almost frothing at the mouth when I rode to his place later that night to check on him."

Silver pulled her wrapper closer around her. Did she have

to keep drawing attention to the fact that she was barely dressed?

Her taffy-colored eyes filled with worry. "You don't think he'd do to Jillian what he did to his wife, do you? He hardly knows Jillian."

"I'm not saying he would. He's lived here for a year and we haven't had any trouble from him. Yet the moment Jillian arrives these things start happening to her."

He rubbed the tension from his forehead. "What doesn't make sense to me is that even if he did do those things to scare her, why not just stop? Why pack up and flee?"

"Unless he plans to do worse and he can't when he knows you're watching."

"Yeah," Shane agreed, though it sure as hell didn't make him feel any better. "That's exactly what I was thinking."

★

HARVEY SWATTED AT the early morning mosquitoes that insisted he be their breakfast. They buzzed annoyingly around his head and ears, adding to his already foul mood. This was the second time in his life he'd been run out of his home by a damn woman who didn't know her place in society.

There was a bloody reason women weren't allowed in veterinary schools!

He'd been sure, so sure, that the town would hold to their belief that Jillian didn't belong. But they were starting to waver. Hell, hadn't he seen for his own eyes Justin's wife come begging for help because Justin, of all people, had asked?

More than once he'd heard Justin's opinion of the lady doctor. He'd sworn he'd shoot an animal between the eyes before calling on Jillian and yet at the first test he collapsed like a house of cards and sent his wife to get her.

Harvey had hoped to go in the barn last night, go in and do some damage so they wouldn't think she was so all-fired special but not only had Jillian stayed the night, so had Parker. Harvey fumed. It was one thing to stick your pecker in her; it was another to encourage her to keep doctorin'.

He snarled as they strolled out of Justin's barn, as though coming out of church on a Sunday morning. There was some discussion, but, even though he held his breath and leaned as far forward in the bush as he could without being seen, he couldn't hear nothin' but the blasted mosquitoes.

Suddenly Mary came out of the house. Harvey snarled as money changed hands. He ground his teeth when Justin, the low-lying rat, shook Jillian's hand. Harvey stewed until Jillian and Wade had mounted up and rode out of sight.

He was tempted to go after Justin for this double cross, but he knew he needed to keep his head. He'd cleared out his things hoping that would cool the sheriff's heels. If he did anything now, it would only get a posse together to look for him.

And he couldn't afford that.

He'd been watching Jillian, but she either always had someone with her or she wasn't without her firearm. It was near impossible to sneak up on her. But, as he retreated through the branches and undergrowth to get to his horse, he couldn't help thinking about the big shindig of a wedding coming up on Sunday.

And everyone knew folks didn't carry no guns to a wedding.

Chapter Sixteen

Though nothing untoward had occurred since Jillian had found her rabbit dead, Scott nevertheless rode into her yard as agreed upon the Sunday morning of Eileen and James's wedding. The pies and cookies Silver had helped her bake were loaded in the back of the wagon. Scott wouldn't hear of Jillian hitching Hope. He accomplished the job quickly, all the while talking softly to her horse and reaching out to pat Hope every few minutes. He then tied his mount to the back of the wagon, helped Jillian up and took the reins.

The day couldn't have turned out better. The stifling heat had given way to a cooler, more comfortable afternoon. The breeze was enough to brush Jillian's curls, but not enough to yank them from their pins. She hadn't been to a wedding in such a long time and not to one where she could honestly say she both liked and respected the couple about to take their vows.

"Oh, look." Jillian sighed as they rolled into Wade's yard.

Chairs were lined in rows on the grass. A wooden archway decorated with red roses waited at the front where the ceremony would take place. The backdrop of Eileen's rose garden added color and scent. *A perfect place for a wedding.*

"Looks pretty, don't it?"

"It suits them."

She accepted his hand and carefully, so as not to snag her dress, stepped down.

"I'll take care of this." He gestured to the food she'd packed. "And then I'll look after this beauty." His large hand stroked Hope's neck.

"All right, if you're sure."

"Eileen, Letty, and Annabelle are inside. Shane will be arriving shortly with Silver. James and Wade are in James's bunkhouse getting ready. We're not expecting the other guests for another hour or so. I'll take care of this then finish getting ready myself. I'll see you shortly."

Jillian hadn't seen Wade since yesterday. True to his word, when Jillian had awakened in Justin's barn, he'd been in his own bedroll in the stall across the aisle, yet she'd smelled his scent as though he were still beside her.

To her surprise, he'd not only ridden her home, he'd kissed her before heading back to the ranch. It hadn't been the passionate kiss she'd come to crave, but the way he'd gently touched his mouth to hers had felt different somehow. Almost as though it were a promise of more to come.

She'd thought of nothing since. Had he changed his mind? Had he come to accept her being a doctor? And if he hadn't, could she really walk away from him? Could she really move to another town and start again? And what if that town didn't learn to welcome her either? Then what?

She'd thought long and hard, really examined what made her happy, where she saw her future.

And she'd come to a decision.

★

FROM THE NOISE behind the door of his ma's and Annabelle's bedroom, Wade knew where the bridesmaids were. Though he couldn't wait to catch a glimpse of Jillian, his mind was on his mother. He knocked on his own bedroom door, having given it to his ma to use for the morning.

She looked stunning. There were no frills or lace on her simple cream-colored dress, just a red ribbon that cinched her waist, which matched the single rose she'd placed above her ear. Her smile stretched across her face and her skin glowed with happiness.

His ma was getting married.

"You look beautiful. James is a very lucky man."

Her gaze shimmered. "I don't know who the lucky one is, but I'm sure glad to have this second chance at love." She took his hand. "I know you said you were happy for us. That wasn't a lie, was it?"

"Of course not," he said with absolute certainty. "Two of my favorite people are getting married; it's hard to be unhappy about that."

She sniffled, ran a hand down the front of her skirt. Annabelle's door opened. There were whispers and giggles as the bridesmaids descended the stairs.

"It's time."

She drew in a breath and exhaled slowly. "Are you ready to give me away?"

He hated those words. And more than anything he hoped to hell that wasn't what he was doing.

"Not giving," he clarified, "sharing."

"Oh, Wade!" She smacked him on the arm as her eyes glistened. "You're not supposed to make the bride cry."

He leaned in, kissed her cheek. "I love you, Ma."

"Oh, well, now you've done it." She sniffled as she pulled her handkerchief from her sleeve.

★

THE SMELL OF roses perfumed the air. John Daniels had set his chair behind the others and when Wade and his ma took their place at the end of the aisle, he smiled over his violin, then let the bow tiptoe over the strings. The crowd stood. A collective "ah" floated over the gathering.

A son was entitled to feel a little melancholy when his ma was marrying someone other than his pa. He squeezed the hand that rested on his arm and though she squeezed back, her gaze never shifted. Her attention was all for the man waiting for her. Wade looked up, saw the sheer joy on James's face, and the melancholy shifted to happiness.

Despite trying, Wade couldn't see Jillian or the other bridesmaids for the standing crowd. It wasn't until he and his ma had nearly reached the end of the aisle that he caught sight of her. He nearly stumbled over his own feet.

Her hair was a beautiful cascade of curls. She wore the same dress she'd worn the night of the dance but today it looked different somehow. She held a single red rose in one hand. In her other, she held his daughter's hand. Annabelle waved at him. Seeing his daughter happy and carefree with her hand tucked into Jillian's made his heart swell. They looked perfect together.

He and his ma reached the front. Wade looked James in the eye, let show the emotion he felt.

"She's lucky to have you. I'm honored to give her to you."

James's grin was a bit on the watery side. "You've always been a son to me. I couldn't love you more if you were mine. I hope I'll do you proud."

Wade shook the hand of the man he adored every bit as much as he'd loved his pa.

"You already have."

★

HE COULDN'T HAVE planned it any better. The whole damn town was at the Parker ranch and he didn't have to worry about slinking about. He let himself into the stable. There was only one horse in the barn but since Harvey had been in often enough to see Justin, the animal recognized his scent and went back to eating.

Heading straight for the tack room where he knew the kerosene was kept, he took the can from the floor. If this wasn't enough he'd let himself into the mercantile. Coming outside he took a moment to stop and listen, but nothing had changed. Marietta was silent as a tomb.

Chuckling, he headed for the feed mill and set to work. When he figured he'd doused it good, he started a flame at the far end of the building. Then, calm as though he were walking to church, he strode out of the feed mill and headed for his horse.

It wouldn't take long for the flames to engulf the building, which was why he didn't bother setting any other fires. He needed to get away before someone saw the smoke, or worse, him. As it was, black smoke was just now beginning to billow from the window he'd opened. Soon it would be seen for miles. No doubt it would create alarm, draw most everyone to town in a panic as they wouldn't be sure which building was on fire. In the chaos and confusion, it would be near impossible to keep track of everyone. It would be easy for one or two to get "lost" in the stampede.

Laughing, he headed for the Parker ranch.

★

"IT WAS PERFECT, don't you think?" Silver asked once the ceremony was over and James had kissed his bride.

Jillian and Silver had stepped aside to allow the guests room to congratulate the happy couple. Since that left many empty chairs, they'd helped themselves to two.

"It was. I'm glad I'd thought ahead and put a handkerchief in my pocket," Jillian answered.

"I noticed the way Wade looked at you." Silver teased.

Jillian had as well. His gaze had been fixed on her from the start of the ceremony. Along with what had happened after Justin's, hope bloomed in Jillian's heart. Maybe she really could have everything she'd ever wanted.

"Has he changed his mind?"

"If he has, he hasn't said."

Silver leaned forward. "But?"

"But…" Jillian laughed. She should have known Silver would see through her. "But I've decided it doesn't matter. I wouldn't be happy without him." She took Silver's hand. "Without all of you."

"Does Wade know about any of this?"

"I only came to this last night; I haven't had a chance to tell him."

"Oh, I can't wait until you do!"

For a moment they watched Eileen and James and Wade and Annabelle receive congratulations and best wishes from the guests.

"Shane looks handsome today."

Silver sighed. "I'm sure Melissa thinks so as well. They sat together during the ceremony."

"But it was you he brought."

She shook her head. "He didn't bring me. He knew I needed to be here early and he escorted me for protection, in case that Harvey fellow is still around."

"Maybe it was more than that."

"It'll never be more than that," she said sadly.

"But maybe—"

"Fire!" someone yelled. "There's a fire in town!"

Jillian and Silver jumped to their feet as those gathered looked to where the man pointed. Black smoke puffed in the air, forming a dark grey cloud in the direction of Marietta.

"My saloon!"

She wasn't the only one worried. Everyone scrambled, leaping chairs and running for their horses. Silver grabbed her skirts and raced after them and, despite her dress and petticoats, easily jumped over a fallen chair.

"Silver, wait!"

But she couldn't have heard. Shouts were flying fast and coming from all directions. Jillian's mind scrambled. Should she stay? Should she go to help battle the flames? Where would she be most needed?

Suddenly the crack of a gun split the air.

Boots dug in for purchase and everyone turned to see who'd fired the shot. Shane was standing on a chair, his right arm and pistol pointing skyward.

"Let's not panic."

"Easy for you to say, that could be my stable!"

"Or my lumber yard!"

"Or my jailhouse," Shane added.

Hell, depending on how bad it was it could be the whole town. With most businesses made of wood except Grey's, the whole town could go up.

"I know we need to hurry, but we can't all go. Men, saddle up. Except you, Reverend," he added. "I'd like you to stay back with the women and children."

Shane had told Jillian what he knew of Harvey and that the man was missing. He'd warned her to be extra careful. As Shane's eyes connected with hers, she knew what he was thinking, that this could very well be Harvey's doing.

The reverend nodded. "I can do that."

But not all the women agreed to stay. Letty, worried about her mercantile, left with John. A few others who didn't have young children to worry about also went with their men. The rest of the women and children fell back, silent and worried, while men saddled horses or rode bareback if they'd taken the wagons. There wasn't time to waste hitching horses and dragging around a wagon would only slow them down. With livelihoods at stake, time was of the essence.

Annabelle came up to her, slid her little hand into Jillian's. "Will Papa be all right?"

Jillian couldn't see Wade for all the scrambling. "I'm sure he will."

As though they conjured him, he suddenly wove through the crowd, heading toward them. His gaze was penetrating but Jillian had no idea if that was a good thing or if it meant he blamed her for this as well.

"Promise me you'll stay here." He demanded.

"I will."

"Good." He held her gaze a moment longer, then turned to his daughter and gave her a fierce hug. "Stay close, all right, Button?"

"I promise," Annabelle said then went to join Jacob on the porch.

Jillian clasped his arm as he turned to leave. Her chest ached with things she wanted to say, but it wasn't the time to tell him. Instead, she pressed onto her toes and kissed his cheek.

"Be careful."

His eyes flashed. Before she knew it, he grabbed her and his mouth was on hers, hot and hard. The kiss was over quickly but its effects lingered. Her head was still spinning and her lips were still humming when Wade ran to join the others.

★

HER HORSE RACED along with the others, its hooves adding to the dust that was already thick as molasses. Dust poured down Silver's throat, burned her eyes. *That better not be my saloon.* Not when every dime she owned was tied to that building. Not when it wasn't only her livelihood, it was her home. Her life. If she lost it…

Suddenly a hand grabbed her reins and her horse was scrambling to a stop while others were forced to veer to the side to avoid a collision.

"Where the devil do you think you're going?" Shane's eyes were darker than the smoke that marred the otherwise blue sky.

"I'm going to save my livelihood, same as those men!" she said, though not a soul could be seen through the curtain of dust.

"We can do that! You need to get back to the ranch."

She may not have been standing on ground, but she dug in her heels anyway. "Unless you're planning on taking me back, I'm going. And judging from that smoke, we don't have time to waste."

His nostrils flared. His jaw clenched so hard he could have cracked teeth.

"I can take care of myself. Now let go! I'm not losing my saloon!"

"Fine," he answered grudgingly, "but don't do anything stupid."

Besides falling in love with you?

Tugging her reins from his grasp Silver charged toward town.

★

JILLIAN'S HEART BROKE for Eileen. It should have been one of the happiest days of her friend's life and instead she was sitting at her own wedding reception, without her groom, staring out at the cloud of smoke that, if anything, was growing.

"Are you sure I can't get you anything?" Jillian asked.

Eileen shook her head, never taking her eyes off the horizon.

"I can't lose him, I can't lose another one," she whispered.

Jillian shifted her chair closer, handed Eileen a handkerchief, but all the bride did was twist it in her hands.

The waiting was going to be torture. Out of respect, and likely out of fear as well, conversations were kept quiet. The food remained covered, but coffee was being made in the kitchen. Other than Jillian, most left Eileen to her worrying.

Reverend Donnelly suddenly spoke from the porch. "I think this would be an appropriate time for prayer."

He led them in worship, and while Jillian believed in God, she found it difficult to concentrate. Her mind was in town and what was happening there. When the reverend finished, he came to Eileen to offer words of comfort.

Allowing them privacy, Jillian decided to see if she could be of help in the kitchen.

Before she could reach the porch a piercing scream rent the air. A hard jolt of fear slammed down Jillian's throat. She grabbed her skirts and along with everyone else, raced toward the sound, which had come from behind the house.

Rounding the corner Jillian gasped. Her knees shuddered. Oh, dear Lord!

Harvey Black held a pale and terrified Jacob around the throat with one hand. And a gun to his head with the other.

"Jacob!" his mother whimpered.

Everyone who'd come running stood in stunned silence, their faces as ashen as Jacob's.

Jillian had no idea how Harvey had gotten onto the ranch without being seen. But with the madness of the men scrambling for their horses, she supposed it would have been easy enough to slip by. Especially when he wasn't expected.

If Harvey was there it could only be for one reason. Culpability settled heavily onto her shoulders. Blowing out a trembling breath Jillian moved forward.

"No!" Annabelle reached for her.

Jillian thrust her arm out to block Annabelle at the same time Mrs. Hollingsworth grabbed the back of her granddaughter's dress. The women locked gazes.

"Keep her safe," Jillian said.

"With my life," Mrs. Hollingsworth added.

Then, despite Annabelle's sobbing protests, Jillian stepped from the group. Standing alone scared the air from her lungs, but she couldn't let anything happen to Jacob.

"I thought this would get your attention." Harvey sneered.

"What do you want?"

"What I want is for you to remember your place," he said as his vicious stare raked over every woman there. "For all of you women to remember your place. It's to get married and birth babies. To obey your man and to take care of his home, the home he works to provide. It's not to be gallivanting around doin' things that ain't your business." His eyes narrowed. "And it sure as hell isn't making noise about the right to vote!"

Jillian had no idea what he was talking about. Of course she'd heard about the right to vote movement that was happening across some of the states and territories, but it wasn't in Marietta.

Yet none of that mattered. What mattered was getting Jacob safely back into his mother's arms.

"Jacob, are you all right?"

She could see the boy was struggling to control his fear.

"I-I'm scared."

"I know you are. Just stand still, all right?"

"I'll give the orders around here!" Harvey yelled, causing everyone to flinch.

"Don't hurt him." Mrs. Garvey pleaded.

"Shut up!" Harvey bellowed.

"It's me you're after. It's me you've been after from the beginning. Let him go."

Harvey pointed his revolver at Jillian's heart. "I'm about done with your orders." He cocked the hammer.

Jillian froze. Sweat ran cold down her back. She didn't know what to do but she had to try, couldn't let anything happen to the little boy who'd defied his father because of his love for a dog. Knowing Harvey hated strong women, she lowered her gaze, raised her hands in surrender.

"I'm sorry. You're right. You have the power here. What would you like me do?"

"That's better," he said.

Though she couldn't see him his voice at least sounded less volatile. But he didn't move, nor did he say anything more. What if he didn't let Jacob go? She counted the passing of time by the thumps of her heart and hoped fervently that the reverend had a few more prayers in him.

"Come here."

Jillian raised her head. As she'd assumed, he was looking straight at her. She took a breath and forced her frozen limbs to move.

The moment she stepped before him Harvey shoved Jacob aside and grabbed her. Though she'd expected it she shuddered when he pressed the cold barrel of the gun against her temple. And prayed her life wouldn't end this day.

He backed them toward the barn. There, next to the bunkhouses was his tethered horse. So he *had* come in during the hullabaloo, which meant he'd known the men weren't going to be there. Oh, God, he'd set the fire.

The men were all in town, and she doubted the reverend would come after her since he was a man sworn to God, not to violence. Which meant Jillian was on her own. If she hoped to get out of this alive, she had nobody to rely on but herself.

★

THEY WERE MAKING so much dust it felt as though his eyes were being scoured with sand. Despite that, Shane smelled smoke. They were getting closer.

Suddenly his reins were grabbed the same way he'd grabbed Silver's moments ago.

"I'm heading back," Wade said, not wasting any time. "I have a bad feeling about this. Harvey disappears and now we have a fire that's drawing every man away? Seems handy."

Shane agreed, but he looked ahead. Through the rumbling hooves and churning dust, Silver plowed on. Dammit, he couldn't leave her.

"Can you spare me?" Wade hollered over the noise of passing riders.

"Do you have a weapon?"

Wade jerked his thumb to the scabbard tied to his saddle.

"I can't go with you. I need—"

Wade slapped him on the back. "Go! I'll see you later."

Before Shane could tell his friend to be careful, he was gone.

★

WADE'S HEART WAS thudding faster than Whiskey's hooves, which was saying something since the countryside was flying so fast beside him it was nothing but a blur. The animal was breathing hard, but he nonetheless gave Wade everything he asked. The wind whistled in Wade's ears. He was over Whiskey's neck until he was almost parallel to the ground.

God, he hoped he was wrong. *Let the fire be just a random thing, and not the trap I think it is.* If it was a trap that meant Black had been ready and Wade could be riding hell for leather toward God only knew what. He nearly choked thinking of those he loved being in danger. Or worse.

Though Whiskey's hooves ate the ground, it felt like an eternity before Wade saw the ranch, saw the crowd outside. Were they all right? He couldn't tell; he was still too far away. They turned as he approached. He knew, holy hell, he knew, something was terribly wrong when his ma burst from the crowd and ran to meet him.

Whiskey's hooves skidded on the road as Wade reined him in. The animal's hide was lathered, its sides heaved.

"What, Ma? What's wrong?"

Her cheeks were streaked with tears. Her lips were white.

"He's got her! He took her!"

The leather cut into Wade's hands. "Who, Ma? Who does he have?"

"Jillian." She pressed her hands over her heart. "Harvey Black took Jillian."

Wade pushed his fear and panic aside. If he was going to help her he needed to keep a clear head. "How long ago?"

"Not long. Maybe ten minutes. They went that way." She pointed in the direction they'd headed.

"Where's Annabelle?"

"In the house with Jacob. Harvey had him first, but let the boy go when Jillian offered herself instead."

Wade knew a moment's relief for his daughter's safety. It was quickly followed by heart-stopping fear for Jillian. He couldn't lose her, not before he told her he'd been a fool. Before he told her he loved her.

"Was Harvey alone?"

"Yes." She wiped her cheeks, but horror lingered in her eyes. "Find her, Wade. She was so brave; she can't-she just can't—"

He leaned down, touched his ma's cheek. "She won't, Ma. I'll bring her back." He wheeled Whiskey around. "Sorry, boy, a little longer."

And once again they were racing over the ground.

★

Terror left a tinny taste in her mouth. Or perhaps that was blood, since she was biting her lip as she tried to think of a solution. Unarmed and jammed in the saddle in front of Harvey, she was in no position to jump off without risking getting her skull trampled. Even if she did manage to keep her head intact, she feared he'd simply shoot her.

Which meant it wasn't escape she needed to concentrate on; it was getting his revolver. A difficult task as it was currently lodged in the small of her back. What she needed was to get them off the horse. Then maybe she'd have a chance.

She turned her head, grimaced as his fetid breath fell over her face.

"I'm not feeling well," she said.

And the more he breathed on her, the truer her lie became. Between being jostled about, the fear of having a gun pointed at her and his terrible breath, her stomach was in knots.

"I don't give a good goddamn how you're feeling." He rasped.

"You want me to be sick all over you?" she asked.

For good measure she made an act of swallowing back hard, pressed her hand to her mouth as though she'd vomit. He jerked on the reins, tossed her to the ground before the horse had even stopped. She landed hard on her hands and knees. Her palms and knees burned but she kept to her ruse. Moaning, she clutched her belly, rocked back and forth. Soon his dusty boots were in her line of sight. She willed herself to be sick, tried envisioning all manner of disgusting things, but she was a doctor and as such had an iron stomach.

"Well?" he said.

She inhaled deeply, wiped her mouth, and met his gaze. "Now that I'm not being tossed about in the saddle, my stomach's settling. Maybe if we stopped for a few—"

His hand came from nowhere, caught her across the cheek, and snapped her head back. When the spots cleared from Jillian's eyes and she met Harvey's, she saw that his were wild, mad. He leaned over her, fists curled.

"You think you're smart? You think you can outwit me? Well, you can't! You're nothing! Nothing, do you hear me?"

Panic filled Jillian until she shook with it. She was out of ideas. She wasn't physically strong enough to best him. He had the revolver. Even if she could get to the shotgun tied to his saddle, she had no idea if it was even loaded.

"I asked if you'd heard me?" he yelled, spit flying from his mouth.

"Yes. I heard you."

He nodded. "Get up. We need to keep going."

She rose to her feet. "To where?"

"Where you'll never cause trouble again."

If she was going to die, Jillian decided with sudden determination, then she was going to die on her terms.

"I'm not going anywhere with you," she said and took a step back. "You want to kill me for being a doctor? For taking on a man's role? Then you can do it here."

Chin high, shoulders back, knees trembling harder than the last leaf hanging in the fall, Jillian stood her ground.

Harvey's lips peeled back. The devil himself looked at her from eyes colder than a rock in the dead of winter. He cocked the revolver, raised it.

"Just remember when you're rotting in hell, that you brung this on yourself."

"I know about your missing wife. It won't be me going to hell. It will be you, for murdering two women."

"Bloody meddlin' sheriff," he grumbled. "Well neither he nor anyone else can prove anything."

"Then you did kill your wife?"

He laughed. "'Course I killed her. Women voting. Whoever heard of such nonsense? Just 'cause Wyoming and Utah did it, don't mean the rest have to follow. But she insisted. Was gathering a group of women in our town, making noise about women's suffrage."

Madness gleamed in his eyes like a sharpened knife. "She needed to be stopped, just like you need to be stopped. All's I need is a place to bury you where you'll never be found." His gun didn't waver, but his eyes left her as he looked around. "Goddammit! How the hell did he catch up so fast?"

His gaze swung round to Jillian but hers was on the rise of dust and the lone rider heading their way.

Harvey reached for her, but Jillian was ready. She leapt back, turned to run.

"No, you don't!" He grabbed her by the hair.

Jillian screamed as pain exploded from every hair on her scalp. Quickly she blinked away the tears that filled her eyes. The rider was gaining. All she had to do was buy time. Drawing back, she plowed her elbow into Harvey's ribs.

He grunted, but recovered quickly. Then, with the revolver still in his hand, backhanded her. She spun to avoid it, but the blow caught her on the temple. A blinding pain burst through her skull. She staggered, blinked furiously, but her eyes had stopped working. She reached out for something to grab but met nothing but warm air. She felt darkness creeping in. Her knees were buckling.

Dimly, as though through fog, she heard hooves. Was it the rider approaching or Harvey leaving? She thought she heard shots fired, but why did they sound so far away? She tried to focus, but it was impossible. Everything seemed too far out of reach. The more she tried to make sense of what was happening, the less it seemed to.

She finally gave up trying.

★

WADE HAD NEVER aimed a weapon at another man. He never would have considered himself capable. But when Harvey hit Jillian, when her body swayed then collapsed from the blow, Wade didn't hesitate. Guiding Whiskey with his thighs, Wade raised his shotgun.

Harvey, however, wasn't going without a fight. He shot; the bullet whistled past Wade's ear. He wouldn't get another chance. Wade adjusted his aim, fired. Harvey jerked, staggered. With shock widening his eyes, he fell dead to the ground.

Wade reined in his horse. Not wasting a moment looking at Harvey's worthless, lifeless body, he raced for Jillian. She'd taken a hard blow to the head, and judging by the bruise darkening her cheek, Harvey had struck her more than once.

Bastard.

Wade knew nothing about doctoring or medicine but he remembered when he'd hit his head after falling from the rafters that Jillian had said head wounds bleed a lot. His fingers carefully skimmed where he'd seen Harvey hit her, but all he felt was the warmth of her scalp. No blood. Was that good or bad?

He lifted her, cradled her in his lap. He took comfort from her even breathing which tickled the hair at his throat. But his heart had yet to beat normally. He'd feared he'd lost another woman he loved. Only this time, she'd die before he could tell her the words.

He kissed Jillian's forehead. "I need you. Annabelle needs you." His heart felt as though it would burst with emotion. He rocked her back and forth. "Wake up, Jillian. I need to tell you."

"Tell me what?"

Her voice was gravelly but it was the sweetest sound he'd ever heard. Relief made him weak.

Gently he set her on the grass. Her eyes seemed clear, her color was good. "Are you all right?"

She brought her fingers to her temple. "I think your whole herd is stampeding right here. Otherwise I think I'll live." She tried to sit up, moaned, and lay back down.

"Easy. Take your time."

"I thought I heard shots. Where's Harvey? Did he get away?"

"No. And he won't be bothering you or any other woman again." He cupped her cheek. "I was so scared."

Her smile was the most beautiful thing he'd ever seen. "Me, too. He killed his wife. Shane suspected so but Harvey admitted it. All because she wanted the right to vote. It's why he came after me, because I threatened what he believed, that women are lesser than men somehow."

"He was wrong. Can you sit up?"

He helped her, kept his arm around her back until he was sure she could sit on her own. Then he took her hand, laced her fingers with his.

"I was a fool. I was willing to let you go because I thought Annabelle needed a mother who'd be home with her, who'd stay on the ranch and never leave her."

He scoffed at his own naivety.

"But what she really needs is someone to love her, to teach her compassion, to teach her to stand up for what she believes in. I want my daughter to feel safe and loved enough to be the woman she's destined to be, whatever that entails. I want her to be exactly like her mother and exactly like you.

"I was wrong to think you weren't good enough for my daughter." His eyes swam with emotion. "I was wrong not to admit that I love you."

Her frown chilled him. Was he too late?

"And if the town changes its mind? If folks learn to accept me as a doctor?"

He raised her hand to his mouth, kissed it. "I hope they do. Justin sought you when he needed a doctor and his horse is fine. It's only a matter of time until someone else will call on you."

Jillian shook her head and immediately regretted the motion. She placed a hand to her head and held up the other when he moved to help.

"I'm fine." She took a moment, drew some deep breaths then lowered her hand.

"What if you change your mind, Wade? What if a horse kicks me or a cow knocks me over? Then what?"

Fearing he was losing the battle, Wade hurried to reassure. "Then you'll scare a few years off my life, but I won't stop you from doing what your father spent so much time teaching you. Jillian, I know you have reason to doubt me. Hell, I've given you more than enough reasons, but I'm saying I've changed. I want you to be a doctor because without it, you wouldn't be happy."

"But with it, will you be? You weren't happy when Amy became a midwife."

He sighed, felt his heart start to tremble. "You were right. When she became a midwife I felt I wasn't enough for her. That I couldn't make her happy. But looking back with fresh eyes, I see what you said was exactly right. She wasn't unhappy with me, she never was. And"—he hung his head in shame—"she'd told me so. I was just too stubborn to hear it."

It hurt to admit. To know that, despite his wife's words, he hadn't believed her. Hadn't believed enough in their love to accept her words were the truth. He'd let his pride get in the way.

He wouldn't make the same mistake again.

He guided Jillian to her feet and then took both her hands. "I love you, Doctor Jillian Matthews, and I'd be honored to be your husband. I promise to cherish you, honor you, and respect the fact that you're a damn fine veterinarian. I've seen your work. I wouldn't be able to live with myself if I kept that talent from helping others.

"Be my wife, be Annabelle's mother, and I promise I'll love you and our life together for as long as I live."

★

JILLIAN COULDN'T HOLD back the tears. They pushed against her eyes as hard as the love that pushed against her breasts. She'd moved west to be a doctor. To work at what she loved, to prove to herself, Clint, and every other person who'd doubted her that she could do it.

And, in the end, she'd gotten so much more.

With her heart bursting, she wiped the tear that crept down his cheek.

His jaw trembled. "I don't want to lose you."

"You won't." She smiled. "I'd already decided that without you, being a doctor wouldn't make me happy. You're my heart, Wade. You're my home. But I had to ask, had to know you were sure."

"I am. I've never been more sure of anything in my life."

He cupped her cheek. "You really would have given it up for me?"

"I really would have." Then she smiled, threw her arms around his neck. "But I'm really glad I won't have to."

★

THE FEED MILL was gone. By the time the men had gotten to town, there was nothing they could do. The buildings next to it had damage but nothing that couldn't be repaired. Four hours after the men had ridden out, they'd ridden back in, faces drawn and clothes smelling of smoke.

Wade had remained at the ranch with Jillian, saying nothing of what had happened to Harvey when Annabelle was within hearing range. She and Jacob, who'd rebounded quick from his ordeal, were busy talking and stealing cookies when they thought the adults weren't watching.

"You going to go get his body?" Wade asked Shane.

Since Eileen had insisted the rest of the wedding celebration continue, Wade and Shane had availed themselves to some whiskey.

"Yeah, but he can wait. He's ruined enough of my day already."

"Amen to that." Wade drank deeply. The burn helped soothe the last of his frayed nerves.

"You all right? I've shot a man before. I know that can linger."

Wade shrugged, his gaze on Jillian, whom he hadn't let

get too far out of his reach. "It was him or me. I figured I have more to live for."

"I can't believe you're getting married."

"Yeah." He grinned. "Think you'll ever do the same?"

Shane froze but he was saved answering when Scott sidled up. "Are we going to eat soon? All that firefighting's made me hungry."

"What fighting? We mostly just watched it burn."

Scott grinned. "Like I said, it made me hungry."

Wade saw Steven and his wife approach Jillian. Though she was with Silver he wasn't sure what the hell Steven was up to and Jillian didn't need any more aggravation.

He got to Jillian's side at the same time as Steven. Silver eased out of the way. Wade took Jillian's hand, felt as though he could walk on water when she looked at him, her eyes brimming with love.

"Miss Matthews."

"Mr. Garvey."

"My wife tells me what you did for Jacob today." He drew an uneven breath. "Thank you. Thank you for protecting my boy."

"He's worth protecting. I like Jacob very much. You're both very lucky to have such a wonderful son."

Clearly overtaken by emotion, Steven nodded. His clothes were sooty, as though he'd been closer to the fire than he should have been. But then Wade knew if his ranch were going up in flames, he'd try everything he could to save it.

"Well, I just wanted to give my thanks," he finally managed.

His wife dabbed at her eyes with a handkerchief. He put an arm around her shoulders and turned to leave.

"Mr. Garvey? I'm sorry for your feed mill. If I—"

He held up a hand. "I had a bone to pick with what you did and was more than happy to get anybody I could on my side. I never meant you physical harm, Miss Matthews, and I'm ashamed you were hurt because I encouraged a man like Harvey Black."

"Harvey Black was evil. I understand that what he did, he did of his own accord. I don't hold you accountable."

Wade hadn't noticed until then that they'd gathered a following. The sudden silence should have given it away. They all watched to see what Steven would do next.

"Then you're a bigger person than I am, Miss Matthews." He held out his hand. "Marietta is lucky to have you."

Epilogue

"I HATE THE waiting," Wade said from his post at the kitchen window. He had both hands braced on the countertop as he stared through the window to the barn across the yard. His guts were in knots. He rubbed the tight muscles; his gaze fixed on the open barn door, the golden light that spilled from it and the two people sitting just outside its entrance.

James came to Wade's side, peered out the window. "Jillian and Scott haven't moved. Hope mustn't be foaling yet."

Wade closed his eyes, prayed this would be over soon. And he prayed that by the end of it they'd have a filly. A filly between Hope and Whiskey would be a good solid step in starting his and Scott's horse breeding program.

It had taken a while to get to this point. When he'd first mentioned to Jillian the possibility of breeding Hope to Whiskey, he'd thought they'd wait until late spring to breed her. With gestation being almost a year, a spring foal would be bigger and stronger and more prepared for a harsh Montana winter than one born late summer. But once he'd voiced his idea, Jillian had leapt on it. They had a brand new barn; the foal would be sheltered from the worst of it.

Then, with an impish smile, she'd reminded him he would be marrying a vet who'd be around to closely monitor things. Of course she'd also told Scott who'd told James and Eileen and even Annabelle and soon everyone was excited and encouraging him to take the leap of faith.

And so, in the midst of planning their own wedding, considering Scott's offer to partner in the ranch and preparing to move his mother and James into Jillian's house, he'd given in. And he'd been thrilled when Jillian confirmed Hope was pregnant.

Since then they'd had their own fall wedding and he'd never felt so complete as he had when James had placed Jillian's hand in his. The one dark shadow had been that Jillian's mother's already frail health had taken a turn for the worst and neither she nor her sister Katie had been able to make the journey west.

But Jillian hadn't let it get her down and, truthfully, she hadn't had time to wallow in the fact that she had none of her own family at her wedding. With most of the town having witnessed her sacrifice to save Jacob, she'd had enough work to keep her busy.

And he'd had time to do some thinking.

Knowing it wasn't only a two-man partnership he was considering, he'd sought Jillian's opinion. Like she had with Hope, she'd encouraged him to accept Scott's offer right away but in that Wade had held firm. Until they climbed out of debt, at least some, he wasn't bringing Scott into it. He'd felt bad enough bringing Jillian into it.

And again, she'd grinned at him, reminded him that with the town's acceptance of her, with her work, there would be more money coming into the ranch. And so, surely but slowly, they had climbed their way up. They weren't in the clear, but he was no longer drowning in debt. It had taken almost a year but he'd finally accepted Scott's offer and the three of them were legally partners in the Triple P ranch. When Wade had offered to change the name of the ranch to include Scott he'd refused.

Wade pressed his hand against his stomach. God, he hoped Scott didn't come to regret everything he'd done to help Wade.

"Why don't you come play cards with us," James said of the game he and his ma were playing with Annabelle. "Jillian will let us know when the foal is here."

"I can't." He drew a deep breath as Jillian took her turn into the barn. She'd been going in every twenty minutes and from his position he could see her stop well away from the stall. She got in close enough to see her horse, make sure the mare didn't need her, and backed away quietly.

Pride filled him as she crept back outside, waved to him that all was right. She'd been keeping an eye on Hope these last few weeks, as it was the mare's first foal. She'd kept her close, tended to her like a mother over a child, ensuring she had the best food, the best care. She'd been the first to notice that Hope seemed uncomfortable, that she kept getting up and down, that she wasn't interested in her food. They'd moved her into the barn right away and she and Scott had taken their posts outside the door ever since.

James clapped Wade on the shoulder. "Hope's in good hands."

"I know. It's just"—he shook his head—"so much is riding on this foal."

"It'll be fine. Besides, if there's a problem, you won't have to wait for the vet to get here like last time."

Wade turned, met James's smile with one of his own. "That was some night."

"Yeah, you got a wife because of that night, and Eileen and I got a house."

"James, it's your turn," his ma said.

As James went to take his turn, his ma took her place at her son's side.

"How're they doing?"

"Nothing's changed. This waiting is going to kill me."

She chuckled, kissed his cheek. "Reminds me of when Annabelle was born. You were the same then, too. As I imagine you'll be when you and Jillian decide to give me another grandchild."

Wade smiled. He'd been considering doing exactly that. He looked at Annabelle, her dark hair so much like her mother's. He hoped his next child would also be blessed to have its mother's coloring.

He kissed his ma's cheek. "We'll just have to see about that."

"In the meantime," she said, smiling as she looked out the window, "looks like I'll have to be happy with a foal."

Wade's head spun round. Scott was waving from the barn. Wade rushed for the door as the sound of chairs scraping the floor rang behind him. They were a crazy group racing across the yard.

"Slow down, for God's sake, you don't want to scare them to death," Scott admonished, though his eyes glowed as bright as the lanterns.

With Scott leading the way, they crept into the barn. Hope was still down. Jillian was rubbing her hand over the foal's nose, but the sac had broken clean and the foal appeared to be fine.

"Congratulations," she said looking at him, then Scott, "you have yourselves your first filly."

Wade's eyes drank in the sight of the filly and damn if Scott hadn't been right. She was a beauty, exactly what their horse ranch needed.

Wade shifted his gaze to his wife. Jillian sat beside her horse, praising Hope for a job well done. Her face shone with happiness. Her eyes filled with love.

At times like these he couldn't believe he'd been foolish enough to think she shouldn't be a doctor. Not when he only had to look at her to see she was doing exactly what she was meant to be doing.

She turned her face to his, held out her hand to him.

Heart full, he took her hand, knelt at her side, knowing to the depths of his soul they were both exactly where they were meant to be.

The End

If you enjoyed *A Rancher's Surrender,*
you'll love the next books in…

The Frontier Montana series

Book 1: *A Ranchers' Surrender*

Book 2: *A Cowboy's Temptation*

Book 3: *A Sheriff's Passion*

Read more by Michelle Beattie

The Sam Steele series

Her Pirate to Love

In the Arms of a Pirate

Available now at your favorite online retailer!

About the Author

Award-winning author Michelle Beattie began writing in 1995, almost immediately after returning from her honeymoon. It took 12 long years but she achieved her dream of seeing her name on the cover of a book when she sold her novel, What A Pirate Desires, in 2007. Since then she's written and published several more historical novels as well a contemporary. Her pirate books have sold in several languages, been reviewed in Publisher's Weekly and Romantic Times. Two of her independent self-published works went on to win the Reader's Choice Silken Sands Self-Published Star Contest.

When Michelle isn't writing she enjoys playing golf, reading, walking her dog, travelling and sitting outside enjoying the peace of country life. Michelle comes from a large family and treasures her brothers and sister as well as the dozens of aunts, uncles and cousins she's proud to call family. She lives outside a tiny town in east-central Alberta, Canada with her husband, two teenage daughters and their dog, Ty.

Visit Michelle at her website at MichelleBeattie.com.

Thank you for reading

A Rancher's Surrender

If you enjoyed this book, you can find more from all our great authors at TulePublishing.com, or from your favorite online retailer.

Made in the USA
Charleston, SC
13 October 2016